Complications in Paris

Complications in Paris

A Belle Époque Novel

MELINDA COPP

TINY PIANO
PRESS

Book Cover Design and Illustration by LA Villavicencio

FIC027200   FICTION / Romance / Historical / 20th Century
FIC027460   FICTION / Romance / Historical / Gilded Age

First edition: February 2025

ISBN: 978-1-964546-03-2

LCCN: 2024926652

For my parents.

Love does not consist of gazing at each other, but in looking outward together in the same direction.

Antoine de Saint-Exupéry

Chapter One

June 1901

The music swung in a wild crescendo to finish the song, and Diane Talbot, and everyone in the crowd around her, erupted in cheers. She'd been dancing on the outdoor floor of Moulin Rouge for nearly an hour. Her legs were shaky from so much kicking, and her heart thumped like a big drum in her chest. All around her, ruffles fluttered and skirts fell back into place. Legs, dressed in stockings with lace trim, settled onto the ground to wait for the next song. Men—some in white ties and tails, others in heavy eye makeup and not much else—caught their breath. Across the crowd, Diane's sister, Catherine, who'd been dancing as well, was weaving through the people to get to her.

"Let's get some water. I'm too thirsty to kick anymore." Catherine's light brown hair fell in wisps around her flushed face. The sisters linked arms and headed inside toward the bar, where a woman in a skimpy sequined dress was singing on the stage, and nearly every eye in the place was on her. She was like a rare, shiny bird. "God, this place never fails, does it?"

"Do you mean Paris or the cabaret?" Diane flicked her feather boa at her sister.

"Both, actually."

"Two waters, s'il vous plaît," Diane said to the bartender.

"I'm ready to go," Catherine said as she slumped onto a freshly vacated barstool in front of them.

"Do you mean Paris or the cabaret?"

"Both, actually."

"Stop it. We settled on three more months before arguing about it again."

"You're the one who brought up Paris." Catherine's chandelier earrings swayed and sparkled with each shake of her head. The bartender set two glasses of water in front of them.

Diane rolled her eyes and took a drink. After so much dancing, she couldn't say another word without something wet.

The debate about staying or going had become so regular for the sisters that they'd had to agree to put off the discussion as well as the departure. Delaying the departure was all that mattered to Diane; she didn't want to return to Woollett or her parents' house in the middle of nowhere. Well, maybe it wasn't exactly nowhere. But everywhere was nowhere compared to Paris, as far as Diane was concerned. She wanted to stay for as long as she could. The sisters had come over for what was supposed to be a season. On the day of their return, they ripped up their tickets and sent the maid home on the steamer alone. Daddy was furious and swift to close his wallet, as Diane expected he would. Granted, being cut off from their father's money had been difficult. But she couldn't make herself care when she could come to the cabaret and dance whenever she wanted. In Paris. Paris!

Leaving made absolutely no sense to Diane. Her sister was the one who didn't get it. But they'd agreed not to talk about it for three more months, so Diane let it go and focused on the part about the cabaret. She wasn't ready to leave there either.

"Can't we hang around long enough for one of these French gentlemen to buy us dinner? I'm hungry."

"We can find something in the kitchen at home. I have to work in the morning." Catherine worked in the law office where Diane was no longer employed. It had been her first job, and she hadn't lasted long. They moved a few steps away from the bar to finish their water, and someone else in need of a drink quickly took the stool.

"You're no fun at all," Diane pouted. She couldn't stay alone —not in France or at Moulin Rouge. As she spoke, one of those French gentlemen sidled up to them, waiting for a turn at the bar. He was taller than everyone else around them and dressed in a black suit, white tie, and black top hat. There was a red rose pinned to his lapel. When their eyes caught, he nodded, smiled, and politely looked away.

"Can I just say one last thing about leaving Paris?"

Diane shrugged. "As long as we note that this time I'm not the one breaking the rule we agreed upon."

"We can't stay forever. We can't do this forever." She waved her empty water glass around as if to suggest everything about the cabaret. "And planning our return is not only sensible but also empowering. We get to do it on our terms, rather than Daddy's."

"I'm not ready to think about it, though," Diane whined.

"She's right, you know," the Frenchman said. He was facing them now, leaning an elbow on the bar like he was holding it up. And involving himself like he was a part of their conversation?

"Excusez-moi," Diane said, dragging out the syllables with attitude.

"Pardon, mademoiselles, but I overheard, and she's right." The man, who looked perfectly comfortable inserting himself, tipped his head toward Catherine. "Planning your departure from Paris will allow it to happen on your terms. As mademoiselle has said."

"Well, no one asked you." Diane narrowed her eyes. So typical. A man inserting his opinions. How original. Every man she'd ever known well had been the same way. "But my terms are not leaving Paris."

"I thought that wasn't possible?" The man was regrettably dashing with blue eyes and golden blond hair—obviously the sort who relied on his looks to cover up for his rudeness.

"Do you always feel the need to comment on topics that are none of your business?"

He looked between the two sisters, confidence and that specific French sort of snobbishness that she both loved and hated oozed from him. His face flushed and his mouth quirked with indignance. "Well, as a Parisian, I have to say the departure of every tourist is a victory. Au revoir, mademoiselles."

Diane's mouth fell open as he moved off to get the bartender's attention. He exchanged a few words with the barman and then nodded at her and Catherine as he walked off into the crowd.

"How rude," Diane said before he was out of earshot. Didn't he know one should ignore other people's arguments?

"Oh, stop, I think he liked you."

Diane hadn't thought of that. Her face grew warm—though definitely not because she liked the idea of him liking her. She was warm from dancing. "I doubt that."

"Didn't you see the way he was looking at you? He didn't even seem to care that your hair's a mess. He barely looked at me because he couldn't take his eyes off you."

Maybe she should have asked him to buy her dinner instead of chasing him off. Then she thought better of it. "Well, I didn't like him."

Diane finished her water and then set her and her sister's empty glasses among a few other dirty ones on the edge of the bar. Just as she was getting ready to relent and leave the cabaret, Catherine pointed across the room.

"Hey. That's Charlotte."

"Deveraux? I can't believe it. Where?"

Catherine grabbed Diane's arm and pulled her through the crowd, calling after their housemate whom Diane still didn't see. Then there was Charlotte in her feathered hat on a man's arm—probably her aristocrat friend she was crazy about.

Charlotte was a regular girl from the provinces who happened to be a wildly talented writer. Diane liked her because she'd also grown up far from city life. As far as most Parisians were concerned, being from America was as backwoods as being from anywhere outside of Paris. They called it backwoods at home, but here it was provincial. Even the word for uncultured was fancier in France.

"I thought that was you," Catherine exclaimed. "Diane didn't believe me."

"It's not that I didn't believe her," Diane said, sizing up the man on Charlotte's arm. He was the one sending all the gifts and messengers to the house. He was handsome, she had to admit. "You never come out! I'm surprised to see you is all."

"We've only just arrived. I was at a party in the seventh, and then we took the metro here." Charlotte looked up at the man and continued, "Catherine and Diane Talbot, this is my friend Antoine de Larminet. Antoine, these are my housemates. They're sisters."

Diane smiled and held out her hand to Antoine, which he kissed. Then Charlotte stepped aside to introduce another person. "This is Monsieur Guillaume Allard, who was hosting the party. A group of us came from his place."

That was when Diane's eyes landed on the rude gentleman from the bar. For a second, she thought she'd made a mistake, or that the interloper was once again interloping. But no. Charlotte ushered him forward.

"You again," Diane raised an eyebrow at Guillaume, who looked as surprised as she was to be reacquainting. He scowled, but the glimmer in his eyes was playful, like he was thrilled to be meeting her again.

"Diane and Catherine Talbot, enchanté." He kissed Catherine on the hand. When Diane held out hers, he leaned past it and air-kissed her on the cheek. A quick, dry brush of his soft mouth and the stubble along his jaw against her skin. And Diane, it turned out, wasn't mad about meeting him again either.

"We were just discussing leaving and apparently met your friend Guillaume," Catherine continued, unfazed by the coincidence. "I'm ready, and she's not."

"Now that Charlotte and her friends are here," Diane said, recognizing her opportunity, "you can take a cab home, and I'll stay with them."

"Can't you stay, Catherine?" Charlotte said.

"I almost feel like it, now that you're here," she said regretfully. "But I have to work in the morning."

"So go home. I'll be fine!" Diane assured her sister.

"I'll keep you company." Guillaume stepped forward, as if his presence might be appreciated. His blue eyes caught Diane's again, and something warm and pleasant stirred in her stomach. Probably because she was hungry.

He continued, charm unabated. "I need to make up for the poor first impression I fear I left."

Diane's annoyance with this man faltered again. Here was another opportunity. "It will cost you dinner, monsieur."

"Good, then it's settled," Catherine said. "I'll get out of here, and you can stay with them. Will you see me out?"

"Of course." Diane turned to Charlotte then. "I'll meet you back here in a few minutes?"

"Okay."

"We'll get a table outside," Guillaume said as the sisters walked away.

Diane groaned. "Can you believe that guy is Charlotte's friend? He's probably a terrible snob."

"So why are you staying with them?" Catherine smiled wryly.

"To visit with Charlotte, silly. She never comes dancing with us."

Outside, the night air cooled Diane's balmy skin like drink of water. People mingled on the sidewalk and foot traffic streamed from one club to another. Montmartre was alive and filled with the energy of nightlife. A cab of revelers was emptying out just as they reached the street. Catherine waved to get the driver's attention.

"Can you take me to 77 Rue de Fortuny?"

The driver obliged with a nod.

Before stepping into the carriage, Catherine turned to Diane. "I'll see you at home."

"I won't be long." For a moment, Diane considered following her sister into the cab and going home to bed. But it wasn't even eleven yet, and all the pieces of an interesting evening were falling into place. First, the nosy and admittedly handsome stranger turned out to be Charlotte's friend. And that Charlotte had turned up with an obviously monied group of friends. Diane just couldn't go home when things like this were happening. She smiled at Catherine. "I still can't believe you want to leave."

"Do you mean Paris or Moulin Rouge, darling?" Catherine didn't wait for a response; the question a tease, anyway. She pulled the carriage door closed and smiled and waved goodbye to Diane through the grimy window.

With a flourish of her feather boa, Diane kicked her leg high into the air and swept it back down to land in a deep bow. Catherine laughed as the cab drove off. When Diane turned back toward the club, the red windmill spun slowly against the dark sky and the night showed no signs of stopping. Diane, invigorated by the possibilities of it, hurried back inside to find Charlotte. They'd said they were going outside to look for a table, so Diane passed through the front of the house where the woman was now on a swing that had lowered down from above the stage. Her audience still watched from their tables.

All the curves and chambers and red reminded Diane of the diagram she'd seen of the human heart. Moulin Rouge was kind of like the heart of Paris. Of course, there were the fancier places and the palaces and the tower that everyone loved. But here—where eclecticism reigned, and people from all walks of life came together to be part of this raucous, creative, burlesque experience—was the real Paris. The heart of everything that made the place so grand. This was why Diane couldn't fathom leaving and going back to dull, boring Woollett. Nothing in that whole town was red.

Outside, the giant elephant loomed over the dance floor, where people carried on in time to the music. Charlotte's orange and purple feathered hat quivered over a table across the room, and Diane headed that way. Around her, the crowd whirled and cheered along to the music. Diane, who'd been to Moulin Rouge a few times, sashayed in time as she walked. When a man wearing lipstick and a lace bodice bumped into her, he smiled and took advantage, twirling her around and kissing her on the cheek before letting her go in a fit of giggles. Diane danced away, thinking her father would be furious if he knew where she was. She'd taken all sorts of dancing lessons when she was a little girl. But her father made her stop when she turned thirteen because, in his thundering words: he was raising a lady, not a dancer. Good thing he was back in America.

At the table, Guillaume rose and pulled out the seat next to him for Diane. She'd cooled off from her marathon of dancing, but her skin tingled with him so close to her again. Close enough to smell cigarette smoke and the perfume of his rose. He was a full head and shoulders taller than Diane, his clothes finely tailored. And he'd placed his hat on the table in front of him, revealing loose waves of sandy blond hair. When he gestured for her to sit, she said quietly so no one else would hear, "You don't have to make up for any previous rudenesses by being overly nice. It won't work anyway."

"Mademoiselle, I am merely using my manners."

"Oh, so you have those in France."

Guillaume laughed, which made Diane laugh too, unfortunately. She tried to hide it by meeting Charlotte's eyes and smiling. "I'm so happy to run into you."

"Were you and Catherine here for long?" Charlotte asked, returning the smile.

"Well over an hour. We were dancing almost the whole time. I must look like a disaster."

"Don't be silly," Guillaume said, butting in again. "You're the most stunning woman here. Charlotte tells me you're American?"

"I am. But we've been here for months and have no plans to leave." She said it pointedly to let him know he wasn't off the hook for taking her sister's side no matter how nice he tried to be.

The server returned with drinks and asked if Diane wanted anything since she'd only just joined them.

"Nothing to drink, thank you. But have I missed dinner?"

"Dinner is still being served inside, mademoiselle. Let me know if you want a table."

"Maybe. Thank you." She shot Guillaume a quick look, and he was watching her.

After the server had gone, Guillaume asked about America.

"I'm from a small place," said Diane. "But New York City isn't far."

"I've never been," Guillaume said.

"There's not much reason to, not when you live here." She said it dismissively, hoping he'd drop the subject. She didn't want to think about Woollett. She didn't want to explain what life was like there to someone like Guillaume. It simply made for dull conversation, and she'd already told that story a hundred times. Not that Woollett was such a terrible place.

She'd had a wonderful childhood, come from a loving and supportive home. Her parents were working-class people who'd built their considerable wealth through hard work and smart business decisions. Their mother died young, and that was still a difficult reality for Diane and her sister to navigate. But by then Daddy could afford to keep maids and tutors who served as positive feminine role models for the girls as they grew up. He was a kind and reasonable man, when they were obeying him. And generous. Most young women from Woollett would never visit Paris or anywhere outside of the States. She and Catherine were so lucky that their father had allowed them to come. Lucky that he could be swayed, after all those years of French language tutoring, to let them immerse themselves with a season abroad.

One of Charlotte's friends, whose name Diane had forgotten already, spoke up. She had gone to Manhattan last year and talked about a show she'd seen there. By now, Diane had spent more time in Paris than she had in Manhattan, so she didn't have much to add. The thing about being a tourist was that everyone wanted to share the most distantly related stories about the place you were from. Nothing revealed a person's misconceptions about places like these exchanges. The awkward part was that the woman was telling the story to connect with Diane. Though perhaps that she'd tried at all was most important. Like never understanding weights and measurements, these were the everyday conundrums faced by an American in Paris, and so Diane had to tolerate it all if she wanted to continue as such.

As the conversation carried on, Guillaume's elbow brushed Diane's as he played with his hat on the table. Casually leaning her way, he looked like trouble. Very handsome. His hands were broad and looked capable enough inside his white gloves. Everyone at the table laughed when he chimed in. If only he weren't so arrogant.

Speaking of arrogant, Diane had read about Charlotte's aristocrat friend, Antoine, a time or two in the gossip columns. All of it pretty tame and only interesting enough to print because of his high society status. No matter who was speaking, Antoine didn't take his eyes off Charlotte. He was obviously smitten with her. Men were so much trouble, with their egos and their demands, but they were also so adorable. Diane had lamented this dilemma countless times. She lamented it now, sitting right next to Guillaume.

Someone told a joke that Diane missed, and everyone at the table laughed. Then Guillaume turned and caught Diane staring at him. Flustered, her face warmed and she looked away. When she ventured a look back at him, he smiled and said, "Let me buy you dinner. Is anyone else hungry?"

Everyone shook their heads.

"We'll probably stay out here with the others," Antoine said. "But you two can go ahead."

"Absolutely." Charlotte shrugged and smiled suggestively. What exactly she was suggesting wasn't so clear. Diane half-hoped Charlotte would save her from Guillaume's company, not encourage it. But she was hungry. So hungry that she had maybe… maybe been a little hard on him. Maybe. If he was willing to buy her dinner, she could give him a chance to redeem himself.

"Okay." Why not?

Guillaume stood and held out a gloved hand to Diane. His thick arm led to a strong set of shoulders. Her stomach grumbled. She was starving now. She put her hand in his and rose from her seat. Then after a quick, temporary goodbye to Charlotte and her friends, Diane let Guillaume whisk her inside.

Guillaume followed the maitre d' and Diane to a small table near the bar, watching her slim ankles underneath the pile of ruffles on her skirt as they walked. He hadn't planned on leaving his friends, but he felt compelled to smooth things over after his intrusion. He'd heard the women arguing in English and started listening for practice. He spoke English well, but still had to translate the words in his head, and so, standing there waiting for the bartender, he couldn't help himself. He started listening, his attention aided by the fact that they were pretty girls. And feisty, it turned out. That they were Charlotte Devereaux's friends was like a little bite from karma. If she was going to be hanging around with them all evening, then the least he could do was feed her. It might put her in a better mood. He'd seen that work with other women. It would work on him.

After she'd slid into the banquette, Guillaume flicked his tails out of the way and sat opposite her. He thanked the host, who passed them menus and departed.

"Have you eaten here before?"

"You know, I haven't. I've been to Moulin Rouge, but I never had the food." She opened her menu and smiled as she read. Her smile was wide and lovely and lit up everything else about her.

"It's not the most memorable part of an evening here." Guillaume opened his menu but closed it again, still full from eating at the party. "But the chicken is delicious. Please order whatever you like."

"Chicken is so everyday, though." She watched him over the top of her menu. Her eyebrows scrunched together as if it were an accusation. "I feel like I should try something new or exotic."

"Maybe the duck, then?"

"What are you having?" Diane pursed her lips adorably and leaned over the menu.

"Another drink. Maybe some of your bread, if you don't mind. But I ate not long ago."

"At your party?" She said, looking up. Her eyes were enchantingly dark.

There was a scantily clad woman on the stage singing and dancing, and yet Guillaume hardly cared to watch. "Yes. My parents', actually. Which was how I was able to slip away."

"I see. And do you know Charlotte well?"

"Only a little. Mostly what Antoine has told me. You two are housemates?"

"We are. But only for a few months now. So you could say I'm her new friend. But I like Charlotte, and seeing that you're Antoine's friend, you need to understand that I'm using this dinner not only to get fed, but also fact-finding. She and I will discuss this later."

He put his hands up in surrender. "I never doubted it."

The server, dressed in a crisp white shirt and red vest, arrived and took their order. Champagne and the chicken for Diane. Champagne and water for Guillaume.

When he'd gone, Diane sighed and sank into the seat. "You have no idea how ready I am to eat."

"The chicken, though?"

"It sounded too good. Plus, if I've never eaten here before, then doesn't that make everything on the menu new to me? Even something as everyday as chicken."

"I suppose it does."

The waiter returned with their drinks, and Diane took a dainty sip. Her lip paint had faded to a berry stain, and her dark hair seemed ready to break free of the pins and tumble around her smooth, bare shoulders.

After the server had gone and a long drink of his water, Guillaume said, "I'm sorry for intruding on your conversation. I'm not sure I mentioned that before."

Her eyebrows rose in two seductive arches, and she pretended to choke on her drink.

"What?"

"I'm surprised is all."

"Why?"

"I think this is the first time a man has ever apologized to me." She tipped her head toward the ceiling thoughtfully.

"Are you joking?"

"There were a few times a cousin had to apologize for violence when we were children, but I'm sure it's never happened in my adult life."

"Stop."

"I'm being serious."

"Well, I'm being honest. I'm sorry. I apologize."

She bit her lip to stop from grinning and squeaked in the most delightful way. "Okay."

"Okay."

"Let's talk about something else, then." She sipped her champagne and eyed him curiously. "Tell me about this party."

"Ah, well, my parents like to entertain and have a party once a season or so."

"How many guests are we talking about? A hundred people?"

"Maybe." He laughed.

"Friends, family. Business associates? Upper-class folks, like yourself."

"All of those, yes. My friends Olivier and Natalie were there. You met them at the table with Charlotte and Antoine. If you're so interested, I can take you." He looked at his pocket watch, though he didn't expect her to want to go. It was nearing midnight. "It will probably carry on for another few hours."

She tilted her head to the side, as if she hadn't thought about it but definitely was now. "Maybe. Let's revisit that after my chicken comes."

Guillaume laughed again. She was funny in an odd way that he found brightly attractive, and without meaning to, he imagined taking her back to his house for more than just the party. But timing was not his friend tonight, and he could not indulge that fantasy or any others involving Diane. At least not until he'd fully disentangled himself from Marielle.

Things with Marielle, his latest petite amie in a long line of recent petite amies, had mellowed to a coolness. She was pretty and nice enough company. She certainly knew how to have a good time. But, as much as Guillaume hated to admit it, perhaps the thrill of new affection was the only thrill of Marielle. The tingling in his groin that happened watching Diane's mouth against her champagne glass was another sign he needed to disentangle himself as soon as possible. If he was truly supposed to be with Marielle, he wouldn't be attracted to the woman sitting across from him.

He'd met Marielle at a ball and had been seeing her for a little over a month. He'd had high hopes for her, but she, like the others before her, had failed to keep him interested beyond a few weeks of courtship. He hated to think that he was incapable of a deeper relationship with any of these women, but he was beginning to wonder if maybe he was. In any case, the answer wasn't Diane. At least not tonight. He'd have to keep everything in the most platonic of waters. He considered telling her he had a girlfriend, but then decided now wasn't the time. He'd tell her, but there was no reason to just yet. He had to decide how he felt about her first. Had to decide why to tell her. He was breaking it off with Marielle first thing tomorrow, and who knew where the evening would lead.

Diane raised her champagne flute then. "We forgot to toast."

"To forgiveness."

"And to friendship." Her dark eyes grew wide with glee. "Because we're friends now, aren't we Guillaume? Because I believe in keeping my enemies close."

"Then it's friends, definitely." Guillaume drank his champagne. "So, Diane. American Diane. Are you a writer like Charlotte?"

"No. I write in my journal and no one can read it until I compile and shape it all in my memoir. But that will be years from now. I am currently employed as a hostess at Bouillon Juillet."

"Ah." He'd never been there, but he'd heard of the place. They had a popular lunch. "And is that why you've come all the way from America to Paris? To work in service?"

"Not exactly. It's a long story."

"I'm in the mood for a story. What city did you say you were from again?"

"Woollett. It's north of New York."

"I see. And you worked in a restaurant there also?"

"No. I never worked before coming to Paris. My father would never allow it, and I never needed to. We came here for vacation—my sister and I. It was only supposed to be for three months. My father put us up in the Grand Hôtel, and we shopped and went to the top of the tower and toured Paris. It was supposed to be a last hurrah before settling into domestic life, but it's still hurrahing. But when we refused to come home, Daddy stopped paying, thinking that because we'd never worked a day in our lives, that we'd never last on our own. Not that it's been easy. It's been the hardest thing I've ever done in my life. But we got jobs. I've worked in a law office, a flower shop, and now a restaurant."

"I see." This painted Diane in quite a different light. She was not exactly a working-class girl. But she was living as one. "And what about your mother? What does she say?"

"She's gone. Died when I was twelve." Her face fell.

"Oh, I'm so sorry." Guillaume winced. He'd embarrassed himself again.

"Don't be. It's an innocent enough question. I have a step-mother, or a soon-to-be-maybe-step-mother. My father has been engaged to this woman for over seven years, and they were together for years before that."

"I see. It sounds complicated."

"I believe so, yes."

"And you've no plans to go home to Woollett." He pronounced the name of the town like it didn't fit properly in his mouth.

She laughed, and the sound was deep and full and quite pleasing. "Woollett, yes."

"I might have to, eventually. But I hope to put it off as long as I can."

"What's waiting for you when you go back?"

"Oh, you know. The usual things. A marriage to someone my father approves of and the rest of my life in Woollett with as many children as I can physically muster."

Guillaume let his gaze linger on her eyes for a long moment. They were so entrancing that the bustling cabaret around them seemed to dissolve. "That doesn't sound so bad."

"Are you joking? It sounds like a trap."

"And so the question is how long you can avoid it."

"Something like that."

"One of my sisters just got engaged. They haven't even announced it yet, beyond telling the family."

"Oh? Well, it's what people do. Congratulations to her." Diane raised her champagne glass. "How many sisters do you have?"

"Two. Josephine is four years younger than me and Juliette is the youngest. She's six years younger than me."

"Two little sisters."

"Yes. They're very close and quite fun."

"I love having a sister. Most of the time."

"And you love dancing?"

"I love dancing! And I love listening to music."

"What kind of music do you like?"

"All kinds. But especially Debussy. Listening to his songs is like living a full day's emotions in five minutes."

"I love Debussy too. Especially on the piano."

"The Arabesques!" Diane beamed.

"Of course, yes!" Guillaume's face ached from smiling at Diane. About Diane. Her enthusiasm radiated off of her, and he could feel himself melting in it. He liked Diane. "Do you play? Piano?"

"I had a few lessons as a girl, but I was terrible."

Her chicken arrived with a flourish of service and drink refills. And she ate heartily. Guillaume watched the show, letting her eat, but not without stealing glances. She was hungry for such a petite thing. But she didn't come close to finishing the meal. Then even though he'd insisted he wasn't hungry, Guillaume volunteered to finish the rest of it for her. He was the sort of man who could always eat. It was wasteful, and food in general was too delicious to leave behind, after all.

"Oh, that was good," she said, sipping her wine and watching him finish. "Thank you, Guillaume."

The server arrived then with the check, which Guillaume paid happily. Happy that she seemed happy, or at least happier than their initial encounter left her. Confident that he'd fully turned things around, he said, "Can I give you a lift home in my carriage?"

Diane narrowed her eyes at him again, thoughtfully rather than with malice.

"I assure you, I have no romantic designs. I'm actually involved with someone. I have a girlfriend."

"Girlfriend? You're full of surprises tonight, Guillaume." A flicker of disappointment—or maybe just boredom—flashed in her bottomless brown eyes.

"Yes. I have been seeing a woman for several weeks."

"And what is her name?"

"Marielle. But, while I'm fully disclosing, I should also say that I intend to break it off with her soon."

"Soon?"

"Tomorrow."

"I see." She smiled like a predator spotting prey. "And what brought this on."

"It's been in the works for a few days. There's been some distance already. She didn't show up to my party tonight, which was where I intended to discuss the matter with her. She wasn't feeling up to it or something like that. In any case, I've already written to arrange a meeting as soon as possible tomorrow."

"So it's not because you have fallen madly in love with me, right? Because we can't have that."

"I suppose not. No."

"Then I suppose it's safe for me to accept the lift in your carriage. Since you have no romantic designs."

Did he imagine disappointment in her tone? "Well, I wouldn't go that far. Designs are incomplete. Only that, I assure you, to avoid complications, I will not attempt romantic action."

Diane laughed. "It's a deal."

Before leaving the club, Guillaume and Diane looked for Antoine and the rest of the group. They weren't at the table outside. And the place was even more full now. It was hard to move around, let alone find anyone. When they couldn't locate Antoine or Olivier, Guillaume left a message for them with the maitre d'.

Outside, Boulevard de Clichy still bustled with carriage and foot traffic. A warm summer breeze came through, rustling the horse chestnut trees above the sidewalks.

Guillaume's carriage was parked down the street, and when they reached it, he held out a hand to help Diane inside.

When her small hand pushed on his, something in his chest dipped. He liked being with her. But this wasn't so uncommon for him. There had been so many girls. Was there any use falling for this one? Could he help himself?

He climbed in after her, sitting close. Her flowery perfume was more noticeable in the closed space. He wouldn't mind smelling her delicate neck, but he could and would resist the intoxication.

"How's she going to take it?"

"Hmm?"

"Marielle. The breakup."

"Oh." Marielle was the furthest thing from his mind right then. "Perhaps not well. Though it's hard to be sure."

"I see." She looked out the window for a moment and then turned back toward him. "Well, good luck to you on that endeavor."

"I appreciate that. Thank you. I'll probably need it."

"So tell me something else about you, Guillaume," she said. "Do you have a title coming to you like your friend Antoine?"

"No. I am not from an aristocratic family. My father started a shipping company that he built and eventually sold. Now he invests."

"Ah. Self-made, then. Very bourgeois."

"I assume an American can appreciate that."

"You're right. My father made his money as well. In toothpicks."

"Toothpicks?"

"Yes. He started a toothpick factory."

"How vulgar. But also quite clever."

"They've really taken off in America. Worth a fortune!" Diane shrugged. "In any case, we weren't always the kind of people who could afford French tutors and seasons in Paris."

They had come to the traffic circle around Boulevard de Batingnolles, where many of the shops were dark and closed, but a few restaurants and bars were still open and serving. There were lights on in some of the apartments above, but many more windows were dark. It was nearing one o'clock, and some in the city of light needed to rest.

"Perhaps your father can appreciate that you and your sister are working then?"

"Oh, absolutely. I'm sure that's the only reason he hasn't sent the calvary after us. He admires that sort of quality in people. Not that he'd ever admit he admires us for disobeying."

"Well, what father would?"

"What about you, Guillaume? Do you work?"

"No. My father always says he worked for thirty years on docks so I wouldn't have to ever set foot there. He's promised to teach me everything he knows about investing. So I'm not averse to working."

"Well, having had several jobs now, make sure you find something you like. And stay as far away from service as you can."

They were turning onto Rue de Fortuny now. And their conversation fell into a lull filled with anticipation. He enjoyed Diane's company much more than he'd expected to when he'd extended the peace offering to buy her dinner. The way the streetlights cast shadows and highlights across her lips and smooth skin, he wanted to end this evening with his hands on her, his mouth on hers. But he couldn't.

He couldn't fall for her while he was still entangled with Marielle. It was one thing to have many girlfriends, and it was an entirely different thing to allow for overlap. He didn't like overlap. He'd seen many arrangements, and they all seemed exhausting. He was terrible at keeping secrets, and he was uncomfortable lying. Of course, sometimes half-truths and even untruths were necessary. But Guillaume was hoping to find a mate and partner, and so he was, under all the good fun and flirtations, looking for a wife. He'd thoroughly enjoyed being a bachelor, but at twenty-seven, he was looking forward to this period of his life being over. He didn't want this lifestyle for himself at fifty or sixty. He wanted to settle—with the right person. And he wasn't interested in unnecessary complications. Overlapping affairs was too messy, logistically and emotionally.

No, he couldn't kiss Diane goodnight. But perhaps sometime soon, in the near future, he could call upon Diane for another evening together.

"I'm right up here," she said. The carriage rolled to a stop in front of a place with iron scrollwork trim and window planters filled with petunias and geraniums. All the windows in the house were dark except one on the third floor.

"I enjoyed meeting you tonight, Diane," Guillaume said earnestly.

A streetlight shone in the carriage window, illuminating her face in a pale yellow glow. Diane's brow furrowed in thought and then broke into a smile. "I enjoyed it too. Thank you again for dinner."

"Well, I'm sorry again for how it came about."

"All's been washed away with champagne and night air."

Guillaume, with nothing more to say, stepped out onto the sidewalk and helped Diane down from the carriage. "Au revoir, Diane."

"Au revoir, Guillaume." She nodded and turned to walk away. Then with a wicked smile, she added, "Best of luck to you and your girlfriend."

He laughed. She didn't believe that he planned on breaking up with her. "Can I write to you, Diane? After the smoke clears."

"Ha. After the smoke clears. That's a good one." She turned away again and took the two steps up to the door. "Have a good night, Guillaume."

Diane produced a key from somewhere in her skirts and, without looking back at him, opened the door and disappeared inside.

Chapter Two

Diane closed the door and locked it behind her. Then she watched through the window as Guillaume's carriage pulled away from the house and disappeared down the street. How absurd her evening with Guillaume seemed in retrospect. Meeting him at the bar in that odd way, and then he turned out to be Charlotte's acquaintance. Plus, all that business about his girlfriend. Diane couldn't have imagined her evening unfolding the way it had. And with such a character. She was also fairly certain she'd never hear from him again. French men always had girlfriends, and they always said they were breaking up with them. But they seldom did. More likely, she'd see his engagement announcement in the papers. Him and Marielle, or whatever her name was.

Hopeful that the pale light in the hallway meant Catherine was awake, rather than that she'd fallen asleep with a candle burning, Diane crept up the stairs. The women's pension was an old, big house owned by Madame Tremblay. Her rooms, along with the servants' were on the opposite side of the house, buffered by a thick wall and the large dining room. All the housemates lived on the upper floors, so Diane didn't have to walk past anyone's door to get to her own. This wasn't her first late-night entrance. She knew how to get to her room without making a sound.

When Diane opened the door to the suite of rooms she shared with her sister, Catherine was awake. She was sitting on the plaid settee between their bedrooms, reading one of her boring books about how to be a better person. The window was open. Lamplight flickered against the faded floral wallpaper.

"So much for going to sleep," Diane said.

"You're telling me." Catherine was dressed in her nightgown and robe, her hair in a tumbling braid that fell over her shoulder. She was the prettier sister, but Diane was used to that. Catherine sat up straighter and gave Diane the look that meant she was steeling herself for something. "When I came back there was a letter from Daddy."

"Well, something's kept you up. A good letter or a bad one?"

"Good question."

"Is he okay?" Diane's first concern, her worst nightmare, was that her father's health might fail. She wasn't ready to be parentless. Daddy had always been healthy, but their mother had been healthy too before the fever. Life could be snatched from anyone at any time. Daddy was getting older. And his business could be stressful for him.

"Daddy? I think everything's fine with him. Well, he doesn't say, actually. But the concern is that Ada and Harry Beall are coming to Paris."

"What? When?"

"Any minute now. The letter is dated two weeks ago." She gestured to the escritoire they shared.

Diane picked up the letter and read it. In their father's tight hand and very few words, there was exactly what her sister had just told her and nothing more.

"You don't think he's sick and just not saying so," Catherine said, worry tightening her jaw. "And that's why he's not coming himself?"

"Maybe. But probably not. You know how busy and important Daddy is," Diane said facetiously. Their father was important, but he had a full staff of people to cover for him if he wanted. Which he usually didn't. "It's just like him to send Ada."

"You know why they're coming, don't you?"

"To bring us home."

"Exactly."

Diane sat down next to her sister, who reached out to pat her arm. So the calvary was coming after all.

Diane and Catherine hadn't defied Daddy with malicious intent. Diane, now twenty-two, didn't dislike her father, but she didn't want to live her life his way either. Her mother had died so young that she never left New York and had only left Woollett a handful of times. She barely had the chance to dream, let alone make her dreams come true. Diane understood from that loss—among other things—that you only got one chance at life. This was it. And so she might as well do it her way. If that meant defying her father and everyone else back at home who had plans for her, then so be it.

Before coming to Paris with her sister, Diane had been in a casual, though long-term attachment with her father's friend's son. They had grown up understanding that a match between them would secure the families' futures, binding them together. It would solidify the sentiment that the men were indeed more than friends; they were family. Alvin Monroe was his name, and he was a perfectly nice man. Diane trusted him completely. He was fond of her, she could tell. She didn't love him, though.

Nothing about him lit her up. The sex was fine, but it wasn't inspiring. It was almost like she knew him too well to really fall for him. Anyway, a marriage to him was what awaited her back in Woollett. They weren't engaged, exactly. But they'd discussed taking that step upon her return from Paris, which hadn't happened and wouldn't for as long as Diane could hold it off. She'd meant it when she said it, that she'd come back and marry him. But everything had changed since then.

If she caved under her father's pressure, which was a real possibility whether Diane acknowledged it or not, her whole life would be laid out for her. All her friends from home were already living it. The wedding, the family home, the pregnancy, the fabric choices, and all that walking around Woollett all day. If she'd gone back to America as planned, Diane would be doing that very thing right now. And if her father's fiancée managed to get her on a boat home, she'd be doing that before the end of the year. That was the life her father had laid out for her. That was what women in Woollett society, such as it was, did.

She hadn't planned on abandoning the return ship and staying in Paris. She hadn't boarded that steamer in New York, intending never to return. It didn't dawn on her that she had escaped until she was installed at the Grand Hôtel in Paris. Their house was one of the finest in town back home, but it didn't compare to the opulence of Paris. Before long, she knew in her heart that Paris would have to drive her out before she would ever get on that boat home. From that realization, it was only a matter of making a plan and convincing her sister without the maid finding out. She'd been a lovely maid with a knack for intricate braids. But she was employed by Daddy, and therefore not to be fully trusted on a number of matters.

With Daddy, it was his way, or he wasn't paying for it. When they didn't come home, his letters vibrated with anger. But they'd avoided stoking trouble by getting jobs and not asking for any money. Diane wrote to him regularly; not as often as Catherine did, but still. And although every one of his letters demanded their return, Diane liked to think that he was secretly proud of them for doing something so bold, for resisting the easy way and embracing the challenge of life on their own in a foreign city. It was exactly the kind of venture an American man like their father would appreciate, though he'd undoubtedly appreciate it more if Catherine and Diane were sons instead of daughters. They hadn't left him alone. He had his fiancée, Ada Beall, and her stepson, Harry Beall, to keep him company, as well as a whole business to run. All of it undoubtedly kept him too busy to worry too much about his daughters.

They were still in Paris because Diane carefully built her case for staying, and both sisters worked to afford it. Catherine had been a real sport about staying overseas, especially considering she was probably still in love with a man she left behind in Woollett—the very man who would be landing in Paris any time now.

Diane nudged Catherine with her elbow. "And Harry is coming. Ooh la la."

Catherine turned as pink as her nightgown. "Stop it, you. He's probably forgotten all about me."

"Yes, absolutely, my dear. That's why he's coming all the way to Paris. Just for fun. Nothing to do with you at all." For all Diane knew, Catherine could have helped them with their travel arrangements. Catherine could keep a secret, even from Diane, but part of the reason she'd agreed to stay in Paris involved her relationship with Harry. Now that he was on his way, perhaps Catherine's plans, whatever they were, were falling into place. "Did you ask them to come?"

Catherine hesitated. Was that a gulp? Then she said, "No."

Diane watched her eyes for any flinch of a lie, but Catherine was too good. There was no way to know for sure. "Are you happy about it?"

"I'm not mad." Catherine had been harder to convince lately that Paris was where they belonged. And she had been helping Diane with money for months because Diane kept losing her jobs. First, the beastly solicitor fired her for "being rude." Then the flower shop fired her because she'd screwed up an important order, even though the customer was being ridiculous. Now she was working at a restaurant, which was terribly hard and didn't pay well enough to keep her, as Daddy liked to say, in the black. If, for all these reasons, Catherine started to think that going back to America was in Diane's best interests, then Diane couldn't trust her. Not when Diane believed, deep in her soul, that her best interests could only be served in Paris.

After a few quiet, thoughtful seconds, Catherine changed the subject. "How was Moulin Rouge after I left?"

"Interesting, but entirely uneventful." Diane let her head fall back on the settee. "The rude man bought me dinner and told me all about his petite amie and then brought me home in his carriage."

"Oh, for goodness sake. I'm too tired for all that. I'm going to bed." Catherine rose from the seat and patted Diane's head before sliding the pocket door to her bedroom closed for the night.

Diane went to her bedroom, lit a candle, undressed, and slipped on a cotton nightgown. As she settled into bed, all her pleasant memories of silly, charming Guillaume were replaced with thoughts of grumpy Ada Beall crossing the ocean to nag them into submission.

The following afternoon, Guillaume was waiting for Marielle at a table along the wall of Chez Henri. It was a small brasserie where Guillaume rarely ate; for this reason, he'd chosen it as the setting for his unpleasant business. When Marielle came in, thirteen minutes late, he rose from his seat. The restaurant staff was setting tables with fresh carnations and folded napkins, preparing for the approaching dinner hour. Other than the workers, they were the only ones in the place.

He'd hoped she'd have broken up with him by now. It was always easier when the girlfriend dumped him first. But seeing as she hadn't, he had to shoulder the burden. Breaking up was often just as hard as being broken up with.

"You look well," Guillaume said. She was lovely in her yellow dress and hat, but not lovely enough to stir anything in his heart, unfortunately.

"You as well, dear."

They ordered drinks, and she settled in, asking about the party she'd missed and making excuses about how she hadn't felt up to it. She was a dramatic sort, Guillaume had learned over the past month. Prone to sullenness when she didn't get her way and moods that she blamed on others. None of this bode well for him, considering what he needed to say to her now. When she started talking about ordering food, and knowing he didn't want to spread this out over a meal, he got to the point. Guillaume reached across the table and patted Marielle's hand, looking her in the sparkling blue eyes that no longer thrilled him.

"Marielle, my dear, I have enjoyed the past several weeks, getting to know you and spending time with you. But I think we should end our attachment." He said it as frankly as he could.

After a sharp intake of breath, her mouth dropped. "What? Why? I don't understand."

"I'm sorry, my dear. I really am. But I just don't see this going any further, and so it is best to end it now."

Tears welled in her eyes, and Guillaume, who hated causing such strife in anyone, gulped his drink. The server came to the table, and seeing Marielle's tears, slunk away.

Marielle's face twisted as she processed what was happening. "But what happened, Guillaume? Everything was so fine."

Guillaume squirmed. The sight of others crying, especially girls and women, filled him with unease. No matter how many times he witnessed this reaction in his younger sisters— whether he'd caused it or not—a painful helplessness always overcame him. He didn't know what to say. Nothing had happened to alter his affection for her. It was just a feeling, a knowing that it wasn't right. How could he explain that without sounding like a mighty jerk?

He watched helplessly as Marielle, happy girl that she was, wailed.

"I bought this dress because I thought you'd like it," she said between sobs. "I told my father about you."

Guillaume cringed. He was desperate for it all to be over. "I'm sorry."

Tears streaming down her face, she looked at him, accusation floating in her watery, red eyes. "Is there someone else?"

The question landed in his ear like a bright idea. Loving someone new was the perfect excuse. It had a finality that all his other excuses lacked. The heart could be fickle and unpredictable. He was uncomfortable lying, in general, even when necessary to preserve peace. But he wasn't as uncomfortable with it as he was about seeing a woman in tears. Why hadn't he thought of it before? He plastered sorrow on his face and looked at her. "Yes. I met someone else."

Marielle shrieked and gulped at the air. The service staff were gathering across the room now to watch. "Who?"

"Her name is Diane." Guillaume passed her his dinner napkin, a useless gesture. A bath towel couldn't stop this. "I'm sure you don't know her. She's American."

Marielle groaned in disgust. Her face had puffed up around her eyes. She swallowed hard as if holding off a fresh wave of agony. Then her face crumpled anew as she spoke. "Oh, isn't that just perfect. How romantic."

Guillaume leaned across the table and said soothingly, "You deserve better than me."

"You're right, I do." Marielle spat the words at him. There was a rage building under her tears now. Then, at a lower volume, she growled. "Just tell me this: did you sleep with her?"

This question, though fair enough, spoke to Marielle's concern that since she hadn't slept with Guillaume, he would lose interest in her. This wasn't a problem for Guillaume, because they'd gone plenty far to keep him interested. But she'd said little things, used throwaway lines, that suggested this preoccupation. Guillaume recognized it for what it was and had tried to reassure her. But now he saw her preoccupation as a convenient opportunity to seal the fate of their relationship. Marielle would get some righteous satisfaction from thinking the other woman was loose. Would it be enough to stop this gut-wrenching emotional display and the worst drink date of his life, Guillaume didn't know.

Guillaume hung his head like a dog and said, "Yes. We slept together."

She sniffed and quieted as if a curtain had fallen on the scene. Then Marielle began blotting her face with the dinner napkin. Finally, she seemed to be pulling herself together. Disgust and an air of superiority replaced the tears, but there was also a hint of understanding. Acceptance. One couldn't deny the forces of nature, the compelling urges, the whims of the heart. And it wasn't all lies. He'd met Diane. Wonderful, fun, bright, American Diane, whom he hadn't been able to stop thinking about with the same fondness of a new favorite song.

"Thank you for your honesty, Guillaume." Marielle sniffed again, already building the wall around her heart.

It worked like a charm. "Thank you, Marielle. And if it helps, there was nothing you could have done to be more perfect."

"Shut up, Guillaume. I don't need your help ever." She stood then, and Guillaume did as well. They faced each other for a moment before Marielle said cooly, "Au revoir."

Then she walked away and was gone. Relief washed over him. It was over. Guillaume paid the check and walked out onto the street. The sun had tilted toward evening, making its slow descent, skimming the city with golden light.

He started walking toward the river. The sidewalk bustled with people. But as that wave of relief subsided, he was left with a gritty feeling of guilt that scraped at his throat and settled into his stomach. He shouldn't have lied about sleeping with Diane. He knew this. It had been the coward's way out, even if he did kind of do it for Marielle's sake.

On the other hand, despite his discomfort, saying he'd slept with her wasn't such a big deal. There was a chance of gossip, but Diane would soon be on a boat back to America. He'd get away with the small lie. But that didn't stop him from feeling bad about it.

He liked Diane, in fact. That was why he'd butted into her argument in the first place. She absolutely glowed, standing there by the bar. Radiated intelligence and fun. Maybe he had met someone.

Just as he was thinking so, Guillaume saw Bouillon Juillet up ahead, the restaurant where Diane said she worked. It was like a sign that he was meant to see Diane again. And Guillaume embraced the fatefulness of it: a newly free man happening by the same place where the pretty new girl worked. So instead of heading home, Guillaume stepped inside.

The restaurant, like the last one, wasn't busy. A few tables of afternoon drinkers were seated around the wide, open dining room. And Diane was right there, standing next to the long mahogany bar, like she was sent by the stars.

But something was wrong. Her face twisted with anger directed at the man next to her, who had his hand on her waist and an insinuating sneer on his face. The only thing Guillaume saw after that was red.

Chapter Three

The unfamiliar and sleazily warm hand landed low on Diane's hip when she bent over to wipe a table. But as she turned to face her assaulter, she barely got a look at him before another, much larger man was lifting him by his collar.

"Take your hands off her at once," the man boomed. And not just any man, but Guillaume Allard, the man from last night at Moulin Rouge.

"Okay, okay," the smaller man said. He backed off right away. He'd had at least three drinks since he arrived, but he wasn't drunk enough to risk a punch to the face. Stumbling backward a step, the handsy patron righted himself quickly and headed for the exit. As he pushed open the door, he called over his shoulder, "You can have her."

"Are you all right?" Guillaume asked, genuine concern in the furrows of his brow.

"I'm fine. It was nothing I couldn't handle, though. And the bartender would have ended it if not." She was almost better equipped to deal with the handsy patron than she was Guillaume. No man had ever stopped in to see her, and she wasn't quite sure visitors were allowed. Could she get in trouble for this? But these fears were coupled with a specific kind of shame that came with working. She wasn't completely used to it. As snobby as it made her, she still felt embarrassed to be working in service. Seeing Guillaume, an acquaintance in her real life, here in the restaurant in her other life, made her skin prickle and her defensive hackles rise. Back at home, this sort of thing would crush a woman's reputation. Her peers, if they had to work at all, became governesses or maybe teachers in respectable homes. They didn't work at the local restaurant. To make matters worse, she hated that she was embarrassed. She hated that women didn't work in service because it could ruin their standing in society and therefore their prospects for marriage. Conditioning like this kept women beholden to men and often miserable because of it. And this was exactly the kind of thinking she'd stayed in Paris to escape. Sure, the lessons of the working life had hit her a little harder than she anticipated. But she didn't like the way she worried what Guillaume was thinking about her, working in a place like this, with a random man's hands on her ass.

"Where is the bartender now?"

"He had to go downstairs for a keg of beer. But merci."

"Of course." He brushed off his arms and smoothed the front of his jacket.

His fine gray suit hung so well on his large, broad frame. He had another red rose pinned to his lapel, and Diane imagined him with a bouquet of them in his room, or maybe a bush in his garden.

"I'm glad I could help. Does that sort of thing happen often?"

"Often enough in this line of work, unfortunately." She dismissed it. The men at the bar could get handsy, and after a few drinks, so could the men at the tables. It came with the job, though she hadn't gotten used to this either—if she ever would. But it no longer surprised her. "And what brings you in?"

Guillaume shrugged. He'd fully settled down from his rescue. "I was actually just walking by here, saw the place, and took a chance that you'd be here."

"Well, it's your lucky day. Have a seat."

Guillaume perched on the stool closest to where Diane was standing at the host stand. The bartender, a scruffy older man from somewhere in the south of France, returned then, manhandling a heavy keg under the counter. He was as tall as Guillaume, a threatening presence that usually inspired guests to keep their hands to themselves. When he saw Guillaume, he asked, "Can I get you something to drink?"

"Merci, whiskey." While the bartender was busy pouring his drink, Guillaume turned to Diane. "I just broke up with my girlfriend."

Diane furrowed her brow. "You're joking?"

"No, I'm not. We just parted ways in a restaurant down the street."

Diane threw her hands up and let her mouth fall open with mock disbelief. But she didn't say anything. If he was the one showing up at her workplace, then he was the one who'd have to do the talking.

"I didn't plan to do it in your neighborhood. It was a coincidence. So I'm here now. To say hello."

"Hello."

"Do you mind if I stay for a while?"

Did she? The bartender didn't seem to mind. Although unexpected, she couldn't deny the pleasure of seeing him. He removed his hat, which hadn't even been knocked out of place in the scuffle to save her dignity.

"You're not here to tell me all about what happened, are you? I don't want to hear about another woman's tears."

He laughed, a hearty and full sound. "I'm not, I assure you."

"Okay, then. As long as you order something, we can visit a little." That was her job. Talk to everyone and be nice. Let the men flirt. It suited her personality, even though the restaurant business, more so than the law or flower business, could be demeaning. She was looking for something else, something a little tamer, like another shop maybe. But until then, rent was due every month, and she needed the work. So that meant restaurant service for the time being. If she had one reason to pack it in and go back to America, it would be that she'd never have to work like this again. That was the only reason. Guillaume would be a pleasant enough way to pass the few hours before she could go home.

After greeting a couple that came in for early dinner and seating them, she circled back to him.

"Did you order dinner?"

"I got the chicken."

"Ha. Did you really?"

"I heard it was good."

"It's chicken."

"I'm looking forward to it."

Her cheeks ached from smiling. At the same time, she didn't want to reinforce his masculine notions of her helplessness. "I could have gotten rid of that guy, you know. I don't need saving."

"You shouldn't have to handle such things. You shouldn't have to endure them in the first place."

"No one should." She nodded and patted his arm, which was broad and firm and quite capable of dispatching creeps.

"You're right."

"I am right. Just because a man can't control himself doesn't mean that I shouldn't work here."

"Of course not."

"And I'm no better than anyone else, no matter what my father says. I can work here."

"Absolutely." He shrugged innocently. "My mother was my father's first secretary."

His chicken arrived. While he ate, she did just enough work to maintain the air of doing work. The thing she did love about working in a restaurant was the atmosphere. The place was clean and gleaming. The food smelled delicious. Everyone was there to have a good time. She didn't know anyone, but they were the kinds of people she might know if she were still the kind of woman who lived on her father's money at the Grand Hôtel. The neighborhood was trendy. Outside, the city pulsed with people out having a good time too. Some weren't, but they were easy enough to ignore when you were in the right mood. Diane loved Paris. Here, she wasn't from a prominent family, she was just a girl. But thinking about it reminded her of her father's ambassadors on the way. They would be there soon. They could be landing right now, stepping off the boat in Calais, a mere train ride from Paris.

Guillaume laughed then at something the bartender said. He had a nice laugh. It wasn't the laugh of a man adrift without love, it was the laugh of a person who relished life. Diane liked it.

There was one way to stay in Paris—falling in love with a French man. A marriage would as good as make her French. French men were different from American ones—less conservative, more outwardly flirtatious. Guillaume was even the kind of fun-loving, easy-going man she could probably fall right in love with. But she wasn't going to do that. She wasn't going to fall in love and get married to Guillaume or anyone else because a shackle was still a shackle in France. She wanted a life of experiences and freedom, not domesticity and servitude. Paris was just the start of her grand adventure. Attachments would only tie her down.

Fun, on the other hand, she was always open for. Which was why, when he was finished eating and getting ready to leave, she said, "Am I going to see you again?"

He looked at her for a long moment. His blue eyes sparkled a little more now that he'd had a drink. He was relaxed. His casual, desirous gaze swept from her face down the front of her. She may as well have been naked, not dressed in her uniform white blouse and cravat.

"Absolutely. Yes. Do you work tomorrow, Diane?"

"No. I have the day off."

"Will you have dinner with me tomorrow night?"

"I don't know, Guillaume." The Bealls were on their way. She wasn't exactly sure when they'd arrive. And despite everything she'd said about not falling for a French man, the tingly elation she felt hearing him ask to see her again so soon sure felt like it. "You know, I find it morally questionable for a man to jump from woman to woman."

"Nothing serious, then?"

"Deal." Another group came into the restaurant then, and Diane had to get back to work.

Guillaume noticed and got up to go. "I'll pick you up at seven?"

"That's fine. But don't come to the door. The woman who runs the house does not allow gentlemen to come around. I'll meet you outside." Madame Tremblay threw one of their old housemates out for taking up with a married man. Hers was a house for respectable, working women, and Madame was always carrying on about the tragedy that could befall a woman in the clutches of a man who had no intentions of marrying her. Diane wasn't about to get thrown out, especially not with the Bealls coming.

Guillaume swooped in close, closer. Close enough to smell the mint and vanilla of whatever manly concoctions he applied to his body. Diane, suddenly weak in the knees, put a hand on the podium to steady herself.

"Au revoir," he whispered. He kissed her cheek and then left the restaurant.

Watching him pass by the front window, she took a deep breath to collect herself and then greeted the guests who'd just come in the door. For the rest of her shift, she smiled to herself. Dinner with a handsome man, having a little fun, was perhaps the perfect distraction from the fact of her impending visitors and the potential disaster they brought with them.

The next day, Catherine and Diane were both off from work. With the Bealls' arrival imminent, lounging in the drawing room at the house on Rue de Fortuny was akin to waiting on the edge of their seats. Diane had filled nearly eight pages of her journal with anxieties about why in the world her father had sent them to Paris. Now she was reading the help-wanted advertisements in the paper and humming softly to herself, even though Catherine had twice asked her to please stop.

Catherine wasn't doing much better with the anticipation. She was fidgety, and she'd sighed dreamily at least ten times since breakfast. She'd been holding her self-improvement book in front of her face all day, but she'd hardly turned a page.

Although she was dying to, Diane didn't mention Guillaume stopping by her work the night before or that they were having dinner together. Plus, Madame had been there most of the day, cleaning and cleaning and cleaning. Diane and her housemates avoided talking about men when Madame was present because she was staunchly averse to men coming around. Madame was a stickler about the women who lived in her pension. They had to be honest women—not prostitutes or courtesans. Prostitution was rampant in Paris; this was Diane's least favorite part about the city. There were opportunities here for women to make a living, but that was, unfortunately, the primary one. It wasn't personal against women who chose those paths, Madame always clarified, but they couldn't stay at 77 Rue de Fortuny. So Madame took a keen interest in who was picking up and dropping off the women who lived under her roof. For this reason, Diane only mentioned that she had plans later for dinner with friends. Catherine was so distracted she hardly cared to ask.

When the bell downstairs at the front door rang, Diane set her newspaper aside and listened to footfalls while someone— probably Cook or Madame—answered it. These were forgettable, everyday sounds that didn't garner much attention, but they were awaiting word from Ada, waiting to hear that they had arrived in Paris, so Diane held her breath. It all whooshed out of her when Madame yelled up that a telegram had arrived for them. Diane and Catherine looked at each other, faces conveying the mutual knowing that this was it.

"Is it for me or Catherine?" Maybe she could ignore it a little longer if they'd only addressed it to Catherine.

Catherine swatted Diane's arm.

"It's got both your names on it," Madame yelled with exasperation.

No doubt either the ship carrying the Bealls had gone down at sea or they were here. After their pregnant pause, both sisters got up and went downstairs.

Madame was standing strong as a statue in the hallway. She wore her summer garb—a well-worn and impressively clean apron over a plain linen dress. There were crescents of moisture under each arm. Her salt and pepper hair was coming loose around her nape the way it always did as the day wore on her. Madame owned the house, but she ran it with as much elbow grease as the people she employed to help her. She passed the telegram to Catherine with a business-like smile. "You're expecting family, aren't you?"

"Oui," Catherine said at the same time Diane said, "Don't remind me."

Catherine read the blue paper, her face conveying nothing. They were standing at the base of the stairs in the hall between the dining room and the drawing room. Finally, Catherine finished and passed the message to Diane.

"They're here. At the Grand Hôtel. They want us to come."

"Come for what?"

"Dinner tonight, but it sounds like they've also gotten us a room."

Diane read the petit bleu:

We've arrived. The journey was arduous, and we'll rest tonight at the hotel. We hope to see you at dinner. We've booked a room for you, if you'd like to join us.

Diane read it again, trying to gain a deeper sense of the missive's nuance. Join us sounded suspiciously like let's go back to America. "Why on earth would we want to stay at the hotel?"

"So we can all be together, I guess."

"Well, isn't that cozy?" Diane scoffed. "But no, thank you. I'm not going."

"You're not?"

"Are you?" The question was loaded. Catherine had denied participating in their travel plans, but Diane still suspected her sister of ulterior motives.

Madame was still lingering there and with her hands in her apron pockets, and she raised her eyebrows. She was a stern, wide, motherly woman, though she'd never had children of her own. Her husband was long dead. And so now she rented out rooms in her giant house, keeping the women fed and nurtured, making sure they followed all her rules. Diane took the rules seriously and used the utmost care every time she broke one. Madame was also generous. She knew the sisters' full backstory, but she never seemed to come down hard on either side. However, she did have parents, so she tended to be sympathetic to the American sisters with their complicated upbringing. Maybe even a little in awe of them.

"What?" Diane asked her. "I'm not ready to spend an evening with Daddy's petite amie. She doesn't even like me."

"That's not true," Catherine protested.

"Either way, we all know the real reason they're here in Paris. I'm not going. You can tell them I'm at work."

Madame clucked her tongue and then turned to go back downstairs. She could only handle so much nonsense.

"Well, I'm going, so I guess you don't have to." Catherine started back up with a traitorous spring in her step. She was obeying and going to the hotel because she was excited to see Harry.

"You'll cover for me?" Diane followed her. She didn't want to go to the hotel, but she also didn't want her almost-stepmother sending off a letter to their father about how Diane had snubbed them on their first night in Paris.

"What do you mean? Tell them you're working instead of what?"

"I'm having dinner with friends."

"Fine. I'll cover for you."

"I had plans, after all. They can't just show up and expect me to do whatever they say."

"I know."

"But that's exactly what they do expect. That's what Daddy is hoping for. That we'll cave as soon as he puts a little pressure on us. We're not starving to death. We haven't come crawling home with our tails between our legs. So he had to do something."

"Or maybe he's sent them just to make sure we're all right." Catherine's voice rose with the escalating tension.

"Maybe. But if we don't stick together, they can use that against us, you know."

"What do you mean?" Catherine flung her hands in the air, exasperated.

"If they can ensnare one of us, then the other will come along easier." Diane raised her volume as well. They were in their rooms now, behind the closed door.

"And you think that if I go to the hotel, that they're dividing us?"

"Aren't they? Shouldn't we stick together?"

"Maybe on this we're already divided."

"Stop it, we are not."

"Listen, I'm not going to argue with you. If you don't want to go to the hotel, I will tell them whatever you want me to as your excuse. And it doesn't mean they're winning if I want to go see them. We don't even know the game they've come here to play. So let's not get worked up about it yet. They just got here."

Diane sighed. Catherine was right. They'd only just arrived. The game hadn't even started yet; no reason to lose her head already.

"Are you excited to see Harry?"

Catherine shrugged. "I'm a little afraid, to be honest. It's been a long time."

"But you've written."

"Yes. We've been in touch. Infrequently. I didn't know they were coming until we heard from Daddy." Catherine leaned against the jamb of her bedroom door. She was quiet and thoughtful for a moment. "I have to get ready for dinner."

"Me too." Diane went to her room and started picking through her piles of clothes.

Catherine and Harry had always been more than almost-step siblings. Diane didn't know all of the details—Catherine always kept some for herself—but she knew the feelings were mutually romantic. Their parents had no idea. Who knew what they'd say about it? Catherine and Harry weren't really related, and they hadn't grown up together as siblings. But because their father and his stepmother were in a relationship, everyone was bound to have feelings about it. It wasn't like she was bringing someone home to meet the family; she was picking from the family table.

Diane didn't envy her sister. Love could be such a complication, such a tether. She couldn't imagine coming all the way to Paris and longing for the boy back at home in Woollett. That, in itself, was a great tragedy, as far as Diane was concerned. Her sister was blowing her chance at a wonderful experience. The full Paris.

When Guillaume's carriage approached the corner of Avenue de Villiers and Rue de Fortuny, Diane was waiting on the sidewalk. He waved to her through the glass, and she smiled when she saw him. But before he could get out to help her, Diane pulled open the door, stepped inside, and sat on the bench next to Guillaume.

A subtle orange blossom perfume filled the carriage. She was dressed up and less disheveled than she'd been the other two times he'd seen her—once after dancing and the other time getting manhandled at work. That she cleaned up so well and obviously didn't lack sophistication pleased him. Not that sophistication was so important to Guillaume, but it was something they shared. Both of them came from self-made families, which was similar in a way to sharing a religion or ethnicity. Most of his friends had inherited their wealth, and many looked down on Guillaume because, even with fortunes being equal, the Allards actually had to earn theirs. He'd not considered that his family probably shared this fact with many of the upstart American tourists who seemed to be everywhere in his hometown these days.

"It's lovely to see you again, Diane."

"You as well, monsieur." She relaxed into the seat and sighed like she was relieved to be there. With him or away from something else, he wasn't sure. Her eyes sparkled and her lips were the color of berries. "Now that I've made my escape, please tell me our plans for the evening."

"Dinner first, and then I thought we'd see what sounded fun. I know some people entertaining not far from the restaurant," Guillaume said, unable to take his eyes away from her. His curiosity about her kept growing. "Escape from what, exactly?"

Diane sat up a little, seemed to weigh her words. "Oh, nothing. Just a boring day at the house is all. I'm starving, by the way."

"I made a reservation at Café Riche. I hope you'll like it."

"Ooh la la! I've never been, but since I started working in a restaurant, I can assure you there is nothing greater than getting to sit in a comfortable seat while being waited on by someone else. I'm sure I'll love it."

At the restaurant, Guillaume gave the maitre d' his name and they were promptly seated at a table in a secluded part of the polished dining room. It was dressed with a candelabra and red tablecloth. Diane arranged herself on the chair. Her dress was so blue that it shined against her pale shoulders and neck. There were blue feathers embedded in her golden brown curls. She ordered champagne, and Guillaume asked for whiskey.

After the server returned with their drinks and left with their dinner order, Guillaume asked, "How was your day off?"

"It was fine." She shifted around in her seat.

"Are you uncomfortable?"

"What? No. But it was the kind of day I need a distraction from. Tell me about your day." She gulped her wine, taking in such a mouthful that she coughed a little as it went down. When the server brought bread, she asked for another champagne.

"I played tennis with Antoine."

"Oh, tennis?"

"Yes. Do you play?"

"I had a lesson or two back in Woollett." She laughed. "And before you make a joke about not believing a place as backwoods as Woollett could have tennis courts—yes, we did have a tennis court in Woollett."

"A tennis court? Singular?"

"Yes! Just the one. So are you a serious tennis player?"

"I am as serious as an amateur can be." He wasn't joking. He lived a leisurely life, thanks to his father's good fortune. He had little that he needed to take seriously. So tennis it was.

Diane laughed. She was lively and bright with conversation. But she finished two glasses of champagne before dinner arrived. Then she drank two more before Guillaume had finished his food and half of hers. She didn't consume them in a celebratory way, but like something was bothering her. No matter how many times he asked if she was okay, she insisted it was nothing. Twice she told him, "I'm just so thrilled to be out." By the time they left the restaurant, she was boisterous and ready for whatever was next.

The friends he knew in the area were hosting guests, which sounded much more civilized than Guillaume knew to expect from them. They were artists, independently wealthy and avant-garde—great company but also usually doing harder drugs than champagne. Even if Guillaume and Diane didn't partake, not every woman would be open to such an evening, but something about Diane made him bet that she wouldn't mind.

They walked the few blocks down the grand Boulevard des Italiens to the building, and they took the stairs up to the apartment. Standing outside the door in the corridor, Guillaume knocked. Muffled music emanated from within.

"What song is that they're playing?" Diane asked.

"I can't tell." When no one answered after a second knock, he pushed the door open. Inside they were greeted with a nod by a disinterested man and woman in a black feathered hat who seemed to have forgotten she was near a door at all. Or perhaps hadn't heard them knocking over the music. They looked drowsily at Diane and Guillaume and then returned to their conversation.

"It's an American ragtime song that I haven't heard since coming to France!" Diane beamed.

Taking her by the hand, Guillaume led her through the hallway and into the open living area. The ceiling was two stories high and a wall of windows looked out over a breathtaking view of the city and Tower sparkling. People, most of whom appeared to be drinking absinthe, were gathered here and there in groups, talking and bobbing their heads to the raucous piano music coming from somewhere deeper inside. Several windows were open, but a haze of smoke clouded the room.

Diane marveled at the sight, and when a glass of absinthe was placed in her hand, she willingly accepted.

"Have you tried absinthe?" Guillaume narrowed his eyes on her.

"Yes, Father," she joked. Then she raised her glass to Guillaume's. "Santé."

"Santé."

She drank and, cheeks bulging, nearly spit the harsh liquor back out. Her eyes welled as she swallowed.

"Are you okay?"

"I am, though now I'll need a cigarette. Do you have one?"

Guillaume nodded and led her out to the balcony, which ran the length of the apartment and was rimmed by a chest-high balustrade. The night air cooled Guillaume's head. He produced his cigarette case from an interior pocket of his jacket, and lit Diane's for her. She inhaled and exhaled a cloud of smoke, and the cool air seemed to refresh her too.

But time sped up from there. After smoking, Guillaume introduced Diane to the hosts—the Bernards, who were rich with inherited money. Guillaume and Diane danced for a while. The pianist—or pianists who were taking turns, rather— weren't professionally trained but equipped with enough knowledge of the instrument to keep the party going. They smoked and drank and met new people and listened to stories. The details of the evening's events became slippery as Guillaume finished his absinthe. The smoky haze in the room swirled with colors. One drink became four, and Guillaume lost track of how much Diane had had. He didn't know anything about her tolerance for imbibing, but based on his experience with other women, who tended to be smaller and more easily affected, she was probably much drunker than he was.

Still, she carried on, conversing enthusiastically on whatever topic everyone was on about. And she became increasingly flirtatious. Touching Guillaume at every chance, passing sultry glances his way, making use of every opportunity for a double entendre.

When they found themselves alone together again on the balcony, she teetered on her heels as she pointed at him with her cigarette, "You, monsieur, are more fun than I thought you'd be."

Guillaume smiled and smoked, watching her wobble. She dropped her cigarette and stepped in close to him, practically straddling his thigh. She took the cigarette from his mouth and dropped it as she leaned into him. Her swimming eyes focused on his mouth like a target, and as drunk and soft as Guillaume had become, he perked up when her mouth met his with a quick, sloppy, sweep of her tongue. She tasted like cigarettes and booze. The orange blossom scent clung to her skin.

When she pulled away, she bit her lip and looked purposefully at him. "When we leave here, Guillaume, you're coming back to my place."

He thought she was joking after all her talk about the strict house rules against gentleman callers. Then she brought it up two more times.

Much later that night, the crowd having thinned, they fell into a conversation with the party stragglers about the Spanish artist who'd been displaying his work in all the cafés that everyone was talking about. Aside from the hosts, there was another vaguely familiar couple—a young man and an older woman—whose names Guillaume had forgotten if he ever knew them at all. On the other side of Diane sat two gentlemen that Guillaume was sure he'd never seen before, and next to them was a woman he was sure he had seen but couldn't place. Guillaume had stopped drinking but he was still pretty drunk, and he was only halfway following the conversation. Then, before he even noticed it was going around, someone passed Diane an opium pipe.

She hesitated like she didn't know what to do with it, but her demeanor suggested she was eager to learn. The man who'd passed it to her showed her how it worked, and she took a hit, coughing as she exhaled the spicy smoke. Guillaume, not one to miss out, hit it too. But this turned out to be the tipping point, after which there were gaps in Guillaume's memory of the evening.

Later, he would barely recall riding in his carriage in the earliest moments of dawn, heading to Rue de Fortuny. Diane had her hand on Guillaume's lapel, and as she slid into his lap, she dipped her head to smell the faded red rose pinned to his lapel. Straddling him, she drew in close. Her face was flushed but not tired. His heart thumped in his chest, pulsing down to his lap under her weight. He had a thought then—a single drunken insight that bubbled up through the haze of booze—that this woman would be his complete undoing. Before he could dwell on it too much, her mouth lowered down to his in a liquid slow motion. Her breath was boozy and warm and lovely on his skin. They kissed and tasted and tugged at each others' clothing, swirling as if they were caught in a drain.

When the carriage came to a stop outside number seventy-seven, Diane insisted that she could get him in undetected. Everyone was fast asleep. All they had to do was make it in the door, up to the foyer, and up one more flight of stairs to her empty rooms. No problem, she said with a wave of her hand. And so he sent his carriage home.

From somewhere in her dress, Diane produced a key and unlocked the front door. They crept inside, and Guillaume followed her up the dark stairs, stifling giggles and failing to keep his hands to himself. He wanted to kiss her again. Whatever she would give him, he would willingly take and thoroughly enjoy. He didn't make it a habit of falling into bed with women he'd only known for a few days because it was, in his experience, often more trouble than it was worth. Feelings developing prematurely and all that. But Diane seemed different. She was bold and unaffected in a way that other women weren't. She didn't seem like the kind of person who'd burst into tears over a break up, certainly not in a restaurant. In fact, she surprised him. Over and over again. Saying the unexpected, seeing things differently. Not only did she light up his every sense, she was fun, natural company as well. Now he was looking forward to getting her clothes off and nestling between her luscious thighs.

Diane led him into a dark room and closed the door behind them. There was enough light streaming in the window to see they were in a small sitting room with a settee and escritoire. Diane swayed on her feet as she lit a lamp, and then with an exaggerated shushing, inspected one of the two dark bedrooms. The door was open and the bed was empty. He wasn't sure how, but he understood that this meant her sister had stayed at the Grand Hôtel. If Diane had explained why her sister was staying there, Guillaume had forgotten. He didn't care to ask now. He took Diane in his arms and thumped his knee against the settee, almost tumbling onto it.

Diane giggled again and pulled him toward the other door, the door to her room. They kissed as they passed the threshold, as if they might not make it if their lips weren't fused. But almost as soon as they hit the bed, they must have passed out cold. Because not even a blur of a memory remained when he awoke the next morning to the sound of someone screaming.

Chapter Four

As if from the bottom of a deep well, Diane heard the click of the outer door to their rooms open, the shuffling of feet, voices. Her eyes cracked open and registered the familiar sliver of morning light coming through her bedroom window. Her head throbbed. It hurt to move. It hurt to be alive.

"Diane." The voice came through the door. It didn't sound like Catherine.

Diane jerked upright as her bedroom door slid open. She blinked, and her almost-stepmother was standing there, eyes as big and fierce as the sun. Her scream—a completely unnecessary shriek of terror—brought Diane fully back to life. Beside her, the sleeping male form sprang up, nearly falling off the bed as he stood. Guillaume. His bloodshot eyes were alert with panic, his face red and creased from heavy sleep.

Catherine stepped past Ada, and her mouth dropped open.

"Please, don't scream," Diane groaned. Her head felt like marbles were rolling around in it, but she quickly pulled together the fact that she was in bed with a man. She didn't remember how exactly they got there. And now the people her father had sent to check up on her had caught her in the act.

"What in the world are you doing? And who is this?" Ada demanded.

"What are you doing here!?" Diane demanded right back. "Catherine?"

"You said she was working?" Ada said accusingly to Catherine.

"I…" Catherine, brow raised in question, looked at Diane. "I thought that's what she said."

"I'm sorry, but what is happening right now?" Guillaume said in English. He was still standing there, trapped and confused. His hair was standing up straight on one side.

"Pardon me, but who are you, monsieur?" Harry said, stepping forward to play the protective, brotherly role. They were all gathered in Diane's room now—her useless sister Catherine, Ada, and Harry—staring at her and Guillaume.

"Guillaume, this is Ada Beall. She's my father's fiancée. And her stepson, Harry Beall," Diane croaked. Her mouth was so dry it felt like it might stick shut. She spoke in English for her family's benefit. Guillaume would have to keep up. "And this is Guillaume Allard."

"Enchanté," he said weakly.

"And who is Guillaume Allard?"

"Apologies." His accent was adorable. "I'm not sure what's going on between you, and Diane didn't mention she was expecting any guests. I know this must look like something that I assure you it isn't. My intentions with mademoiselle are purely honorable. You see… something happened… I ran into her this morning. Earlier. Much earlier. And then something happened, and we came here, and we…"

He trailed off. This was bad. Madame would throw her out. Ada would tell her father. Her father would probably force them to marry. But wait…

Watching Guillaume stumble for an excuse brought the perfect one to Diane's mind. It was so perfect that it arrived on her tongue fully formed and ready to go.

"Stop. I can explain," she said, holding up her hands. She was sitting on the edge of the bed, which was rumpled but fully made, thank goodness. Catching Guillaume's eye, she nodded, hoping he'd play along. "We're engaged."

"What?" Ada, Catherine, and Guillaume erupted at the same time into a cacophony of questions and outrage, of which Diane could only catch a few discouraging words here and there.

"Diane, what are you talking about?" Ada yelled loud enough to break through everyone's chatter.

Looking again at Guillaume, pleading with her eyes that he wouldn't say anything to the contrary, Diane said, "It's true. We're engaged. We've only just decided. But, everyone, this is my fiancé. I didn't mean for you to meet him like this, certainly, but we were out late celebrating and ended up here. Nothing untoward happened, as you can see. We're fully dressed. But it was quite a late night."

To his credit, Guillaume didn't argue. Poor thing, he stood there puzzled, no doubt lost piecing together the evening and trying to keep up with her lies.

Diane stood up from her bed and for a moment the ground swayed beneath her. She had been so drunk. So very drunk. And now she maybe was still a little drunk. A rush of nausea rose from deep in her gut and climbed to the back of her throat. She swallowed against the will of her gritty tongue. Her clothes were strewn about—a corset dangling from the chair, a dressing gown and feather boa in a pool on the floor, her cancan skirt from the other night draped over her chair— adding to the unseemliness of the scene. There was no way she could prevent Ada from telling her father about this. She was probably composing the letter in her mind already. Diane had to think fast. Shepherding them toward the door, Diane said, "If you'll just give us a moment."

Without a thought toward propriety, she closed the pocket door and turned to Guillaume.

"Engaged!?" He looked as sick as she felt.

"Just follow my lead, please." She brought her hands together in front of her chest, imploring him to help her.

"Follow your lead to where, exactly?" He whisper yelled the words.

"Pretend that we're engaged."

"And then what? Marry you?"

"No, no. Just until they go back to America. A couple of weeks at most. Please." Diane touched his arm. "If they think we're engaged, then there's no way they can get me to go with them. I'll be able to stay in Paris. It will be perfect. And Harry won't have to challenge you to a duel for finding you in my bed."

Guillaume wrinkled his brow and raised his hands as if in retreat. "I'm not so sure—"

"Please, Guillaume. You won't even have to do anything except come for dinner once or twice. Then they'll leave, and we can stop pretending."

"A duel?" He ran a hand through his hair, appearing to be in agony. She couldn't blame him. This was certainly more than either of them bargained for when they agreed to have dinner.

"Please, Guillaume. There won't be a duel, but we can't stay in here. Just help me."

"Okay, okay. I'll help you."

"Oh, thank goodness." Diane rose on her tiptoes and kissed his cheek. The blond stubble scratched her lips. If she didn't feel like throwing up, she'd want to feel that scratchiness elsewhere on her body. He was cute even when he looked like he'd been trampled by a horse. He'd make the perfect fiancé.

"I feel like the biggest idiot in the world that this is happening."

"It's fine. But you should go." Diane went to the door. When she pulled it open, she said, "I'll explain more later."

Everyone was waiting for them in the sitting room. Catherine and Harry on the settee, and Ada in the chair at the escritoire, all with expectant eyes on Diane and Guillaume.

"Yes," Diane said. "Sorry about that again. And Guillaume has to go, but I'm sure you'll see him again later. Since we're getting married."

"You must join us for dinner tonight," Ada said after a chilly silence.

Now that Diane was awake and functioning just above survival, she noticed that Ada looked fresh and well. Her graying hair was pulled back in a high, tight bun, and her cotton floral dress was modest and plain but not completely unfashionable. Her dark eyes were bright and viciously alert, like those of an owl. She must have recovered from her arduous voyage. But did Ada believe the engagement story? Diane couldn't tell.

Ada smiled warmly and continued, "We're all eager to get to know the gentleman who has captured Diane's heart. Can you come to the Grand Hôtel tonight?"

Guillaume looked from Ada to Diane, his face twisted with panic. A bead of sweat fell down the side of his forehead. Goodness, he was a terrible actor. Bad enough to blow the whole plan. Diane sighed and nodded to encourage him.

"It would be a pleasure," Guillaume finally said.

"Let me walk you out." Diane was eager to end this awkward scene. When Guillaume didn't go for the door, Diane reached for his arm and moved him along. To her family, she said over her shoulder, "We'll be right back."

Diane closed the door behind them and looked at Guillaume hard.

"I'm sorry. I am so ill from drinking that I feel like dying, and I just wasn't prepared for this."

She pulled him toward the stairs, wary of Madame, who could be lurking and listening from anywhere. With Ada and Harry already visiting, there was a good chance Madame wouldn't notice Diane slipping Guillaume out. Diane was banking on it. "It's fine. Just go home and sober up. I'll need you to make it through dinner, unless you want me to make excuses."

"No. I can do it." Guillaume looked tired enough to pass back out.

When they reached the bottom of the stairs, Diane checked for Madame but didn't see her or anyone else. She might be able to trick the woman into believing he'd come in with her guests, but she'd rather not tangle the lies with any more threads. They crossed the foyer and went down to the front door.

Outside on the stoop, the street was quietly carrying on with the morning. People on their way to work, delivery trucks making their stops. The heat would come later, but now the air was still pleasant. Diane dropped Guillaume's arm and faced him.

"Thank you for this. I promise to make it as painless as possible. They'll be gone in no time, and then we can part ways."

Guillaume looked somehow more tired, blinking in the sunlight. He said solemnly, "It's fine. But listen, about last night. I'm sorry to say I don't remember a lot of it. I'm not even sure how we got here."

"We took your carriage, and then I insisted you come inside. I don't remember much after that, but we're both fully dressed, so it couldn't be much."

"I remember kissing, quite fervently."

Glimpses of that flashed in her mind, now that he mentioned it. "So maybe if we're going to do this, we agree that there won't be any more heavy drinking."

"Or drug use."

"Or drug use. Yes. There was that too, wasn't there?" A flicker of a memory of smoking with an unfamiliar group at the tail end of the party started taking shape in her mind. "And no more fervent kissing."

"Ah, yes. Perhaps that's not a good idea."

"Though some affection might be necessary to carry on the ruse."

"Yes. Well, I can be publicly affectionate."

"I appreciate that." Diane smiled. This might be fun. But her head hurt so much, it was hard to be sure.

"Who are these people again?"

"The woman is my father's fiancée. He keeps telling everyone he's going to marry her, but it's been over seven years. And the man is her stepson. My sister is in love with him."

"And your father has sent them to bring you home."

"They haven't said as much, but yes. I'm sure that's what they're up to."

"This is all quite complicated."

"Alas. Welcome to the Talbot family." She smiled even though her stomach churned inside her like an oar pushing through water. "I'll see you later, then?"

"Yes." He nodded and walked up the street. He would probably catch a carriage, but Diane didn't have time to ask or care. She needed to find a glass of water and get back upstairs to control the damage.

Guillaume walked up Rue de Fortuny and caught a cab on Avenue de Villiers. The carriage swaying made him queasy, and so he closed his eyes. Pieces of the evening replayed in his mind. Diane getting so drunk. Him getting so drunk. The drunken kissing and the feel of her warm neck and shoulders in his hands. He'd gotten carried away, to say the least. They both had, and they'd created a sticky mess to wake up in. And Diane's family! Guillaume laughed at the memory of their faces; he could do so now that he was away from it, safely on his way home. The woman—Diane's almost-stepmother—had looked like she wanted to kill him. The way she'd screamed. It was funny, but also deeply shameful. Guillaume never wanted to see those people again. And yet he'd agreed to do just that. This had trouble written all over it.

He should never have allowed Diane to drink so much. Not that he could have stopped her. And if he'd understood the situation correctly, she'd told them all she was at work. No wonder Diane had seemed anxious when they were out. She was probably looking over her shoulder the whole time.

But he'd told Marielle that he'd slept with Diane. As an excuse for breaking up with her. It was a cowardly exit to the relationship, and he wasn't proud of himself for taking it. At the time, it felt like a convenient excuse. A name he could give to satisfy Marielle and get himself out of an uncomfortable situation. But he hadn't thought it through. Then he spent the evening with Diane. He'd enjoyed her company greatly. He liked her, and his misdeed had begun to weigh on him. His lie didn't exactly paint Diane in the most respectable light. Although it was unlikely, he'd feel terrible if word somehow made it back to her. Or if her reputation suffered for it. It sickened him to think that he'd potentially harmed her in this way. He'd done a bad thing. The least he could do was help her with this. It was the gentlemanly way out. He could do it. And he couldn't deny that Diane knew how to have fun.

The cab hit some morning traffic, but Guillaume was home in under thirty minutes. He went straight to his room, where he undressed and promptly fell into a fitful, sobering sleep.

After the scene with Guillaume, Catherine and Harry went for a walk to Parc Monceau a few blocks away, and Ada went downstairs to wait for Diane to get cleaned up and dressed. In her room, Diane took a pill for her headache and drank a cup of coffee, which muted the throbbing. She brushed out her hair and braided it. And she washed her face with cold water. Although she began to feel as if she could live, embarrassment and anger still roiled in her gut like nausea. Her shame was hardening. She couldn't believe they'd come to the house and found her like that. It made her want to crawl into bed and stay there until they were on the boat back to America. But she couldn't do that. She dawdled in her room as long as she could, and then Diane went downstairs to face her mess.

She found Ada in the drawing room, sitting on the toile bench by the unlit fireplace and primly sipping a cup of tea. Madame or Cook must have made it especially for her because usually everyone in the house drank coffee. Ada raised her eyebrows when Diane came in, but didn't say anything. Diane poured herself a cup from the teapot on the sideboard and sat in the armchair across from Ada.

"That's better, isn't it?" Ada said as Diane settled in.

"What is?"

"Being clean and freshly dressed and presentable."

Diane let her head fall back against the chair and let out a long, dramatic sigh. The pressed tin ceiling was clean but old, like everything in the house. Paint had flaked off a few spots, faded in others. Diane didn't have the energy to argue with Ada right now. She didn't want to find the words or muster up the determination to express them. In fact, Diane had never existed anywhere she wanted to be less than sitting there across from Ada. But here she was, in quite a mess. A mess that could get worse if Ada said something about Guillaume being in the house to Madame. Surely Ada wouldn't risk offending Madame. And as long as they were engaged, then probably the events of the morning could be swept under a rug. The problem now was maintaining the ruse. Diane lifted her head and decided that the best way out was through.

"I'm sorry, Ada. About this morning."

"I appreciate the apology, I suppose. But you gave us all quite a surprise."

"That was never my intention."

"I should hope not." Ada sipped her tea. "Your father will be quite surprised as well."

"Well, isn't love always surprising?" Diane said, a snide smile spread across her face and then disappeared as she let her head fall back again. Clearly one thing hadn't changed since Diane had come to Paris: the fact that Ada annoyed her so deeply and thoroughly.

Diane had a long history of being hard on Ada. Ada started spending time with their father about a year after their mother's death. It was an appropriate length of mourning, as far as society was concerned. But Diane disagreed. After the trauma of watching her die, Diane hadn't stopped mourning her mother after a year. Much of her teenage angst derived from the fact that so many people around her had stopped. She didn't want to move on. Her whole world was an ocean of grief, of longing for a loved one who would never return. A hole in her life that she couldn't fathom filling. Her sister understood. But obviously her father didn't because, as far as Diane was concerned, he'd replaced their mother as if she were a pair of worn-out shoes or a horse that got too old. This feeling only worsened the more Diane got to know Ada.

Compared to their mother, Ada was dull and humorless. She wasn't as beautiful as Mama had been. She never joked or seemed to have fun. Diane could still remember the way her heart sank when her father told them at dinner he had asked Ada to be his wife. Diane had been almost fifteen. That was seven, nearly eight years ago. What kind of woman would tag along with a man and tolerate being engaged for years without a wedding in sight? Either get married or don't, but don't hedge around in limbo. The fact that Ada, who had only partially succeeded at worming her way into the family, couldn't seal the deal spoke volumes to Diane about Ada as a person. It also spoke something of how their mother's death may have affected their father. The sisters didn't know the details, but maybe Daddy was only willing to take it so far. Maybe he was reluctant to marry another woman because he was still in love with Mama. This was how they excused their father.

"Diane," Ada said mildly.

"Yes?"

"I didn't come all this way to argue with you. I don't even really care about the ways you debauch yourself out of sight of your father. But now that I'm here, and tasked with spending time with you, all I ask is that you maintain some level of decorum so that I—and your father—can remain ignorant of your transgressions."

Although she wouldn't have described her lifestyle as debauchery, Diane let that pass and focused on Ada's task. "So what did you come here to do, Ada? What is your task?"

Ada rarely scolded Diane, even when she was a child and sorely deserved it. She always left that to the governesses and nannies, which was fine. Maybe Ada wasn't interested in replacing their mother, or maybe she didn't feel she had the right. But Daddy had sent Ada here to say something. Come home now, maybe. Or what do you think you're doing. Diane crossed her arms, readied her defense. Regardless of Ada's mission, Diane wasn't going to make it any easier for her.

"Like I said, spend time with you and your sister. You can't just expect never to see us again simply by not getting on a boat. You didn't come home, so we came to you."

"On Daddy's behalf."

"Your father has to work, Diane, you know that."

"And the goal is to bring us home?"

"Are you ready to come home?" Ada raised an eyebrow. Now she was the one with the snide smile.

Diane, not as sharp because of the lingering effects of alcohol, relented. She'd argued all she could right now. So instead of answering Ada's question, she asked about her trip. "You mentioned it was arduous."

"Oh, it was. I don't like to complain, and the ship was well-appointed. But I am much happier at home than anywhere else. And I still feel like the ground is swaying underneath my feet after bobbing around the ocean for so long."

"I remember that feeling. It lasted for two days when we arrived."

"Well, it is not my favorite sensation."

"No seafaring life for you then," Diane said, jokingly.

"Of course not." Ada pursed her lips.

"How long are you staying?"

"Almost four weeks. Twenty-six days."

Too long. "And what are your plans for your time in Paris?"

Ada shrugged. "Oh, well, I'm not sure. We just want to spend time with you and your sister. At the hotel. And here, I suppose, if that's what you prefer."

Diane would prefer they hadn't come at all. And she didn't buy what Ada said about wanting to spend time with them. "I will have to work most days, you realize. Catherine may have more flexibility at her job, but I only started a few weeks ago at the restaurant and my schedule is different every day."

Ada's wide eyes blinked a few times in rapid succession, like she wasn't sure what to say. The woman probably had no idea what it was like to work or hold down a job. That was why she'd latched onto Daddy, after all—so she wouldn't have to reduce herself to getting a job after her first husband's money had run out.

"Maybe you could see a show or go to the museum? Of course, you'll want to see the Eiffel Tower. There's quite a view from the top." Diane rattled off the possibilities, careful not to imply that she would accompany them on any of these excursions. And because she couldn't help herself, she added, "Or maybe a cabaret. You'll never forget a night in Montmartre!"

Ada cleared her throat and nodded. "A museum sounds nice."

Just when Diane's annoyance with Ada had reached new heights, they were saved by the return of Catherine and Harry. Her pretty striped dress complemented Harry's light gray suit. He was tall and dashing, and his light brown hair looked golden and bleached from the summer sun. And, most noticeably, he'd grown a beard since they left America, making him even more appealing to the eye. They were pink-cheeked and smelled of warm air from being outside.

"What were you two up to?" Diane said as they settled into seats.

"Oh, nothing. Just catching up," Catherine said. Her smile lit her whole face.

Harry and Catherine had always been close. How close depended on a number of factors that Diane wasn't privy to. Diane hadn't given Harry much thought since she'd been living in Paris. The few times she'd asked about him, Catherine had been vague and evasive. Now, sitting with the two of them in the drawing room here in Paris, Diane couldn't guess what the next twenty-six days would mean for them. It could be their end or their beginning.

"The park was lovely," Harry said. "You should visit it before we leave, Ada. I think you'd like the statuary."

"I'm sure," Ada said, dryly. "But I'm glad you're here. I'd like to head back to the hotel so I don't miss lunch. They're serving it soon."

"That's fine," he said. "We can go now, if you like."

"Good." Ada stood and smiled at Diane then. "It's lovely to see you again, dear. And I'm looking forward to seeing as much of you over our visit as possible with your busy schedule."

Diane nodded curtly.

"What time should we plan on being at the hotel for dinner?" Catherine's eagerness to please oozed from her whole person.

"Six?" Harry said.

"Dinner is served at seven," Ada said solemnly. She placed her empty tea cup on the sideboard and headed out into the hall.

"I'll walk you out," Catherine said.

Without further ado, Diane was left alone in the drawing room, listening as the company went down the stairs and out the door.

In a moment, Catherine was back. "I'm going upstairs to bathe and set my hair."

"I'll come too." Diane hoisted herself up from the chair. As they climbed the stairs to their rooms, she said to her sister's back, "That was the worst morning of my life."

"I'll say. You gave us all quite a surprise."

"I'm sure I did."

"What happened?" Inside their sitting room now, Catherine closed the door behind them and faced Diane, sizing her up.

Diane looked away. She hadn't considered how much to tell her sister about the situation with Guillaume. Diane had made it quite clear that she wasn't ready to face Ada, and still Catherine had allowed them to catch her unaware. "Why did you bring them here without warning me?"

"They wanted to see you." Catherine shrugged innocently. "So why are you marrying a man you don't know?"

Maybe, probably, at least for now, the less Catherine knew about Guillaume, the better. "I told you I wanted to stay in Paris. If I marry him, I can, regardless of what Ada and Daddy say about it."

Catherine's brow furrowed, eyeing her sister even harder. If anyone was capable of spotting a lie, it was a sister. "You can't be serious."

Diane scoffed, being careful not to show herself. "I'm absolutely serious that Guillaume and I are engaged."

"Fine. What did Ada have to say while we were gone?"

"What does Ada ever have to say?"

"She's not that bad." Catherine removed her hat and set it on the corner of the escritoire. Then she sat down and started removing her shoes.

"Now you're not being serious." Diane rattled off her list of petty grievances—the judgmental looks, the suspicions, the accusations.

She wasn't done when Catherine stood up and stopped her. "Oh, don't be a bitch. She's just tired from traveling, is all. Plus, you traumatized her with your gentleman friend. Give the woman a break."

Chastised, Diane pressed her lips into a line. "I see you're falling all over yourself to do so."

"I'm ignoring that. I didn't sleep much last night, so I'm going to rest." She headed for her room.

"Oh, and why didn't you sleep? Speaking of gentleman friends, how are things with Harry?" Diane waggled her brows suggestively. Catherine was Miss Perfect in Daddy and Ada's eyes because she was never the one in trouble. But Catherine was far from perfect. She was just better at not getting caught.

Catherine blushed but didn't crack. "That's none of your business."

Chapter Five

When Guillaume stepped out of his black lacquered carriage, Diane was smoking a cigarette outside the Grand Hôtel. She looked radiant under the glow of the streetlamp. Her hair was twisted up and spilling back down in curls that Guillaume immediately wanted to touch. Her pale green dress clung to her curves in the most appealing way. Everything about her reminded Guillaume that he was a man. When she saw him, she dropped her cigarette in the ashtray and came toward him.

Since sobering up, small pieces of their previous evening had come back to him. The conversations he'd had, the people he'd seen, Diane. They'd kissed, he remembered that. Quite a bit. His lips were still tender. But he had some regrets. He usually preferred to know a woman a little better before sneaking into her bedroom. He'd have much preferred all of it to have happened sober. But if he'd been sober, he would have slept with her, if she'd have let him. That was the other thing—she probably wouldn't have let him in her room if she'd been sober.

"Were you waiting here for me?" He kissed her once on each cheek, lingering against her soft skin for an extra second both times.

"I was." She smiled. Her eyes sparkled with genuine pleasure at seeing him.

There was undeniable chemistry between them. Even seeing her now, when he was about to walk into a hornet's nest of a dinner with her family, there was nowhere he'd rather be. And he regretted that they'd agreed to keeping their hands to themselves.

"Everyone's waiting for us inside, unfortunately. We better go."

Guillaume offered her his arm and they walked together inside the palatial hotel.

The luxurious lobby was busy with guests dressed in dinner attire coming and going. The expansive room was decorated in rich red and gold carpet, giant bouquets of flowers, and fringy potted palm trees. Guillaume had had dinner here a few times. The food would be good even if everything else about the evening went to hell.

"We stayed here when my father was still paying for our Paris vacation," Diane said as they headed in the direction of the restaurant. "It's quite nice."

"I've never been upstairs."

"They've booked a room for me. Did I tell you that? Me and my sister."

"I think I caught that."

"Well, nice as it is, I am not going to stay." She squeezed his arm. "And now that I have you, I won't have to worry about them breaking down my resolve."

Diane's family was seated at a round table surrounded by windows and green palms. When Diane and Guillaume walked up, Harry stood. "Monsieur Allard, you made it."

Guillaume nodded to him and pulled out a chair for Diane.

"He arrived right on time," Diane said, as if she were building a case for him, punctuality being an obvious virtue.

Guillaume smiled and drummed up his most convincing charms. Before sitting down, he kissed a hand of both Ada and Catherine. He shook Harry's. He made eye contact and spoke in English to make them feel comfortable. He gathered that they didn't speak much French.

Guillaume occasionally met the parents of his romantic attachments. This was obviously different. And fake. Nonetheless, the pressure was on. She was depending on him, and he wanted to rise to the occasion. He didn't like it when people didn't like him. Not even his fake fiancée's American almost-family members. And he still felt responsible for the behaviors that led her to such a predicament.

Not long after sitting down, the server arrived with a bottle of champagne. While he popped the cork and served the wine, Guillaume caught Diane's eye and smiled encouragingly. So far so good.

"We were just talking about what Harry and Ada should do while they're here," Catherine said.

"Oh? What's on the list?" Guillaume asked.

"Notre Dame, I think," said Harry. "And the Tower."

"Guillaume has lived in Paris his whole life," Diane said. "He can probably suggest some interesting activities."

"Ah, yes," Guillaume said. "I always recommend a trip down the Seine this time of year. If you go early in the day, it won't be so hot. And the tour companies usually serve a lovely lunch."

"Oh, dear, I'm not sure I can stomach another boat ride," Ada said, dramatically. "Though I did read about a cruise to Notre Dame."

"Seeing it from the river is spectacular, but you could always take a fiacre to the cathedral if you're not up for a boat."

His magnanimity surprised even him. Was he trying too hard? Harry seemed distracted by Catherine. So much for challenging him to a duel. And so this performance was largely for the almost-stepmother, Madame Beall.

It was strange that she and the father hadn't married yet. Guillaume wasn't sure what to make of that. Once those decisions were made, people usually wanted to get things sorted out and move forward accordingly. Maybe this wasn't so in America.

Their Americanness was apparent. When they addressed both him and the restaurant staff, they slowed and enunciated their words in a way that suggested they thought the French were dumb. Did they not know that almost everyone in France spoke English? Guillaume had to listen carefully, but not that careful. Although well made, their clothes were simpler and therefore more conservative, especially Madame Beall's dress. Not quite as modern, perhaps, considering most fashions went from Europe outward. They were the kind of clothes made to cover rather than enhance. She was probably in her early fifties, judging by the swaths of gray in her dark hair, but still a handsome woman. Plain, though, because everything she wore understated her natural features. And based on the other Americans he'd encountered—which admittedly wasn't so many, at least not close contact—they seemed to equate this sort of plainness with virtue.

Dinner was served, and Guillaume's first bite of steak tasted as good as it looked. The meat was tender and perfectly seared, and his potatoes were buttered and salted to perfection. He became so absorbed in eating it that he didn't notice Madame Beall's displeasure until Catherine asked what was wrong.

"It's so rich, it's almost too much. I'm not sure I can finish. What a waste." She tittered on with complaints, her face scrunched and sickened. Guillaume ungraciously wondered if her tendency toward complaint might be part of the reason Diane's father hadn't married her. Spending the rest of your life with someone who complained all the time would be torture, though he didn't know Diane's father. He could be just as miserable. Maybe they complained together.

When the server came around to check on them, Guillaume asked for two more bottles of wine. When Madame Beall protested, he insisted that it was his treat.

They drank one bottle of wine and opened the other. And even though he was hesitant to drink too much, the alcohol did seem to loosen everyone at the table up, Madame Beall in particular.

"The French just seem to be less than thrilled that we're here, is all I'm saying," she said when Diane asked her thoughts on the country so far.

"I don't think we can expect people to roll out the red carpet for us just because we're Americans."

"We're paying to be here, aren't we. I'm sure this place isn't cheap."

"Perhaps if you don't know, then you can't really say that you're paying," Diane said.

"You know what I mean," Madame Beall said, dismissing Diane's jab with a wave of her hand. She took a large drink of her wine. Her lips and teeth were stained now from the dark grapes. She hadn't eaten much of her dinner to counteract the alcohol. "We're the guests, aren't we?"

"Has the hotel been unwelcoming?" Guillaume asked. Like a good fiancé, he could humor his almost-mother-in-law, or whatever she was.

"Oh, of course it hasn't," Catherine said, rolling her eyes in the loving way any daughter might about a parent's faux pas. "She's just tired."

"The thing about France that I keep marveling at is that everything is so old," Madame Beall continued. "Like these chairs could be a hundred years old, and here we are still sitting in them. I'm not sure I like that."

"That's a silly thing to say while visiting France, Ada," Diane said. Her face had flushed. "I think it's lovely. The depth of culture here in France is superior to new, shiny America in many ways. Some of the streets and buildings have been here since medieval times, which is fascinating and sophisticated. There's a sense that the French are further ahead than the Americans because America is just getting started doing what France has been doing for a thousand years already."

"Well," Ada said, undeterred. "That's your opinion, dear. We all have one of those."

Thankfully, the subject dropped and they spent the rest of dinner talking about people back in Woollett. The evening seemed to be going fairly well. The Bealls were self-important, but not unbearably so. His sense of relief, however, turned out to be naive.

As coffee and dessert wines were served, Madame Beall said, "I haven't seen your engagement ring, Diane."

"Oh, well…" Diane looked at her hand.

"I'm planning on giving her a family heirloom." Guillaume jumped in, pleased with his own quick thinking. It was true though; he had an antique ring for when he did marry. "I'm having it resized."

"Ah," Madame said, delighted. "You see what I mean about the French loving their old things. Doesn't a new bride deserve a new ring?"

Guillaume wasn't sure what to say to a complaint like this. His translation could be off. Did Americans really eschew heirlooms?

"I think it's nice," Diane said, turning her dreamy gaze toward Guillaume. Her eyes were as dark and alluring as night. In her gaze was a pleasant place to be, he had to admit.

Ada turned to Diane and said, not so nicely, "I wrote to your father about your new fiancé. Sent a telegram. He's probably reading it right now."

"Oh. Well, news travels fast, I see."

"It does, doesn't it."

Guillaume didn't know Madame Beall or her moods, but she seemed to have come alive during dinner. Maybe the exhaustion from travel had worn off. Maybe the wine was bringing it out.

She was sitting up, smiling, playful. "My only question is what are you going to do about your engagement to Alvin Monroe? Because he came to the house the day before we traveled. He brought a letter. I left it upstairs, but I can give it to you later, Diane. And I'll be honest, no one will be more surprised by this new development in your life than him."

Madame Beall was talking fast, and Guillaume had to translate as she spoke. But even as he sorted the words in his mind, he couldn't believe he was understanding them correctly. "Who is Alvin Monroe?"

"She didn't tell you about him?" Madame Beall said in disbelief.

Silence fell around the table. Catherine and Harry were listening with full attention now. Diane, next to him, put a hand on his forearm, as if bracing him for something. She had a panicked look on her face.

"He's her almost-fiancé back in Woollett." Madame Beall said it with nonchalance, as if it was strange that Guillaume didn't already know. But the table fell silent, all eyes expectantly flickering between Guillaume and Diane.

Guillaume tugged at his collar and cleared his throat. "Almost-fiancé?"

"Didn't she tell you?" Ada asked again. Her eyes were bright and smug. "I assumed since you two were close enough to marry, you must know such a fundamental detail of her background."

"What point are you trying to make?" Diane asked, her mouth drawn.

"My point is that we've come all this way, and you've surprised us with this engagement that has seemingly come from nowhere." Her voice grew more shrill with each word. "We all thought you were marrying Alvin. So it's only natural for me to ask for clarification."

"Clarification? Okay." Diane, fury in her eyes, turned to Guillaume. "I have an almost-fiancé back in Woollett."

Something in his chest sank with a painful thud. Guillaume was unsure how to play this, considering the engagement was a sham anyway. But he was disappointed by the revelation. Deeply so. How could she not have told him? Especially when he'd been so forward about his entanglement with Marielle when they first met. He was hurt because he cared. But how would a real fiancé react? Madame Beall's revelation seemed to change the fake fiancé game they were playing. Why had he agreed to do this again? "Is this how Americans do everything? Almost?"

"Ha. That's quite funny, Guillaume. I didn't know the French were funny." Ada raised her volume and enunciated her words.

Diane's eyes were on her hands in her lap. No help at all.

Anger rose in Guillaume now. It dawned on him that this shocking revelation was the perfect excuse to extract himself from the whole mess. These people made a challenging first impression. Not one of them had even attempted to address him in French. It would feel fabulous to be away from their company and drinking with friends somewhere in a vibrant conversation. A complete and total relief. A real fiancé would be upset by the revelation. He wouldn't even need to break character to get himself out of spending another minute with these people. And he took the opportunity.

Guillaume removed the napkin from his lap and placed it on the table. Looking at Diane for dramatic effect, he said sternly, "That you are promised to another is troubling news so early in our engagement. I will need some time to reconsider things."

Guillaume rose from his seat, followed by Diane and then Harry, who stood because a lady had.

"Good evening, and thank you for a most enlightening meal." Guillaume walked away from the table.

"Wait," Diane cried behind him.

At the same time, the insufferable Madame Beall said, "Is he leaving? I thought he said he'd pay for the wine. Did I misunderstand?"

Guillaume kept walking, but as he was crossing the wide lobby, Diane caught up to him.

"Guillaume, where are you going?" She grabbed his arm.

He turned and faced her. Her eyes were wide and unsure. He shrugged. "Home, probably."

"But that's a little dramatic, don't you think? Walking out like this?"

"I'm behaving as any fiancé would upon receiving such news." He was, wasn't he?

"Yes," she said. "I suppose you are. Will you sit for a moment?"

He nodded and followed her to a set of armchairs by the wall. When they were seated, she said, "Are you upset about this?"

"Maybe."

"What do you mean maybe?"

"I don't know, Diane. You could have mentioned the boyfriend back at home before we went out to dinner. Before any of this happened. If I'd known, none of this would have happened. Now I look like a complete jerk in front of your family. That can't be helping your cause."

"You're right. I should have told you."

"So tell me what is an almost-fiancé."

She groaned. "He was my friend, my best friend, for a long time. We grew up together. Our fathers are friends and colleagues. Anyway, everyone assumed we'd marry, including us. When I left America, I told him we'd make the engagement official upon my return. Almost-fiancé."

"I see. So you've made promises to another man?"

"I suppose I have."

"And even though you've overstayed your plans, you still haven't broken it off with him?"

She dropped her head. "I haven't. Not explicitly."

Guillaume scrubbed his face with his hands, frustrated at how complicated this fake engagement was becoming. "I'm wildly uncomfortable getting involved with people who are involved with others, you realize. This was why I told you about my entanglement the night we met."

"Yes, I understand that."

"And this changes the arrangement between us, I'm afraid."

"Guillaume, I need your help!" Urgency strained her words. "I can't tell them my fake engagement is off, that my life is such a screwed-up mess. Then they'll definitely take me back to America."

"I understand, Diane. But I don't see how it's my problem."

She flinched, and he immediately regretted being so harsh. But he was beginning to believe whatever debt he owed to karma for lying about sleeping with Diane had been paid. She lied to him, and so he was off the hook.

"You're really upset," Diane said.

"It seems I am." He shifted to leave, but she put a hand out to stop him.

"Guillaume, listen." She established eye contact with him, even though he tried to avoid it. "I didn't tell you because I don't usually tell anyone. Yes, I made promises to him. But I left him to come to Paris. And I'm obviously not in a hurry to get back. That's all you need to know about him."

"I'm not sure I agree, Diane."

"We had an agreement, Guillaume. What about that? You're just going to let them haul me away?"

"I'm sure you'll come up with something." He stood then, and she did too.

"You'll be hearing from me, Guillaume. I'll write you every day until you change your mind."

"Au revoir, mademoiselle."

Guillaume walked out of the hotel while the concierge called up his carriage. What a mess he'd just escaped from. It was almost unbelievable. Diane looked so surprised by her almost-stepmother's revelation, as if she'd forgotten all about the guy back home. And maybe she had gotten caught up in the moment and not considered it. But that didn't exactly reflect positively on her, lovely as she was. Lovely was only the half of it; she was clever and fun and gorgeous. He definitely didn't mind the thought of her trying to woo him back into their fake relationship. But at the same time, he didn't believe her when she said she would.

Chapter Six

When Diane returned to the table, everyone's eyes were on her—Catherine's concerned, Ada's smug and satisfied. Harry's curious.

"Well, I hope you're happy. You've fully embarrassed me." Diane stood behind her chair. The older couple at the table next to theirs was watching her, but she didn't care. She wasn't going to sit with them for another moment. "You've chased off my fiancé. The only fiancé I have, I should note. I'm not engaged to Alvin Monroe. I never was. And I'm not spending another moment of my evening in this hotel, either."

"What about the letter from Alvin? We can go up together and get it."

"I'll get it later. I'm leaving."

Catherine made no moves to follow Diane. The traitor. And so Diane walked out alone and caught a fiacre back to Rue de Fortuny.

The wide, tree-lined Boulevard Haussmann passed by the carriage window. All the pretty apartment buildings were lit from within, alive with dinner parties and other evening activities. Diane sighed and sunk deeper into her seat. There had been a time when she thought she'd marry Alvin Monroe. The families were so close; a marriage bringing them all together would have been perfect. But now that Diane was away from all that, she could see how, as much as she liked

Alvin as a person, being with him would mean going along with what he wanted. Befriending the people he wanted to befriend. Attending the parties he needed to be seen at. Her friend had grown into a man who needed a help meet. Someone to win over the wives of his business associates, make the right impression, host the parties, look nice. That was what Diane had run away from. Not that the domestic life of a society wife would be terrible—not like factory work or prostitution—but it didn't feel like it was for her. She wanted to go out dancing without worrying what everyone would think. She could do that here. Coming to Paris had given Diane a deep sense that her life could be different.

All the same: how had she neglected to tell Guillaume about Alvin? She should have known someone was bound to bring it up. And Guillaume was right; he had been forthright with her. Such an oversight on her part was foolish. Stupid. Had she even been thinking? One thing certainly hadn't changed since she'd come to Paris—she was still making a mess of things.

The house on Madame Tremblay's side was dark, but a faint glow came from the drawing room window on the tenants' side, which meant someone was still up and perhaps willing to hear all about Diane's evening. Catherine wasn't going to be around, so she couldn't talk to her. Diane wasn't sure what to make of her sister lately. She certainly didn't help tonight when Ada started yapping away. Diane wanted nothing more than a friendly ear.

As she climbed the stairs, the sound of giggling women was an instant relief. She took the last few steps two at a time.

"Bonsoir, mademoiselle," Nadine said, blotting her eyes with a corner of her silky sleeve. Her other hand held a crystal tumbler of a brown liquid that was most likely whiskey. She was sitting in one of the two battered Louis XIV chairs, dressed in a nightgown and kimono with her hair piled on her head. Nadine was an actress at Comédie Française and was often working in the evenings. That she was home was more than enough reason for them to be gathered together for drinks in the drawing room. As much as Diane loved going out, she also loved that spending an evening at home with her housemates could be just as fun.

"I've had a horrible evening, mademoiselles." Diane sprawled on the open half of the settee and sighed. "You have no idea how glad I am to see you all."

"Tell us what happened. We're always up for a tale of woe." Charlotte was perched on the other end with a pillow in her lap and a cup of tea. She reached toward the little table next to her and then held aloft the bottle of what was, sure enough, American whiskey. "Care for a drink?"

"That does sound good," Diane said.

Vanessa, who was sitting in the other Louis XIV chair, passed an empty tumbler. Her blonde hair was down, and she was also dressed for bed in a plush, stuffy-looking robe that covered her from neck to toe.

Charlotte poured and then passed the drink. She splashed some whiskey into her tea cup before setting the bottle down.

This surprised and delighted Diane, who had assumed the tea cup held only tea. Charlotte seemed more reserved than the rest of her housemates. Nadine said it was because Charlotte was from the Provinces, but Diane didn't know enough about France outside Paris. Diane was from a smaller town too, but she wasn't nearly as serious a person as Charlotte. She was always up early, working away at her desk, applying herself in a way that Diane couldn't fathom. She'd never been dedicated to anything the way Charlotte was to her writing. All of her housemates were dedicated—Vanessa was serious about her work in journalism, and Nadine had always known she was destined for the stage. They worked so hard and with such direction. Diane was constantly in awe of them. And she had no idea how to find that same level of passion in herself.

"Did you lose your sister along the way?" Charlotte asked.

"I'm starting to wonder if that wouldn't be a bad thing," Diane said. "Can you ladies keep a secret?"

They all three spoke at once.

"No!"

"Absolutely not."

"Are you crazy?"

"Well," Diane laughed. "Try this time."

Then she told them the full story—everything from the fake engagement to the explosive dinner at the Grand Hôtel. They all listened intently, nodding and sipping their drinks.

When Diane finished, she sighed again. "I don't know what to do now."

Charlotte, whose mouth had dropped open and hung there through the duration of Diane's story, held up her hand as soon as Diane stopped talking. "I have so many questions, Diane, about all of this. But the most pressing one is: does Madame Tremblay know you had a man in the house?"

"Not that I know of." Diane grinned thinking about her brazenness. Sneaking Guillaume into the house undetected was remarkable, considering she'd gotten him in while she was falling-down drunk. Too drunk. But Charlotte, being new in the house, was still very concerned about the rules. Now, finally, Diane could talk about her shameful morning. "And I walked him out in broad daylight."

Her housemates gasped and squealed, but Diane didn't exactly feel good about what she'd done. Madame Tremblay, no matter how much she loved Diane, would make her leave the pension if she found out. She needed to convince Ada that she had her life together here in Paris; losing her lodgings would be a disaster. And she'd have no one to blame but herself.

"Catherine doesn't know the engagement isn't real?" Nadine said.

"No. So don't tell her. At least not until I have time to explain everything." She would explain everything to Catherine, eventually. She just had to make sure she could trust her first.

"Why didn't you tell him? About this man back in America?" Vanessa asked. She worked at a newspaper and so had a knack for pointed questions. "Maybe it's not really over?"

"Yeah, why didn't you tell him?" Nadine leaned in with interest.

"I don't know. When he brought up his girlfriend—ex-girlfriend now—Alvin maybe flickered through my mind. And not even because I thought I should tell Guillaume. It was truly a flicker."

"And why didn't you break it off with the American?" Charlotte asked.

"He hasn't written in weeks." Diane shrugged. "And I still can't bring myself to go home. So I guess I just don't think about him all that much these days. I had no idea that he'd speak to Ada."

"This is the crux of the matter, Diane. It's why you're here and not in America right now, isn't it?"

"I suppose it is. I thought we would drift apart. Maybe I wanted us to drift apart. And I thought we had until my father's ambassadors showed up."

"Oh, this is messy, Diane," said Charlotte.

"It is, I'm afraid," said Vanessa.

"So what are you going to do now?" Nadine asked.

"Well, I guess I need to write to Alvin. Tell him the almost-engagement is off." She should have done that a long time ago, she knew this now. But what to do about Guillaume wasn't so clear.

"And what about your handsome and charming French fiancé Guillaume?" Nadine asked.

Diane's face warmed. "I don't know. Have any girls ever left the pension to get married?"

Nadine shrieked and tossed a throw pillow at Diane.

"I'm only teasing. I'm not really going to marry him." Diane smiled and winked mischievously.

"You should get some rest. All your problems will be easier to solve in the morning." Nadine swallowed the last of her whiskey. Everyone's glasses were empty now. "I'm off to bed."

"Me too. I have a lot of work to do tomorrow morning," Charlotte said. "But I'm sure this will all work out, Diane."

Vanessa rose, patting Diane's shoulder as she followed the others out.

It was late, but Diane didn't feel tired. She wished Catherine were there to help her figure out what to do. Just when she'd thought she found the perfect solution to her visitor problem, he was breaking off the fake engagement, which was terribly inconvenient. With that turning into a mess, her Paris life looked more unhinged. And she was all the more weak against Daddy's persuasion to come home. She couldn't do that. She wasn't ready. And so she needed to fix this thing with Guillaume.

Diane hoisted herself up from the settee and crossed the hall to her room, humming a few notes of a Debussy song as she went. As she slid her pocket door closed and began to undress, a hopeful plan started to formulate. Forget sending a letter; she'd send a telegram first thing in the morning to break it off with Alvin. She'd show Guillaume that she'd broken off whatever was left of her commitment to Alvin, then she'd try to convince him to come back. The fake engagement was still salvageable. As far as her family knew, Ada really had ruined a real engagement. She'd do everything she could to fix it as if it were. She'd even get to mope around and be snide to Ada to make it all the more real. It was another perfect plan. At least she hoped.

Guillaume was alone at breakfast the following morning when a letter arrived. His sisters had spent the night at a friend's house. His father, anxious to get to his office before the traffic became unbearable, had already left. And his mother hadn't come down yet. The housekeeper, Benoîte, brought the pink envelope in and set it on the table next to him. It was from Diane.

Guillaume didn't open the letter immediately. He finished his eggs en cocotte first, fearing whatever she had to say might ruin his appetite. Then, when his plate was empty, he slid a finger under the envelope flap and tore it open.

Dearest Guillaume,

I apologize again for not being forthright about my situation from our start. I write to tell you that I arose with the sun to send a telegram straight to the hands of my former romantic entanglement. He will receive word today about my desire to break off any attachments. I am no longer entangled! And I hope that, knowing this, you will reconsider our arrangement. It would be most helpful to me.
Diane

Guillaume read the letter twice and set it aside. It was nice to hear that she had taken care of her business, but he couldn't help thinking the only reason for doing so was that she'd been caught. In any case, he didn't have time to worry about it.

After the last gulp of his now-tepid coffee, he left for an appointment on the tennis courts with Antoine. He and his oldest friend had been playing tennis against each other since they were boys at Lycée Bonaparte. Although Guillaume won more often, Antoine put up enough of a fight to keep it interesting.

They'd agreed to play for best of three games. Guillaume won the first quickly, but not without breaking a sweat. Before starting the second game, they were resting and getting a drink on the side of the outdoor court.

Antoine took a mouth full of water and then grunted like he'd just remembered something important. "I ran into Marielle the other day. Did she tell me that you're seeing a woman named Diane?"

"Did she?" Guillaume had almost forgotten about Marielle. Almost. But of course she was still out there, talking. Hearing her name reminded him of what he'd said to her about Diane and stirred up the guilt he still felt about it. Not that it mattered now.

"She did. And I presume this is Charlotte's housemate Diane Talbot, the American."

"It is. Or rather it was. We've seen each other a few times since you introduced us at Moulin Rouge. But I'm fairly certain that I won't see her again." Guillaume picked up his racket and pointed it at the court. "Ready?"

"Sure." Antoine didn't mention Diane again, and neither did Guillaume.

Lately, Antoine, who was in line to inherit the title of vicomte, had fallen for Diane's housemate Charlotte. It wasn't going well between them, as his mother was pushing for a society marriage that she'd conveniently lined up for him. Most of their conversation that morning revolved around Antoine's messy love life. For this reason, Guillaume didn't have to say much about his own.

After mopping the court with Antoine, Guillaume arrived home to find a second letter from Diane.

Guillaume,

I understand that you are out of reasons for helping me. But because I still find myself in need of your assistance, I must appeal to your sense of duty. One would hope that after we were discovered in such a compromising position—a position that risks not only my home but also the respect and safety net of my family —you would be more inclined to make the situation right. I await your reply, knowing you will do the right thing.
Diane

She was getting desperate, resorting to blame. But he still wasn't ready to budge. She could have so easily told him everything when he'd been so forthright with her when they met. That night at Moulin Rouge, before his split with Marielle, he didn't touch Diane. He didn't venture a kiss. He was a perfect gentleman. And their conversation had given her multiple opportunities to share the truth of her situation as well.

It was disappointing too because he liked Diane more than he'd liked any other petite amie. Ultimately, Guillaume wanted a wife who was fun to be around and would challenge him. And even though it was premature to think it could be love, he'd loved everything about Diane he'd seen up to the deception. It could have been love, the beginning of it. Now he wasn't sure he could trust her.

The third letter arrived just as Guillaume was preparing to leave the house with his family for a party. Benoîte found him in the foyer, dressed and waiting for everyone to come down.

"This just came for you, monsieur," she said. "By messenger."

Guillaume thanked her. By now, there was no question who had written to him with the delicately monogrammed pale pink stationery. But he was surprised that she was still trying. He opened the envelope.

Guillaume,

Please forgive me. Desperation has me in knots. Would it help if I offered to make it worth your while? I ask only half in jest. Help me get through these next few weeks, and I will be forever indebted to you, monsieur.

Wink, wink

Diane

Guillaume laughed reading it. She was funny, he'd give her that. But humor couldn't sway him either.

His mother came down then, dressed and ready to leave. She was wearing a new dark blue dress and her signature diamond earrings and necklace. A lush peach rose was pinned to the lapel of her cropped, fitted jacket. Her hair, blond in her youth, was now silvery gray.

"You look lovely," Guillaume said when she'd descended. He tucked the letter into the breast pocket of his jacket and promptly forgot all about Diane.

"Thank you, dear. Where's your father?"

"I haven't seen him yet."

Just then, the man in question emerged from his study. Papa was dressed in his black evening suit and white tie. "Are we ready?"

"I believe so," his mother said.

"I've asked them to bring around the landau so we can enjoy the night air."

"Oh, what a lovely idea."

They walked together outside where the open carriage was waiting.

Guillaume's family lived in a sprawling house in the seventh arrondissement. It wasn't an ancestral home, but a place his father purchased. Guillaume had grown up here, never wanting for anything. His father had made most of his money in his shipping enterprise in Marseille before Guillaume was born. After the war, he'd been in the right place at the right time on a number of investments. And although his father dismissed his accomplishments as mostly luck, his forward-thinking approach helped him choose projects and opportunities wisely. Guillaume's mother was younger, his father's second wife. The first died during childbirth, along with the baby, Guillaume's older brother. Now Guillaume had younger sisters, and he liked to think his father had found happiness after such tragedy.

"Are Juliette and Josephine joining us?"

"Not tonight," his mother said. "Their friend is having a little birthday dinner party. They're already gone."

"Ah." Guillaume would miss their company and commentary on all the people at the party.

"How's the tennis game?" Papa helped Maman into the carriage.

"Not bad. I beat Antoine this morning." Guillaume followed his father up and took a seat.

"And how is Antoine?"

"He's fine. Sends his love." Guillaume was relieved to be getting out. After being so disappointed about how things turned out with Diane, he was looking forward to a fun evening seeing his friends. For the first time in several months, he was unattached and free of the drama associated with keeping a girlfriend. As much as he loved them, girlfriends could be a lot of work.

The landau took off. The party was at the Bettencourts' house, a short ride away. Summer wasn't a big season for parties, but this was a fashionable event that they held every year. With July 14 coming up, it was festive and patriotic. And while they rode, his parents talked about their late summer plans. Most society families—those who could afford it, Guillaume's included—left the city after Bastille Day and spent the hottest part of the year at the beach. Over the next few weeks, the city would empty out and every hotel on the northern coast would fill up.

The garden in front of the Bettencourts' pale stone house was filled with people mingling and enjoying the cooler night air. The sounds of a string ensemble floated through the open doors and windows. Inside, a swan ice sculpture and elaborate flower arrangements decorated the wide, tall foyer. Monsieur and Madame Bettencourt were welcoming everyone in. Madame Bettencourt wore a pale mauve dress with layers of pearls around her neck. And Monsieur Bettencourt, breaking with the traditional black, wore a mustard yellow jacket with his white shirt and tie. Guillaume's parents had known them for many years.

After greeting the hosts, Maman and Papa went looking for friends. Guillaume, who was starving, headed toward the food. All around people were dancing and eating. Most of the faces were familiar, and Guillaume nodded and greeted friends and acquaintances with la bise as he made his way to the buffet.

After procuring a glass of champagne and making quick work of a plate of mini quiches, Guillaume scanned the crowd. He was fairly sure Antoine would be there, but he'd been so tangled up with his literary lover that his attendance wasn't guaranteed. Guillaume was considering stepping out for a cigarette and to see who might be in the garden when his eyes landed on Marielle. She was dressed in a dramatic black and pink gown. And she was staring so intently at Guillaume that he could nearly feel her eyes boring into him. He nodded cordially and looked away. He hadn't expected to see her, though now he wasn't sure why. She was often at fashionable events. And like him, she might be reveling in her new freedom. Still, Guillaume didn't want to talk to her.

With his head down, he started for the door. But just when he thought he'd made it, she was right there in front of him, blocking his path.

"Ah!" He exclaimed, a little too loud. "Heading me off at the pass."

"Excuse me?" Her brow furrowed.

"It's an expression. Never mind." Guillaume kissed her quickly on each cheek in greeting, and she allowed him. "How are you, Marielle?"

"I'm fine, Guillaume, considering. And you?"

"Just fine." He nodded. "You look lovely. And it's a pleasure to see you. But if you'll exc—"

"It's lovely to see you too," she interrupted. "But you're not getting away that easily. How are things with the new petite amie?"

"They're fine, Marielle." He didn't want to be rude and walk away, even though he itched to do so. He had broken things off with her, the least he could do was give her a moment at a party.

"Is she here?" Marielle looked past Guillaume then, like she expected to see that he had a woman in tow.

"No, Marielle, she's not here."

"What was her name again?" She put a finger to her chin and tapped it in thought. "Oh, I remember. Diane. Diane the American."

Marielle was a somewhat fanciful woman. They'd never really gotten serious, but she played at seriousness with him, making their connection bigger than it could possibly be in so short a time together. It had been cute at first, but now that version of her was coming out again, and it made him uneasy.

Guillaume regretted ever telling Marielle about Diane. What was she playing at now?

"So where is she?" Marielle asked. Her eyes took him in from head to toe like she was window shopping.

"I suppose I'm not sure." He was intentionally vague.

"Oh? Is that because it's over? So soon? Or is she on a boat heading across the Atlantic where she belongs?" Marielle laughed, and Guillaume wondered how many times the empty champagne flute in her hand had already been filled that night. Then she touched his arm and doubled over. "I'm joking."

"That's good, because it certainly didn't sound very nice." He needed to get away from her. "I'm headed out for a smoke."

Marielle didn't like cigarettes. Guillaume stepped around her, confident this would deter her from further conversation.

"I'll join you," she called after him, unrelenting.

He didn't wait for her, but she followed him out to the garden. They stopped next to a white lilac bush in full, lush bloom, and Marielle continued her line of inquiry.

"So why isn't your American Diane here, again?"

"I don't know, Marielle. I didn't invite her?"

She smiled mischievously. "Well, that's just fine, isn't it. And your best friend, Antoine, didn't even know you were seeing her. He was quite enlightened when I told him."

"So?"

"So, things must not be going well, then. I can't say I'm sorry to hear it. I've been unexpectedly torn up about you, Guillaume. And to be honest, I wasn't going to come out tonight. I've been such a sad mess. But now I know that getting myself together to be here was all worth it."

"And why is that?" Guillaume smiled, biting back his annoyance. He patted the breast pockets of his jacket, looking for his cigarette case. He didn't feel it there.

"Because if there's one thing I know about you, Guillaume, —firsthand information, I might add—is that your heart can easily be tempted. And I don't intend to go down without a fight."

"A fight?" His side pockets were empty also. Had he forgotten his cigarettes?

"That's right, Guillaume Allard. I intend to win back your heart." As she said it, she pressed her bosom forward, showing off the deep cut of her gown. Perhaps chosen with this exact move in mind.

"Listen, Marielle, even if things don't work out between Diane and me, I'm not interested in reforming any previous attachments."

"Why not? If she's the reason you left me, and she's gone, then I don't understand. I don't harbor any ill will toward you."

"Marielle, dear..." Guillaume searched for the right words. Hadn't he already broken up with her once? How in the hell did he end up here, having to do it again? He'd never noticed Marielle was so irrational, though perhaps he'd not been paying close enough attention.

"No, no, Guillaume. I won't hear it. Just allow me to try and win you back." She advanced then, eyes locked hopefully on his, and she almost got close enough to rub up against him. But Guillaume, still looking for his cigarettes, stepped away and reached inside his jacket to check his interior pockets.

That was when he felt the envelope. He pulled it out before his mind registered what it was. Seeing the pink paper, he immediately remembered.

Marielle saw it too. "Is that from her?"

"Marielle, what are you talking about?" Putting it away, he tried to stall her so he could think.

"That pretty pink letter in your pocket?"

"Marielle, listen, it is a letter from Diane. An important one, okay. And while I'm flattered to have won your continued attention, I must firmly decline."

She narrowed her eyes. "Why don't I believe you, Guillaume?"

"I'm not sure. But Diane and I are still attached."

Marielle pursed her lips, disappointment flickering in her eyes. But with an almost imperceptible shake of her head, she strengthened her resolve. "I won't believe it until I see it."

"Marielle, be serious. You think I'm making her up?"

"Maybe. To put me off."

"Forgive my bluntness, but why won't you just be put off then, regardless?"

She tilted her head, considering this. "Because, Guillaume, whether you know it yet or not, we are meant to be together. I had two tarot readings that strongly suggested this to be so. It's only a matter of time."

"Well, you're wrong. The cards too. Diane and I are getting along quite nicely. In fact, she'll be attending the Prévots' ball next week."

"Oh, will she?" The strangest uncertainty shone in her eyes. "So I'll meet her then?"

Guillaume thought of the letter, of Diane. Her family would be gone in a few weeks. And then, despite his inkling that he'd live to regret it, Guillaume nodded his head. "You'll meet her then."

With a flick of her hair, Marielle was gone.

Guillaume let his head fall back. The summer stars sparked in the inky dark sky. A hint of a breeze rustled the flowering shrub at his back, sending the perfume wafting anew. The heady scent was almost sickening. He usually loved lilacs because they reminded him of his grandmother who passed when he was a teenager. What had he done? What was he doing? How did he keep ending up in these sticky situations? His romantic complications were ruining even his memory of Mami.

A laugh carrying from somewhere on the other side of the lilac brought him back to the party. A cigarette. He needed a cigarette in the worst possible way. He found a group of smokers gathered around a circular seating area further out in the garden. He knew one of the gentlemen through his father and introduced himself to the others. He procured a cigarette, and while he smoked, he began thinking through the letter he'd write and send to Diane first thing in the morning.

Chapter Seven

Diane marched into the Grand Hôtel for lunch with Ada, armed with the knowledge that Guillaume would continue to help her with the fake engagement. He'd sent a messenger first thing to let her know that her letters had convinced him, and she could count on him for full participation in whatever she needed. He mentioned something important he needed to confess to her. She'd been too elated at the time to question that or what part of her letters finally changed his mind. But now that she'd had some time to process her victory, she wondered if it had been her little joke about making it worth his time. She'd intended innuendo; had it been received? Or was there some other motive behind his change of heart? In either case, it didn't matter.

Diane had been so tense since Ada's arrival that she was ready to explode. First, Ada found them in bed together. Or, rather, on the bed. Then the fake engagement. And then the fake engagement was thrown into upheaval. Diane could only imagine the telegram updates that were certainly being tapped out between Ada and her father. They'd have her back in New York in no time if she didn't get her life together, even if it was just for appearances. Guillaume's cooperation was critical. And now she had it.

The lobby was peopled with well-appointed guests and liveried staff. She remembered hotel life well, and now that she wasn't worried about her situation, she could appreciate it. When she'd been staying here with Catherine, the hotel culture and community had surprised her. So many guests—many of them American—were staying longterm. Everyone knew everyone; cliques formed around the most impressive people; gossip was rampant. It was like an outpost for American society. She'd been glad to leave it behind.

Diane headed for the restaurant where she was supposed to meet Ada. She'd no doubt requested this lunch so she could convince Diane to come home. But when Diane spotted Ada seated in the busy dining room, a man was at the table with her. A handsome man. And it wasn't Harry.

Diane slowed and ducked behind a potted palm tree, sure Ada hadn't seen her. Then she peeked around and watched as Ada tipped her head back in a full, joyful laugh. Never in all the years Diane had known this woman had she ever seen her laugh in such a way. Tolerant chuckling, maybe, at one of Daddy's silly jokes. Never like this. As Ada regained her composure, the man leaned closer, nearly to her ear, and said something obviously private. Then Ada, honest to goodness, blushed from her neck to her hairline.

What was going on? Diane's skin tingled with suspicion. Was she having an affair? Ashamed, but also angry, Diane swallowed hard and stepped out from behind the plant. Her feet stomped the ornate carpet as she crossed the dining room. She was close before Ada noticed her presence and immediately straightened in her chair. Now who was getting caught, Diane mused. "Ada, who is your friend?"

"Diane, honey, I didn't see you come in." Ada recovered herself quickly. "This is Mister Andrew Glover. He's also an

American. We met on the ship and both happen to be staying here at the same hotel."

Diane looked between them. The man was younger than Ada and handsome in a bland sort of way. He had brown hair the color of the deer that roved around their neighborhood in Woollett. And he was pale like he spent most of his time indoors. But he had a bright, pleasant smile and intelligent eyes.

Mr. Glover stood and extended a hand to Diane. "It's a pleasure, my dear. Ms. Beall has told me so much about you and your sister."

Diane sat, but Mr. Glover did not.

"I'll let you ladies enjoy your lunch." He bowed and was gone before Diane had settled into her seat.

"Making friends, Ada?" Diane said, imbuing her words with as much suspicion as possible. "It looks like it's my turn to send a telegram to Daddy."

Ada's mouth fell open, but there was an unmistakably guilty glint in her eye. Ada was so prude that she'd probably feel guilty just getting caught sitting with the man. Especially with Diane the one catching her. Ada narrowed her eyes at Diane. "Don't try to catch me out because I already discovered you in bed with a man on this trip, Diane."

"You looked awfully cozy for friends," Diane said churlishly. After what Ada had done to Guillaume, Diane was justified in being hard on Ada. Sure, it was probably a harmless flirtation. But who would want to flirt with Ada? It was baffling.

Ada gasped. "You're blowing this completely out of proportion. I guarantee you that whatever you saw isn't what you think it is. I was on a boat for six days, for goodness sakes. I'm allowed to make friends."

"It's unfaithful regardless. I saw you flirting and blushing."

"Oh, Diane, it is not." Ada gaped and blinked furiously. She was completely flustered, which Diane rather liked. Ada folded and refolded her napkin. "An attached woman can enjoy another man's company and even flirt a little without it being unfaithful. Love isn't a jail."

"Isn't it, though? A jail? Every one of my friends back in Woollett is married and pregnant and stuck in Woollett. That sounds like jail to me." Diane's indignation rose. "And you've been hanging around my father for years, and yet he still won't marry you. That sounds like jail too."

"That's ridiculous, Diane. You don't know what you're talking about."

The server arrived then, but neither of them had looked at the menu yet. They'd been too busy arguing.

"Hot tea for me," Ada said.

"I'll have wine. Something red."

When the server departed, Ada chastised Diane. "It's a little early, isn't it?"

"That's part of the reason I love France so much. It's an indulgent culture."

Ada clucked her tongue. Then with a disapproving look said, "Go ahead and tell your father that you saw me speaking with another gentleman, Diane. I'm curious to see what he'll say. Maybe I'll have to stay in Paris then too."

The server returned with their drinks, and they ordered: soup for Diane and an omelet for Ada. The interruption and thinking about food cooled both of their tempers. And Diane refocused on the fact that she'd already won whatever argument Ada was here to present. The engagement was back on.

"Look," Diane said after a few quiet moments. "It's fine if you're making friends and flirting. I don't really care what's going on between you and my father."

"Your father and I are fine. In love. And perfectly happy with the course and pace of our relationship."

"Understood." Diane sipped her wine and was immediately thankful she'd ordered it. It was warm and summery in her mouth. She extended an olive branch by changing the subject. "So how is Daddy?"

"Your father is well. Busy with work, which is why he isn't here." Ada paused and sipped her tea. "But he's worried about you and your sister."

"As you can see, we're doing just fine."

"Your father misses you. He wants you to come home, if I'm being perfectly honest. And he's disappointed to hear that you have no intention of doing so."

"Have you talked to Catherine about going home?" Diane hadn't really spoken to her in days.

"I have, and I think she agrees that the vacation is over."

"Oh, does she?" This wasn't exactly news, but it still stung. She and her sister had always been united on most matters, but they were divided on this. If Diane wanted to stay in France, then she'd have to do it alone. She'd never done anything alone.

"I believe so, yes. And I got a telegram from your father this morning. Even with the engagement, he'd like you to consider coming home for a visit. You can leave with us and stay for as long as you can."

Come for a visit? That sounded like a trap. "Well, for now, I am not in a position to leave France. My engagement is new, and so there is much to be done. Plus, I have to work."

Ada nodded but didn't argue.

"What did he say, exactly?"

"Your father?"

"Yes. You said he sent you over here to fetch us. What did he say?"

"To bring you home. He obviously didn't think it would be so difficult. Or that you'd be engaged to a Frenchman. Otherwise, he might have come himself."

Diane hadn't heard from her father since Ada arrived, but surely she would soon. She expected a telegram at any moment. But since Ada had already gotten one, she asked, "And what did he say about my engagement?"

Ada drew her mouth into a line and looked away. She didn't want to say it.

"That bad?"

"Honestly? He doesn't think it will last."

"What? The engagement?"

"The engagement. The marriage, if it gets that far. I mean, honestly, Diane. Have you really thought this through? America is your home. You spent your whole life there, and much of it attached to Alvin. No one understands how you could just throw it all away to live in squalor in a foreign country."

"I'm not living in squalor, Ada. And I resent you saying so. Is that what you've told my father?"

"Well, no, your rooms are nice enough. Hardly squalor. And Madame Tremblay seems wonderful. But working in service? Really, Diane? What will you do when your sister is no longer around to share rent? How much longer before you're out on the street?"

"Aren't you the snob? But I am no Fantine, Ada. And I am engaged to a very wealthy man from a prominent French family. Have you forgotten that little detail?"

"Like I said: no one expects that to last."

The engagement wasn't going to last, but it still hurt to hear that everyone expected her to fail. Even coming from Ada, the words cut. Diane swallowed her emotions in a lump and narrowed her eyes. "Guillaume and I have every intention of living the rest of our lives together. But even if it doesn't work out with Guillaume, I'm not marrying Alvin. Time and distance have muted my feelings for him, and I don't imagine they'll ever return. And I resent being held to something I said before I'd ever left the town I was born in. How should I have known that the world is so big and so interesting? How should I have known that there is so much more available than what was presented to me in Woollett? I didn't know what life was until I came to Paris. How can I be held to a commitment I made in complete ignorance? It hardly seems fair."

"And Guillaume is so different from Alvin?"

The difference between the two men was like night and day. Marriage was still marriage, though. Diane hesitated, but only long enough to remember that the whole thing was a sham anyway. "Yes. He's different. Paris is different. I am a different person since I've come here. And I can't go back to Woollett right now."

"I don't see why not."

"Why do you care if I come home, Ada? Really?"

"You know your father. He misses you, as I've said. And he feels strongly about you marrying Alvin, that he knows best. He sent me over here to convince you to come home. If you don't come home, it will mean I've failed. And he will be most displeased with me if I don't get him what he wants." Her words came out fast and urgent. Then she stopped for a moment and sighed. "And I care about you, Diane. Believe it or not. French men are different, and not necessarily in a good way. I think you will learn a hard lesson that could be avoided altogether."

"Please, Ada. I am not interested in taking advice about men from you. My father is not perfect, but your relationship is the opposite of aspirational."

Ada flinched and placed a hand on her chest.

Diane hadn't meant to be so mean. But she'd been observing Daddy and Ada for years, and so all Diane's unkind thoughts were right there, ready. They were the kind of words that, afterward, shamed the person who fired them off as much as the target. "I'm sorry. I don't want to hurt your feelings. I only want to win my case."

Ada sipped her tea and seemed to regain some strength. "Your father and I are not unhappy the way things are. If that doesn't suit you, well, that's not really any of your business."

"Then perhaps you and my father should extend the same courtesy to Guillaume and me." Diane put her chin up triumphantly. She'd won this battle, for sure.

Ada shrugged, but didn't verbally concede. A minute later, she perked up. She blotted her mouth with her napkin and made a show of pulling an envelope from a skirt pocket and sliding it across the table. It was the letter from Alvin. Diane recognized the neat, uniform script. Fighting the surprising urge to tear it open and read it right away, Diane nodded and tucked it into her own skirt pocket. She'd read it privately, where Ada couldn't judge whatever reaction might come. Still, no matter how much she liked hearing from Alvin, her mind hadn't changed.

They finished their lunch in silence. After the server cleared their plates, Ada asked Diane if she'd like to come upstairs.

"No, thank you," Diane said. "I'd like to run a few errands. But I'll come for dinner tonight."

"Will Guillaume join you?"

"No. He has prior engagements."

"Then let's plan on the river trip he suggested. Maybe tomorrow?"

"I have to work tomorrow."

"Okay, well, whenever you like then. Ask him when he's available."

"I thought you'd had enough boating."

Ada shrugged. "If I'm to convince your father that this marriage is a good idea, then I need to get to know Guillaume."

Even in her grumpy mood, Diane recognized this as a concession. Spending more time with Guillaume wouldn't be a problem. As long as they could pull off the ruse. Ada would no doubt be looking for any crack in their fledgling relationship that she could exploit to further her argument. Diane may have convinced her today, but this was far from over. The work of the fake engagement was only beginning.

On her way out of the hotel, she found an empty seat in the lobby. Diane sat and pulled the letter from Alvin out of her pocket. She took a deep breath and slid her finger under the flap to open it. Her heart thumped as she read, but it didn't waver. He missed her. He still loved her and wanted a life with her. But it was still all about him. She read it once, folded the paper back into the envelope, and then she caught a cab home to Rue de Fortuny.

Four days later, Diane left the house on Rue de Fortuny and walked toward the meeting spot that she and Guillaume had planned. It was mid-morning, and so most of the traffic had already cleared. Big old houses similar to Madame's lined the street; some were divided up and rented out to several tenants, others were occupied by single women or couples. A young family lived in the place on the corner. The only other people on the sidewalk this morning were domestic workers heading out on errands. Diane turned onto Avenue de Villiers.

The Bealls had booked a daytime cruise, which included lunch and champagne, rather than the dinner cruise, which included heavy drinks. The earlier in the day, the less likely Ada would be to drink and create drama like she had at dinner. They were all to meet at Quai Malaquais to catch the boat.

Diane didn't want Guillaume to pick her up in his carriage in front of the house because, as far as she knew, her secret was still safe with Nadine, Vanessa, and Charlotte. Madame didn't know about the engagement, and Diane wanted to keep it that way. That meant not letting Guillaume hang around. Not that he'd been hanging around. He'd written only to confirm their arrangements for the boat ride, and the correspondence had been brief and impersonal. No gifts or special messengers to raise suspicions.

Catherine also still didn't know the engagement was fake. She had not been gone from the house on Rue de Fortuny for all that time. She spent two nights away at first, then came home. Then Catherine went back to the hotel the night before the cruise without giving Diane any sort of explanation aside from it being closer to the water.

Diane wasn't sure what was going on between Catherine and Harry, only that Catherine said they weren't rushing into anything. Catherine could be so open about some things, but also so secretive about matters of her heart. Catherine and Harry became fast friends when Daddy and Ada started spending time together. He had his real mother, who lived in New York City. But he and Ada, perhaps in their mutual grief for his father, remained close. So he'd come around for a few weeks every summer and for holiday dinners, like a cousin but not. Catherine and Harry were inseparable on these visits. For a long time Catherine insisted that nothing was going on between them, until she stopped denying it and refused to talk about it at all. The sisters came to Paris not long after that.

Guillaume was waiting at their meeting place on the corner of Avenue de Villiers and Rue de Fortuny when Diane walked up. He'd dressed in a lightweight tan suit and straw hat, and his mouth cracked into the most perfect smile when he saw her.

"You look lovely." He took her hand and kissed it without making eye contact.

"Thank you. I like your hat." His breath tingled on her skin, and her face ached from smiling so hard. Something like relief flooded through her. She was glad she didn't have to take this family boat ride without him. She was stronger. Her lie was stronger.

"I like yours." She was also wearing a straw sun hat, one of her sister's, that was decorated with large silk flowers. Her seersucker dress was simple and lightweight. Together, they looked like summer embodied in a couple, which was good because if today went well, then they'd probably be off the hook for spending more time with her family for at least a few days. The less time they spent together in front of their audience, the less likely they'd slip up and reveal their false affections.

"As much fun as this exchange of niceties has been, we should go." He helped her into the carriage and it moved off, entering the flowing traffic and heading toward the river. The day was well underway, with bakeries busy and offices open for business.

"I want to thank you again for helping me with this," Diane said after she settled in. "And I'm sorry again about Alvin and all that mess. It was so over in my mind that I never imagined Ada would bring it up. I would have prepared you otherwise."

Guillaume nodded. "It's fine. And you don't have to be so apologetic because I have an ulterior motive for helping you."

"Oh?" She hadn't really considered his motive, aside from wondering whether or not he was doing so because he liked her. She kind of hoped he did. His acting skills hadn't impressed her, and so it would help if he really did like her. But that might make things tricky later when she ultimately broke it off. She would rather not break any hearts.

"Yes. I ran into my previous attachment the other day, and she's become, perhaps, fixated on the idea of us getting back together."

"Oh." A needle of jealousy pricked her, but she was always a little territorial. This didn't mean anything.

"I'm afraid so. I was disappointed, you know. That you hadn't thought enough of me to be forthright and clear about your situation. I was ready to write you off completely." Guillaume brooded. Was he mad about this because he was jealous? And why did this delight her in the sultriest of ways? He continued, "But then I ran into Marielle, and she started acting weird. With your charming letters in mind, I realized that continuing our arrangement would have some obvious mutual benefits."

"So you told Marielle about me?"

"I did."

"Huh." This was interesting. "And what did she say?"

"She was quite difficult to convince, actually. But in any case, I told her that she could meet you at an upcoming ball. It's a big event every year, everyone still in the city will be attending. I hoped you would come with me. To ward her off."

"To ward her off? Guillaume, who were you seeing? A vampire?"

"I'm beginning to wonder."

Diane gasped and covered her mouth with a hand to stifle her laugh. She liked that he could play around with her like this. "That's terrible to say. If I feel bad for her, I'll want to be friends, just so you're aware. Things could actually get far more complicated if Marielle and I like each other."

"That is probably not a good idea. Maybe try not to like her." Guillaume squinted and drew his mouth into a hard line. "Because that's not all I told her."

"Oh?"

"As I said, she was difficult to convince. Telling her about you made it more final. But I also told her that we slept together."

Diane's mouth fell open. "And that was the reason you gave her for breaking it off?"

"Well, when she didn't accept my first handful of reasons, I got desperate. I'm sorry. She was crying, and it just came out."

"You know, Guillaume, I have felt so guilty about roping you into my scheme, when you've been scheming on your own."

"I have. Regrettably." He brought her hand to his mouth and kissed it. "I'm sorry. And I'm hoping we can call it even."

"When is the ball?"

"On Saturday. Do you have to work?"

"I don't."

"So you'll go?"

"I suppose we can call it even. I'll certainly owe you one after today."

"Or your life."

"Oh, wow, Guillaume." Diane feigned insult. "You really sized up my family accurately."

"I'm sure it won't be that bad. I'm only joking."

Diane fingered the upholstered seat under her. It was a lovely dark green brocade and the carriage walls and ceiling were lined in matching green satin. Across from her, Guillaume's long body nearly took up the whole seat.

"Will the ball be fancy?"

"It will be formal, yes. The hosts are both from aristocratic families."

"Okay. Pretty fancy then."

"And my parents will be there. I'll introduce you to them, but we won't make a big deal out of it."

"I see. Parents do raise the stakes. Any chance you can buy me a dress? So I'm ready for Marielle's critical eye."

"I suppose that is important," he said thoughtfully. "I'd be happy to buy you a dress. Though maybe I should stipulate that the budget will be set according to how miserable this cruise ends up being."

"Is that some sort of challenge? As if I have any control over what these people will say."

"I seem to recall something in a letter about making it worth my time." He raised a mischievous brow and a zap of curious pleasure passed through Diane. He was flirting with her. But before she could respond, the carriage stopped and swayed as the driver jumped down. They were there. Now their flirtations would have to be on display. Needed to be. So she decided to save it for the boat.

Chapter Eight

The carriage dropped them off at the top of a cobblestone ramp that led down to the water. Guillaume offered her his arm, and she took it. His muscles were firm under his layers of clothing, and touching him filled her with a pleasant, relaxed confidence. The sun was up, but the clouds hadn't burned off yet. And the gray river sparkled and reflected vibrant pastels. They walked together around the bend and down to where a man with a white hat and striped shirt was helping Ada onto a sleek, shiny wooden boat. It was a private tour, and that lovely vessel waiting for them filled Diane with glee. It would be hard not to have a wonderful time on a day like this.

She'd been working so hard lately, trying to keep up with expenses and save as much as she could. Her financial difficulties started as soon as her father stopped paying. Diane and her sister both started working at the law office shortly after deciding to stay in Paris. Diane got fired after a few months for her attitude. It had been harder than she expected to adapt to the working world. And she hadn't realized that, no matter where she worked, she'd have to endure some degradation of pride. Now she'd give almost anything to have her job at the law office back. She didn't like waiting on those self-important men. But never having worked before, she had no idea just how good she'd had it there. Self-important men were the least of her worries.

The irony that she was now working in service hadn't escaped her. Not at all. But she was determined to get what she wanted, and so she'd been watching the papers for another office position. If her sister left Paris with the Bealls in twenty days, then money would be even tighter. She'd grown accustomed to sharing her sister's larger and more stable income.

In any case, she'd worry about all of that later. For today, one of her precious few days off, she was going to enjoy this boat ride as much as she could. She'd be nice and flirt with Guillaume and be a woman who had her life in Paris under control.

The captain offered a strong, weathered hand to help Diane step onto the yacht. And when everyone had made it aboard, he explained the plans for the day. Traveling west, they'd take the northern route around Île de la Cité and Île Saint-Lous, looping back around to have an early lunch at Notre Dame. Then they'd continue down the river to the Eiffel Tower before heading back to where they started mid-afternoon.

La Trappe du Jour was a brand new commercial vedette made in France, fully outfitted for their comfort. The back side of the boat was open, with a seat for the captain behind the wheel and a bench that wrapped around. The canvas upholstery was crisp white, and square pillows with nautical stripes sat in each corner. Mounted to the stern, a little French flag fluttered to life and settled again.

Inside the cabin had more seating, a table, and a mirror-lined miniature bar where three bottles of champagne were sitting on ice. Another door led out to another seating area in the bow. The rich golden wood had been polished to a high shine.

"This was such an excellent idea, Guillaume." Diane smiled up at him.

"I hoped you would like it."

After introducing himself and the quick tour of the vessel, the captain went over some safety guidelines and made quick work of untying the boat and departing from land. As soon as they were on the water, the breeze picked up.

"Let's have some champagne," Harry said. He stepped inside as everyone else settled into the seats at the back of the boat. After passing around flutes and a bottle, they toasted to family and new adventures. Everyone drank and watched the world pass by.

Ada was sitting on the opposite side of Guillaume. After a few quiet moments, she touched his sleeve and said in her enunciated English, "I hope you'll forgive me for letting slip the secret. Or, rather, the old news. And although your engagement is a surprise, I am looking forward to spending the day with you, Guillaume, and getting to know you."

"Thank you," Guillaume said. "I'm looking forward to a fresh start as well."

"Guillaume grew up in Paris, didn't you?" Diane shifted the conversation away from the drama.

"I did," Guillaume said. "Not far from here."

"I hope I will get to meet your parents and see your home," Ada said pleasantly. She was dressed in a crisp, white cotton dress and sun hat. "Diane has assured me it's lovely."

Diane had never seen Guillaume's house, but once she got going, the fake engagement story seemed to write itself. She knew enough about him to know the place was big and fancy.

"We'll have to see," Diane said quickly. This conversation needed to be shut down.

As many questions as Ada had been asking about Guillaume's family over the past few days, Diane should have known that she was working up to spring this request on them. Guillaume turned to Diane, a question in his eyes. But there was no way Diane would allow that to happen. There was no need to wrap anyone else up in this tale. She'd weave an epic of lies before she allowed Ada to meet Guillaume's parents. She still wasn't sure what to do about meeting them at the ball herself.

"Guillaume, let's go sit up front. I want to see the rest of the boat."

Guillaume turned back to Ada and nodded respectfully. "Excuse us."

They made it up front and settled into the v-shaped seating area just in time to pass under Pont Neuf. The mascarons snarled at them as they passed into the shadowy coolness underneath the bridge and then back out again. Poplar trees and weeping willows dotted the banks, and the clouds were starting to dissipate.

"I've been in Paris for almost a year and this is my first time on the river."

"Really?"

Diane nodded. "Do you spend much time on the water?"

"Not as much as I'd like."

They watched the scenery for some time, which for Diane, also meant stealing glances at Guillaume while he wasn't looking. The front of the boat could comfortably seat three or four people, but he took up so much space with his long, tall body that she couldn't avoid being close to him. He was leaning on an elbow against the bow, and she was leaning into the bow on the other side. Even with the breeze and riverine aroma of the air, she could smell his mint and vanilla cologne. His face was tan and lightly freckled from playing tennis outside. His eyes as blue as the sky on a clear day. He'd adorably missed a small spot on his neck when he'd shaved that morning. She couldn't have picked a more appealing fake fiancé. Diane didn't find proximity to him to be a chore or challenge of this arrangement at all. Her whole body tingled with anticipation and full agreement. "This isn't going at all badly, is it?"

"What's that?"

"Today. The arrangement. It's not so bad."

"Not at all. In fact," he quirked a mischievous eyebrow, "I'm rather enjoying it."

Diane smiled and warmed as soon as his attention was on her. Then she noticed they had an audience. Through the cabin windows, Ada was watching from the seating area at the back of the boat. Her watchfulness was a steady observation devoid of emotion. Her gaze didn't falter when she was caught looking either. She was just watching.

Diane put a hand on Guillaume's sleeve and smiled at him. "Don't look now, but someone spies us."

"Oh?" He shifted in his seat, acting casual. After a few seconds, he looked and then turned back to Diane.

"I don't think she believes us."

"Are we not acting engaged enough?"

"I can't tell if she doesn't trust us, or if she's just completely dumbfounded by the fact that I snagged a Frenchman."

"Perhaps." He stole another quick glance in Ada's direction and then turned his attention back to the shore.

"Perhaps we should give her a little show," Diane said, scooting closer on the bench to Guillaume.

That mischievous eyebrow shot up again, and his blue eyes seemed to catch fire. The heat swept over her. No one—not even Alvin—had ever looked at her like that. So convincing. Could Ada see that?

"Maybe I should touch you like this, so she'll think we're having an intimate conversation." Diane moved her hand from his sleeve to his chest and gazed into his eyes. He was solid and warm under her hand. They were inches apart now.

"You're quite convincing from my point of view," he said, watching her intently.

"Maybe I should laugh and look away, like what you've said has scandalized me." Diane started pulling her hand away from him, but he caught it and held it.

She gasped, and her body flooded with another wave of heat. They passed under another bridge and the echoing sounds of carriages overhead barely drowned out the thump of her heart.

"What if we were to kiss right here in front of her? Do you think that would convince her?"

His face had flushed as red as hers felt. And his eyes—darkened by his dilated pupils—locked on hers. He licked his lips. His perfect, pink mouth. Then he groaned and moved away.

"Diane, I think we should stop the show now, before I get too caught up in my role and kiss you for real."

"That wouldn't be so terrible." She swallowed her disappointment. She was having trouble looking away from his mouth. "We've kissed before."

"That was different, and I'm not sure either of us remembers enough of that for it to count. And I am not trying to get thrown off the boat."

"Who would throw you off the boat?"

"Her." He tipped his head at Ada, who was still watching at them from the back of the boat.

Diane laughed out loud. "You might be right about that."

Guillaume lifted a hand and sheepishly waved at Ada, who responded in kind. "She is shameless in her observation."

"It wouldn't hurt, you know, for her to catch us stealing a kiss."

Guillaume narrowed his eyes at her. "If I didn't know any better, Diane, I'd say you want me to kiss you."

"Just look around, Guillaume." She spread her arms and gestured at everything around them. "Paris. This beautiful boat. What girl wouldn't want to be kissed here?"

They were coming up on Notre Dame, and the captain slowed the vedette. The plan was to dock here for two hours of picnicking and sightseeing before continuing the ride. Guillaume stood then and offered her a hand. "Let's rejoin the others."

"The adventure continues." Diane, regretful that the kissing opportunity had passed unfulfilled, let him pull her to her feet. He didn't drop her hand as he led her through the cabin toward the stern, where everyone else was gathering themselves and their belongings together in preparation for going ashore.

Stone walls lined both banks of the river. The scalloped arches of the Pont de l'Archvêché spanned it up ahead. The cathedral's spire pricked the sky. They waved at pedestrians on the Pont au Double as they passed underneath. The river narrowed and walls on either side seemed to close in a little, the closer they got to Notre Dame.

With professional efficiency, the captain had the boat tied to the dock near a stone staircase up to the cathedral grounds.

The gentlemen helped the ladies across, and then the captain jumped back on board to pass the picnic baskets to Harry and Guillaume. Then the little group mounted the stairs and joined the crowds of sightseers gazing at one of the city's loveliest landmarks.

Diane had seen Notre Dame before in passing, but up close it was breathtaking and strange. With so much complexity and fine, lacy detail, it didn't look like something that could stand for centuries. Even with all the lovely scenery, she couldn't stop thinking about kissing Guillaume.

"Do you come here often?" Diane asked Guillaume while everyone in their group oohed and ahhed.

"I have been here many times, yes. I think every Parisian has."

"This has got to be why France is so different from America. We don't have anything like this. Nothing at all. And it affects us, makes us categorically different from people like you, who have lived around such depth of culture for your whole life."

"If you're saying the French are superior to the Americans, I'm not going to argue with you." He was only half-joking.

"Not better, exactly, but definitely different," Diane said thoughtfully. "And I've no business arguing on America's behalf. After all, I want to stay in Paris."

The tour company had assembled a simple cold lunch of charcuterie, cheese, bread, fruit, and wine. There was enough of a breeze to keep the flies away, and it hadn't reached the hottest part of the day yet, so the outdoor dining wasn't as rustic as it could have been. They ate at small round tables, fixtures of the green space in front of the cathedral, and then walked around the whole structure before touring the inside.

Guillaume stayed attentively by Diane's side, guiding her with light touches and stealing sweet glances, convincingly smitten.

When they'd finished, they had a few minutes before their departure time, and so Diane and Guillaume walked on the Pont au Double to see the view from over the water. When they reached the center, they stopped and looked over the side facing away from where the others were gathering to leave. And so they had a quick private moment alone. A tour boat similar to theirs slid through the water underneath them. Next to her, Guillaume waved as it passed. His shaggy hair parted around his ear where his hat pressed it down. And his sideburns reached the sharp angle of his jaw. After a moment, he looked down at her and caught her staring.

"We should get back down there," he said, his eyes taking her in.

They were side by side and close, and she didn't want to get back on the boat and ride next to him for the next few hours not knowing—not being able to remember—the taste of his breath. His pink mouth curved into a sideways smile, almost like a dare.

Quickly, before he could get away, or she could think better of it, she put a foot on the bottom of the metal bridge railing and pushed up to his mouth for quick kiss. She'd intended a peck, but he caught her and held her. His broad, strong thigh settled between her legs, and if he hadn't been holding her, she'd have collapsed into a swoon. Staring at her, curiously delighted for a moment before he dipped his head and kissed her again. He firmly held her in place, while he pressed her lips apart and swiped at her tongue with his. Tasting and sipping like a man who had all the time in the world. Diane, meanwhile, melted into his hold on her. His body was firm and strong, insistent. If kissing him had been like this that night after the party, she knew now it was a crime that she'd been too drunk to remember. An absolute crime. When he stopped and pulled back slightly, Diane groaned.

"Don't stop." She didn't want him to ever stop doing that to her with his mouth. His perfect, skilled mouth.

"Ha. I have to, or they'll come looking for us." Guillaume righted Diane and released her from his glorious arms.

Diane, blinking and looking around, regained her composure. She tucked an errant brown curl behind her ear and said, "My goodness. That was quite… believable."

Guillaume laughed and led her back down to the waiting boat.

Once aboard, Guillaume sat next to Ada and Harry because a good fiancé would probably make some attempts to bond with Diane's family members, especially after spending all morning in such close togetherness.

He also needed space to process what had happened on the bridge. His desire to kiss her had been palpable. It had been there all day and ramped up considerably on the boat ride when she'd been staring at him like she was ready to eat him. And then she kissed him, as if she'd been thinking the same thing all along. Being a fiancé, even a fake one, did have some benefits. Still, he was apprehensive. He had not forgotten about her tendency to keep him in the dark.

So instead of sitting with Diane, he chatted with Harry, who happened to play tennis. Guillaume promised to add him to his guest list at the club and gave Harry his card. "Send word anytime you want to play."

Harry promised he would.

And Guillaume did his best to charm Ada by pointing out all the monuments and naming the bridges on their way east. They passed where they'd boarded and kept going, passing under the Pont Saint-Michel and Pont de la Concorde, heading toward the Eiffel Tower. It came in and out of view as they traveled, until they were so close it couldn't be missed. It had been a magnificent addition to the city, everyone Guillaume knew thought so. Truly the statement piece of a city covered in jewels.

He caught Diane smiling at him with a mixture of confusion and amusement on her face. Her hat shaded her eyes but enhanced her delicate profile. And the light sparkling off the water skimmed over her like a painting. They opened the last bottles of champagne as the captain turned the boat around Pont de l'Alma and steered them toward the end of the trip.

At the boat landing, they all thanked the captain and came ashore. Now they were sun-kissed and more closely acquainted. As the party made their way up the ramp to street level, Guillaume slowed to match Diane's pace.

"My carriage is waiting for me up here. I can give you a ride back to Rue de Fortuny."

"That's okay." Diane looked tired from being on the water all day. A little pinker than she had been earlier. "I'm going to the hotel for dinner. I'll ride with them."

"Thank you for today."

She smiled. "Thank you, Guillaume. I really enjoyed myself."

"Me too. Much more than I imagined."

"Oh really." She laughed. "Are we Americans so terrible?"

"I meant the kissing, not so much the company. Though that was pleasant too."

"The kissing, huh?" She grinned devilishly, and her eyes flicked to his mouth. The small gesture sent desire deep into his loins.

"Why don't you come back to the hotel for dinner? Ada will be thrilled, and then perhaps we can sneak away for another kiss."

"I thought we were only supposed to be doing that for show."

"Pardon me, monsieur, but you kissed me back even though no one was around to see it." She shrugged. "Plus, I'm not sure it matters at this point. They found us asleep in my bed together. Maybe the kissing is something to keep between us."

"Maybe." Guillaume growled out the words. Maybe the kissing wasn't a good idea at all. The last thing he should do is give into his urges for this woman. "Which is why we should hold off on any more of that. Besides, I have a previous engagement."

"Okay. Just leave me to fend for myself then," she said wistfully.

"Au revoir, Diane."

"Au revoir."

"I'll write," he called as he walked away. Then he couldn't resist turning around one last time. She was still standing there watching him. She smiled and waved and then blew an exaggerated kiss. It was silly and affectionate. And it wasn't at all for show.

Chapter Nine

That night at the Grand Hôtel, Catherine and Harry excused themselves from the dinner table as soon as they'd finished eating. Harry said he was going to smoke, and Catherine said she was going upstairs. They'd hardly spoken to each other, and the tension between them was so palpable that Diane could almost see it vibrating between them. But Catherine and Harry were very careful. They'd gotten quite good at hiding their feelings. No matter whether they were madly in love or ready to kill each other, Daddy and Ada never seemed to notice. Or if they did, they ignored it.

Their departure left Diane alone with Ada. A server came to clear the last of their plates from dinner. It had been a long day on the water, and so the meal had been thankfully subdued. Guillaume had a prior arrangement and hadn't come. Now Diane was finishing her coffee and looking forward to home. But she also wanted to know what Ada would write to her father that night, now that she'd spent the day with Guillaume.

"Today went well," Diane said to Ada. "Guillaume enjoyed himself."

"He's a fine young man," Ada said sternly. "And very knowledgable about the city."

She spoke of him more like the boat captain than the man her almost-stepdaughter was marrying. "You don't like him?"

"It's not that. Your father isn't convinced that this marriage is a good idea, and I can't say I am either."

"What could you possibly not like about Guillaume? He's nice. He's rich. What's the problem?"

"He's not you, Diane. He's not your life."

"I don't know what that's supposed to mean," Diane grumbled.

"I get the appeal, Diane, I do. Paris is beautiful. Guillaume is handsome and cultured. But you're an American. Your home is in America. Your family is there. Your best friend, the man you've promised to marry, the man who truly knows and understands you is in America."

"You're wrong. Daddy's wrong too, if that's what he said."

"Be honest with yourself, Diane. This is a fling. A dalliance. A defiance. You've always been a good girl, and now you're rebelling against your father."

"Ada, please. You and I both know that I've never been the good girl. That's Catherine."

"That's what you don't understand, Diane. This is big. Refusing to come home from a vacation is huge. Much bigger than you think." Ada glared at Diane. "Are you really throwing your whole life away? Because that's what this is. Your whole life is in Woollett. By staying here, you're a stranger in a strange land. You'll be alone among people who are not like you. Who don't value the same things as you. Who don't understand you. Who don't care. The shine will wear off this Frenchman, no matter how handsome he is, because he's not like you. And then you'll be stuck here."

"Oh, please. Boats leave for New York every day."

"Maybe so, but what if Alvin moves on? You and Guillaume are too different, and when it doesn't work out, you won't have the option of going back to Alvin. You could lose out on the real thing by chasing something false.”

“What do you mean 'false'?” Diane straightened in her chair. Ada was cutting close to something in Diane that was uncomfortable to examine.

“I mean is this thing with Guillaume really real? More real than your life at home?”

“We're engaged.”

“I'm not arguing that. I'm asking you if the feelings underneath it are real enough to make this choice.”

Diane didn't want to answer. There was no point in examining her fake engagement for the sake of winning an argument. She was too tired. She swallowed the last of her coffee.

“With that reductive and, frankly, wrong assessment of my life, Ada, I believe I'll be going. I am too tired to argue any further.” Diane stood up from the table, and Ada didn't try to stop her. But before walking away, Diane paused and said, “You know, Ada, you and Daddy think you know me so well. But you don't really know me at all. You never did, and you definitely don't know me now. Make sure you tell him I said that in your next telegram.”

Diane faltered as she walked away from Ada and out of the hotel. Was she making a terrible mistake? Because Ada was right: the thing between her and Guillaume was fake. Her sister was ready to hop on a boat back to New York. And Diane would soon be alone in a foreign country. She loved it here and didn't feel unsafe. But she'd never been truly alone before. Not the way she would be when everyone but her got on the boat to go home.

For a long time, she'd believed that marriage was a trap. But what if complete freedom was a trap of another kind? What if she was making a decision that she'd soon regret? What if Paris was the real trap? A shiny, exciting place that lured her in and was seducing her into her own ruin. French books were filled with that sort of thing. Downfall.

The concierge caught Diane a cab, and within minutes she was pulling away from the hotel. But Ada's words stayed with her all the way across town.

Back on Rue de Fortuny, Diane let herself in and walked up the stairs. There were no letters for her on the table in the foyer, and the drawing room was empty. She continued upstairs, where her and Catherine's rooms were dark. She hadn't expected to find Catherine here, but when she left the table early at dinner, Diane wondered if she'd come home. And so Diane was disappointed.

The carriage ride across town—and ruminating about her confrontation with Ada—had reenergized her. She wasn't ready to go to bed or to be alone. Light was coming from upstairs where the others lived. Relieved that someone was home, Diane went to see who it was. The only open door was Nadine's. She was standing in front of her mirror, tying a ribbon into her intricately braided red hair.

Diane knocked. "Bonsoir."

"Bonsoir. Are you just coming in?"

Diane nodded. "I had dinner with our visitors at the Grand Hôtel."

"Ah, fancy."

"Yes, fancy and annoying. I've had my fill today."

"Did Catherine stay there again?" Nadine spritzed her neck with perfume from a cut glass bottle with a red bulb and tassel.

Where the floral mist hung in the air, Nadine moved her arms to catch it on her skin.

"I think so. She apparently hasn't gotten her fill yet." Diane stepped inside and sat on the bed. It was covered in a soft, worn quilt that had been sewn from old dresses—a rainbow of satins and velvets. Nadine's wardrobe doors were splayed open with a gush of gowns streaming from it. Layers of tulle and poufs of taffeta in every color. Nadine was an actress and the oldest of the housemates at twenty-seven. Her personality was as colorful and warm as her room. One of the greatest parts about living in Madame's pension was that Diane had a few extra sisters when her own wasn't up to the role.

"She's with her gentleman friend from America, though, so perhaps she's getting her fill right now." Nadine waggled her eyebrows suggestively.

"Don't remind me. I'm mad at her because she's going back to America."

"Is she?"

"I think so, but I can't tell for sure. She and Harry have been hot or cold since he arrived. Who knows what they're up to while the evil stepmother sleeps."

Nadine gave herself one last look in the mirror and stood up.

"You're going out?"

"I am. I had rehearsals all day, then I came home and napped. Now I am ready to dance," she said with a flourish of her arms. "Come with me?"

Diane, still buzzing with nervous energy, didn't hesitate. "I'll be ready in ten minutes."

She went downstairs to her room and lit a lamp, flooding the space with light. Everything was as Diane left it when she'd gone out that morning—in a state of utter chaos. All her clothes strewn about, dirty dishes here and there. Catherine habitually spent time every day straightening up their shared rooms, but she'd been at the hotel so much that it had gotten out of control. Diane, who didn't have the tidying up habit, picked through her piles of clothing, ignoring the fact that Catherine was right: a messy space was uncomfortable and frustrating. How had she let it get this bad? She just needed to get out. An hour at the dance hall could work wonders on a weary spirit. She dressed in her ruffled things and dancing shoes, and then went out to meet Nadine.

To avoid attracting Madame Tremblay's attention, they didn't talk on the way down, and they went out through the kitchen service entrance.

"I can't be out all night," Nadine said as they hurried toward Avenue de Villiers. The night was warm, and the houses glowed from within. Nadine was the one who'd introduced Diane and her sister to cancan dancing. They'd all gone out right after the sisters moved in. Diane learned fast that there was nothing so wonderful as a dance hall close to home.

"Nor can I."

Nadine hailed a fiacre without any trouble, and gave the driver the address in Montmartre. Moulin de la Gallette was one of their favorite dance halls, and Diane had been several times. As they rode through the city streets, Diane's chest began to ache. There were no dance halls in Woollett, and even if there were, her father would know as soon as she set foot inside. Everyone in that town knew everyone and kept up with all the business. Here in Paris, she was free to slip out and dance whenever she wanted. There were friends in her house and cabs on the streets and music playing all over. She wasn't ready to go back to a small town, and that night, she danced with her friend like she'd never get another chance.

The next morning after breakfast, Diane ran into Cook in the hall as she was leaving the dining room.

"A messenger just brought this for you, dear." Cook was one of the two house staff Madame Tremblay kept on full-time. Claire, the maid, was the other. This was a considerably smaller staff than Diane was used to at home. But the house itself was smaller. They didn't host parties or dinners the way Daddy and Ada did. The way her mother had loved to do when she was alive. And here their interactions were far less formal. They staff were more like house mothers than hired help in Diane's eyes.

"Oh, thank you for bringing it up."

"The boy who brought it said it was important. And I wanted to see if it was from the gentleman I saw you escorting out of here one morning last week."

Diane gasped and put a hand on Cook's elbow, both to draw her in and steady herself. "You saw me?"

"Don't worry. Madame didn't notice. But you be careful now. That's asking for trouble."

"I know. I'd had far too much to drink and been bold. I hardly remember it now. Please don't tell."

"If I were going to tell, I would have done it already." She passed over the envelope and went back down to the kitchen.

It was from Guillaume. He'd made an appointment for her at the modiste that afternoon and would meet her there. Diane pressed the letter to her chest and smiled to herself. She'd almost forgotten about the dress. She hadn't been able to buy anything since they'd lost their father's support. All her dresses were slightly out of fashion, which was noticeable in Paris, the fashion capital of the world. Diane made conscious efforts not to let this bother her. She couldn't afford to live any differently. So a trip to the modiste was like her birthday had come early. And for the rest of the day, she kept telling herself that all the excitement and expectation she was building up for the appointment had nothing to do with the fact that Guillaume was meeting her there.

Guillaume arrived at the dress shop a few minutes early on purpose. He waited on the sidewalk for Diane to arrive and was happy he did because she was there minutes later in a cab. When the fiacre came to a stop, Guillaume came forward and helped her down. She was dressed in white gloves and a lightweight gray suit and hat. Simple and elegant. Her hair was curled and held up loosely by jeweled pins.

"Bonjour, monsieur," she said after he paid her driver.

"Bonjour. I'm glad you could come on such short notice." He was also pleased she'd arrived on time. Her life seemed a little chaotic, and people like that were often perpetually tardy. Not Diane though.

"It's not every day a girl gets a new dress. At least not this girl."

"Well, I'm happy you're here." He held out a hand toward the shop door. "Shall we?"

Ornate, colorful gowns were displayed on forms in the wide, spotless front windows. The door had been painted a charming red. Guillaume held it open for Diane, and watched her face light up as she stepped through. Guillaume, as a boy, had been shopping a handful of times with his mother and sisters. They all got like this too. Something about all the fabrics and lace and trimmings thrilled them the way a competitive tennis match thrilled him. As much as he hated to admit it, he'd been looking forward to shopping with Diane, seeing her like this, and watching her make her choices.

A sparkling chandelier hung in the center of the well-appointed shop, and an attendant welcomed them as soon as they were inside.

"I'm Guillaume Allard," he said to the shop attendant, suddenly aware that he was going to have to keep up appearances. After a few seconds of hesitation, he continued, "And I made the appointment for my fiancée, Diane. She needs a dress for a ball."

Playing along was easy enough once the pretense had been established. There was a comfortable-looking bench near the three-way mirrors, which Guillaume headed straight for. He knew from being around his sisters that choosing a dress was complicated. He didn't know the different names for the styles and cuts, but he knew distinctions were important. Most importantly, he knew better than to offer opinions unless they were solicited, and then only cautiously. He planned to lay low until he was truly needed: when it was time to pay. He'd brought a paper to read.

But as the appointment unfolded, he had trouble focusing on the words on the page. Although most of what they said was more or less meaningless to him, Guillaume smiled at the sound of their girlish chatter. He learned that Diane liked to wear red. She worried about her waist looking thick. And she wasn't shy about exposing her décolletage.

"This," the seamstress said, gesturing at Diane's bust, "is one of your greatest assets. You're too young not to show it off."

"Merci," Diane said primly. Over her shoulder, she caught him watching her. Her cheeks were pink and blushing, but her eyes glimmered with happiness.

When the seamstress asked her to step onto the platform to be measured, she assured them that she didn't need to undress. Even though she was fully clothed, as the measuring tape tightened and then fell away from Diane's various parts, Guillaume imagined removing her clothes and putting his hands in those very same places. And that kiss on the bridge. That surprise. Not a minute had passed since that it wasn't flashing through his mind. They'd talked about kissing on the boat, but only in the context of faking their attachment. That was not the context of their actual kiss. It had been stolen in a romantic moment alone, which was a different kind of kiss entirely. He shifted in his seat. Maybe coming along had been a mistake; he should have just told them where to send the bill when he'd made the appointment. He flipped to the next page in the paper.

A little over an hour after arriving, they were finished and back out on the street. Diane had her hat and jacket back on, and the smile hadn't left her face yet.

"Can I drop you at home?"

"No. Although it's one thing to tell the ladies at the shop that we're engaged, I'm not ready to have that conversation with Madame Tremblay. So I'd rather not raise her eyebrows with your gilded carriage." It was parked not far from where they stood.

"I see. Well, let me hail you a cab." There wasn't much traffic on the street, but he'd seen a few cabs pass while he'd been sitting inside. As he stepped to the curb, she followed him.

"Thank you again, Guillaume, for the lovely afternoon. It's been so long since I've gotten a new dress. I didn't even realize how much I'd missed it."

"It was my pleasure." And it truly had been. "Are you sure you don't want the ride?"

She was standing close now, and although it was covered in cotton and silk, his awareness of her great assets had heightened to near urgency over the course of the afternoon. Her eyes fell from his, all the way down his body, like she was licking an ice cream cone. Delicious, undeniable tension sparked between them.

At just that moment, a cab came along and stopped when Guillaume raised his hand. "Will you be joining Harry and me for tennis tomorrow morning?"

"You've planned something?"

"We have. He wrote to me this morning."

"Well, I wouldn't miss it." She gave the driver her address. Then Guillaume offered a hand to help her, and she took it, putting her precious weight on him when she stepped up. When she was seated inside, she smiled. "I'll see you tomorrow."

Guillaume nodded and closed the door to the carriage. He waved her off and then went home.

The next morning, Guillaume arrived at the tennis club early. Although he didn't harbor any superstitions about success on the court with his actions beforehand, Guillaume did have his routine. He pressed through the doors to the club thirty minutes before his court time. He smiled and greeted the attendant at the reception desk and then headed to the locker room. Seeing an acquaintance in the corridor, he nodded without stopping to chat. The other man didn't stop either; it was too early for anything but passing greetings. Guillaume entered the locker room, which was quiet and empty. The symmetry of the space and rows of lockers were unremarkable and soothing in their regularity, especially when no one was around banging the metal doors. He picked up two fresh towels off the stack and went to his locker in the corner closest to the courts.

Inside his locker, Guillaume kept his racket, his new canvas and rubber gymnasium shoes, several balls, and a minimal toilette for cleaning up afterward. He carried his clean tennis whites in a compact duffel bag. While he dressed, he liked to think through several perfect swings. This helped him clear his head and get ready to play. Sometimes, between removing and putting on various pieces of clothing, he'd pause to act out the swings he was working on in his mind. Backswings, serves, whatever he wanted to focus on for the day. He'd breathe deep and envision the ball whizzing through the air, hurdling, ideally, just out of his faceless opponent's reach.

Despite going through his usual motions, this morning he couldn't quite clear his head. He was looking forward to spending time with Diane and her family, especially without her pill of an almost-stepmother there watching them. As Guillaume understood it, she was staying back at the hotel; Diane, Catherine, and Harry would be joining him as guests. But he couldn't truly relax because Diane didn't want Catherine to know that their engagement was fake. Diane didn't trust that Catherine wouldn't tell Ada. Guillaume wondered if she wasn't being a little dramatic about all of this, but it surely made things interesting. He liked family drama, especially when it didn't involve him. Still, overly dramatic or not, he had to keep up appearances and watch what he said. These extra concerns didn't bode well for his performance on the court.

When he was dressed and ready to play, Guillaume locked up his locker and went back out to the lobby. His guests were waiting for him when he got there. Diane was like an exotic flower in a pale pink cotton blouse and fluttery white skirt. She wore the same straw hat from the day on the boat. Catherine was dressed similarly in a white skirt, yellow blouse, and straw hat. They were standing at the back, looking out the windows at the courts, facing away from Guillaume as he approached.

"You made it," Guillaume said when he reached them, and they all three turned at the same time. He greeted Diane and Catherine with la bise. When he moved to greet Harry the same way, the way he might greet any almost-stepbrother of a fiancée, Harry startled and backed away. Guillaume had forgotten that American men supposedly found the gesture too intimate. So he smoothly recovered and extended a hand to Harry instead.

"This is a lovely club," Harry said, skipping over the awkwardness and gesturing out the window. There were six clay courts lined up two by three across the yard. A line of trees secluded it from the street, but the mansard roofs of the sixteenth arrondissement were just visible over the leafy barrier.

"I like to play here," Guillaume agreed. "I'm glad you could come."

Only Harry had his own racket, so Guillaume borrowed two from the club and then led them outside.

"You know all three of us will be rusty," Diane said to Guillaume as they walked along the edge of the courts. Then to

Harry and Catherine, she explained. "Guillaume plays almost every day."

"Rusty? Speak for yourself. I play three times a week back at home," Harry said.

"We could play doubles? Me and Harry versus Diane and Guillaume?"

"Before anyone claims me as a teammate," Diane said, holding up her racket. "I have to confess I pulled a muscle dancing the other night. It's still sore. It might hamper my movements on the court."

"You were dancing?" Catherine and Guillaume said at the same time. His heart dipped when she'd said it. Not because she'd been dancing; he wasn't the sort of man to be put off by a woman who went to dance halls. He regretted missing out on the fun. And the thought of her hands on another man's shoulders gave him a possessive jolt of jealousy.

"I was. At Moulin de la Gallette with Nadine." She shrugged and grinned.

"I wish I'd have known you were going dancing. I might have gone," Catherine said.

"Would you?" Harry said grumpily.

"What was I supposed to do, send a messenger to the Grand Hôtel? You weren't home." There was a sharpness in Diane's words. She and her sister weren't getting along.

"Even if your game is subpar, you can be on my team," Guillaume said. He didn't want to spend his court time thinking about Diane dancing with other men in a crowded club, and he didn't want to watch her argue with her sister either. Splitting them up might keep the peace.

"I would have gone dancing too," Guillaume said as the two teams headed for opposite sides of the net. She hadn't mentioned dancing when they were dress shopping. But why would she? He hadn't asked. He hadn't fully considered Diane's social life outside of his arrangement with her, which was silly. Of course, she had an active social life. That wouldn't change because of him. But the jealousy was different from the territorial pangs he'd feel with any other girlfriend in a situation like this. Everything Diane did affected him more than anyone else ever had. He liked Diane. A lot. And, on some base level, he considered her to be his. So much for faking it.

Diane groaned and rolled her eyes at Guillaume. "Why can't a girl just go dancing without sending out a stack of petit bleus?"

"I'm not saying you need my permission," Guillaume argued. "I just would have gone with you. If I'd have known. If I'd have been invited."

Diane eyed him suspiciously. "I'll keep that in mind."

He was relieved when they spaced out on the court. And like most problems, all the tensions brewing among the four of them worked themselves out during the game. Diane turned out to be competent enough to keep up. Harry and Catherine had played together before, though mostly in adolescence. In the end, Catherine missed a serve, and Diane and Guillaume won. Diane threw her arms in the air to celebrate. Then she hugged Guillaume and patted him on the back, making a show out of beating her sister. It was the sort of thing he'd seen Josephine and Juliette do a million times. When someone had a competitive disposition, the first and most obvious opponent was always a sibling.

"This is fun," Guillaume said when she released him. They were facing each other in the center of their side of the court.

"It is." Diane was flushed and pink from the exertion of the game and the growing heat of the day. Her eyes sparkled.

"It's fun seeing you with your sister. You remind me of mine." He twirled his racket between his palms. "Have you told Catherine that our engagement isn't real."

Her brow furrowed, and she leaned in and spoke softer. "I haven't, so let's not talk about it now."

"You don't think she'll keep it a secret?"

"I don't know."

"Is that why you two look like you're ready to kill each other?"

"There are a hundred reasons for that." She laughed. "I'm joking. I love her, but we're not happy with each other right now. That's the best way to put it."

They crossed the court to where Catherine and Harry were standing and talking.

"Do we have time for another game?" Harry asked.

"Of course. Me and you?"

"Sounds good. Ladies, do you mind?"

"Not at all," Catherine said.

"We can get something to drink inside."

After a quick drink of water, Guillaume trotted back out onto the court. Harry squared off on the other side. Harry served and Guillaume easily returned it, setting the fast game into motion. Guillaume scored the first point, then the second. Harry scored by narrowly sneaking one past Guillaume. But Guillaume easily fell into the flow of the game, watching Harry, responding to his returns almost before he made them, and enjoying the satisfying thwack of the ball against his racket. It wasn't easy, but Guillaume proceeded to beat him.

Guillaume didn't pay much attention to Diane and Catherine when he was so focused on the game. But when it was over, Diane jumped up from her seat and cheered. He liked seeing her there, watching him do the thing he enjoyed the most. It felt natural and fun to have her around. His immediate thought was to get her signed up for a lesson. He could meet her here any morning. If she were his real fiancée, that's exactly what he'd do. But she wasn't, and so he hugged her and let her celebrate his win and offered to buy them all a glass of wine at the club before they parted ways for the rest of the day. He told them about the club and the new indoor courts they were building. He listened to their stories with interest. And he was humble about beating Harry. Guillaume was his most charming self, but he held back a little too.

Spending more time with Diane and her family at his club brought the fake engagement closer to home. He hadn't told his family about her, but soon he'd be introducing them all. He wasn't entirely sure he was ready to bring Diane into his world.

When they were leaving, Diane rose on her tiptoes to kiss him on the cheek. Her lips were a warm, dry brush that sent a ripple of desire for more through him. Her lips were so pleasant, so perfect. But they weren't really his. In the seconds her face was so close to his, time seemed to slow and thicken. And then she was pulling away, an absence like a throbbing ache, and time sped back up to normal.

"Until the ball, darling," she said breezily.

"Until the ball."

Chapter Ten

A week later, Guillaume's carriage rolled to a stop in front of 77 Rue de Fortuny at precisely eight o'clock. Diane normally wouldn't let Guillaume pick her up here because the madame of the house was strict about male visitors, but he had gathered from her last letter that somehow the word of their engagement had reached her. Now that Madame Tremblay knew they were engaged, Diane had written, it would be strange if he didn't come to the door and present himself properly. And so here he was.

He stepped out of the carriage and crossed the sidewalk and mounted the two steps with purposeful strides. Then, faced with the door, he raised his fist and knocked. But before he could pull back for a second knock, the door swung open. Diane and a stout older woman with a creased brow were standing there.

"Bonsoir, mademoiselles," he bowed to them.

"Bonsoir, monsieur," Diane said, sounding exasperated. Or maybe just nervous. "This is Madame Tremblay; she owns the house and has promised Ada she'd look after me."

"I see. It's a pleasure, Madame Tremblay." He bowed to her again. "I can assure you I'll bring her home in one piece, and the ball we're attending is a family affair. Nothing to worry about."

"I'm happy to hear that," Madame said. "And Diane tells me she's marrying you to stay in France. Is that so?"

Guillaume gulped reflexively but then smiled. "I have proposed to mademoiselle, yes, and we're working on gaining the approval of her family."

"I see."

"I'll see you later, Madame," Diane said, kissing her on the cheek and then turning toward the waiting carriage.

Guillaume nodded and followed her, while Madame Tremblay retreated inside. Once they were settled next to each other and the carriage moved off, Diane sighed and fanned her face with her hand.

Guillaume said, "She's quite stern, isn't she? I thought you weren't telling her about the fake engagement?"

Diane laughed and swatted his bicep with the back of her hand. "I was avoiding that, wasn't I?"

"So what happened?"

"I am trying to keep everyone on a need-to-know basis, as far as this whole thing goes. But I did tell my housemates. They're in on the secret. Madame Tremblay overheard us talking and confronted me right away. She's not in on the secret. As far as Madame Tremblay is concerned, our engagement is quite real."

"I see. So the housemates all know the truth. The madame of the house knows about the engagement, but like your family members—Catherine included—she thinks it's real."

"That's right. Believe it or not, when I told Madame Tremblay, I thought it might actually alleviate some of the complications with my current situation."

"Alleviate the complications?" This amused him.

"Maybe? I had to tell Madame something. I do live under her roof. And I had to mention that Catherine is probably leaving. She's basically moved into the Grand Hôtel."

"Has she said she's leaving?"

"We haven't really talked about it. She's been spending so much time with Harry that I've hardly seen her. But if she leaves, I don't know how I'll be able to afford my rent."

"I see."

Diane groaned, and although it was meant in exasperation, it landed erotically in Guillaume's ear. She smoothed her hands over her skirt. "Let's not talk about it anymore. I can't stand it. Tell me about the party."

"It's at a lovely place in the sixteenth. Friends of my parents."

"And you still want me to meet your parents? You told them about me?"

"They know I'm bringing a date. But we can't pretend we're engaged, or tell them we're pretending to others."

"I'm not good enough for that?"

"Ha. It's not that. My sister just announced her engagement. And it's real. So I don't want to distract any attention from her. If my parents think I'm getting married too, they'll want to announce it, which will mean gossip. But not telling them makes it easier, doesn't it? You're just a friend meeting my family."

"Will that be enough for Marielle? Because she might not back off until you're officially off the market. Hell, she might not stop trying until you're married. We might actually have to go through with it to save you from her."

"That's very funny. Just don't tell my mother."

"What's that supposed to mean?"

"Telling her would drastically complicate my life, not alleviate the complications."

Diane stiffened and crossed her arms over her chest. "She won't hear it from me."

He'd irritated her, but he wasn't sure why. When Diane didn't say anything else, neither did Guillaume.

The sky was fully dark when the carriage slowed and fell into the arrivals line at the party. The face of the stone house had eight cheery windows with shutters and ironwork details. Tricolored buntings draped each one. The house was illuminated from inside, and the garden was filled with guests arriving and streaming inside. Torches lit the landscaped paths, where roses bloomed on lush shrubs.

When it was their turn to disembark, two attendants came to their aid, took their names, and ushered them toward the front door. Diane took Guillaume's arm, and they walked in together. She seemed to have recovered from whatever had been bothering her before.

The Prévot family greeted Guillaume with air kisses and firm handshakes, and they nodded approvingly when he introduced them to Diane. They got flutes of champagne from a passing server, and Guillaume showed Diane around. The foyer opened onto a wide ballroom where a string quartet was playing and people were dancing. A wall of glass doors opened onto an outdoor patio, so guests could step out without actually leaving the party proper. And there was another formal garden filled with statuary and seating. People were all over, enjoying themselves.

Guillaume didn't see his parents anywhere, which was fine because he was still apprehensive about introducing Diane to them. It felt different than it had with other women, and not only because of the fake engagement. So he didn't mind delaying it. But they ran into Marielle right away.

"Guillaume," she said with a faint note of shock.

"Ah, Marielle. Surprise, surprise. It's lovely to see you again." He kissed her hand, even though she tilted her head in preparation for him to kiss her there. He did not. "This is my friend Diane Talbot, whom I mentioned."

"You did mention her." Marielle examined Diane in her stunning red dress. It had fine peach lace overlaying the bodice and parts of the skirt, which made for a striking color combination that even Guillaume knew to appreciate.

"And Guillaume has told me so much about you, Marielle. The pleasure is all mine." Diane confidently went in for the kisses that Guillaume hadn't, which softened Marielle up a little. Diane continued, ignoring any hesitation or negativity from Marielle, plowing straight through as if they were destined to be friends. "I understand that it's you I have to thank for breaking Guillaume in. He's such a wonderful man that I know you must be impressive."

Diane's French was nearly perfect, which Marielle would appreciate. In fact, Diane charmed Marielle in no time. They chatted in that friendly, happy way women did when they liked each other. And they completely ignored Guillaume. By the time Marielle left them, she was smiling. And Diane had gotten her calling card and an invitation to go skiing that winter at Marielle's family's chateau.

Marielle left so peaceably, so charmed by Diane, that Guillaume held no more reservations about her meeting his family. Introducing this woman to his mother would be easy. Maybe too easy.

"Let's dance, and then I'll find my family," Guillaume said close to Diane's ear. She nodded and took his hand, following him to the dance floor. The ensemble started up a waltz, and Guillaume put his hand on her waist. It heated her skin through her dress. Holding her just closer than respectable, they spun in tight circles together. He was so much taller than her that the bottom of his white cravat was at her eye level. Her nose even with the rose on his lapel. Its perfume was intoxicating. His broad chest made such a pleasing view, such a natural resting place for her hand.

The music swirled lightly and filled the ballroom. Diane, out of habit, counted in her head to keep track of the steps, even though she could waltz in her sleep. The room was warm, but with the doors propped open, it wasn't stuffy or uncomfortable. His strong arms enclosed her so near to his body. Being there, dancing with him, thrilled her more than anything she'd done in a long time. Then they spun apart in time with the music, and the room full of people came back to her attention. They weren't alone, but she wanted to be.

"That went well with Marielle," she said when the waltz brought them close enough to talk.

"I am impressed by how quickly you two became friends."

"Sometimes ladies have to stick together."

"I see that." He smiled down at her, watching her intently. "In any case, I appreciate it. I think she likes you so much that she'll let you have me."

"I'm sure she has some other options. Not that any of them compare to you."

"You don't have to say that, you know." He leaned in close and whispered, "Since we're faking it."

"Hey," she said as the song came to an end. "I am nothing if not loyal. And proud."

As they were leaving the dance floor, a young woman waved to them. She was with another young woman who looked very much like her.

"My sisters," Guillaume said, steering Diane toward them.

"We heard you were bringing a guest, Guillaume."

"Bonsoir, mademoiselles," Guillaume said, kissing each of them. Both girls were blond like Guillaume, but they were so petite compared to their much larger brother. "Diane, these are my sisters Josephine and Juliette."

"It's lovely to meet you," Diane smiled and nodded at each sister. "And congratulations, Josephine. Guillaume tells me you're getting married."

"I am. Thank you." Josephine beamed at Diane with a smile so similar to her brother's. Each sister was dressed in a shade of pink, and both wore pearls. And the way Juliette and Josephine looked at their brother, they obviously thought the world of him.

"You're American," Juliette said, eyes wide. "Where are you from?"

"A small town that no one's ever heard of north of New York City."

"What's the name of the town?"

"Woollett."

"Woollett?" Juliette said, copying Diane's American accent, making the word stand out against their French. "That's a strange name. But now I've heard of it!"

Juliette was delighted. Both of Guillaume's sisters were so adorable and so French that Diane liked them immediately.

"Ah! You have."

"Do they have cowboys where you're from?"

"She's obsessed with cowboys ever since we saw the western carnival." Josephine rolled her eyes playfully at her sister.

"They don't have cowboys in Woollett, unfortunately. There we just call them farmers."

"I'm not sure those count."

"No," Diane said. "I'm not sure they do."

The sisters both laughed. They seemed close enough to fill in each other's thoughts, much like Diane and Catherine always had been. At least until recently. They were still close, they always would be, Diane was sure. But close looked different the older you got. Josephine was getting married, a huge life change that would change her sister's life too.

"Where are Maman and Papa?"

"They're somewhere, no doubt looking for you," Juliette said. "We're walking outside to see who else is here."

"And maybe find my fiancé." Josephine giggled. "It still feels so surreal to say that!"

Juliette rolled her eyes this time.

"All right, well, I'll see you later then. I'm going to introduce Diane to Maman and Papa."

The sisters waggled their brows at their brother as they sashayed away.

Diane sighed with relief watching them go; if their parents had raised those two, then they had to be delightful. Guillaume wasn't so bad either.

"I see them," Guillaume said, nodding toward a well-dressed couple on the other side of the room who looked like an older version of Guillaume and his sisters. Then he turned to Diane. "Are you ready?"

"To meet your parents?" Diane gulped down the last of her champagne. "Did Marielle ever meet them?"

"She did. But I introduce my parents to everyone I'm with at every party. They've met almost all of my friends."

"So this doesn't have to be a big deal?"

"It doesn't. Not like the time I met your family. Or almost-family. We don't have to pretend."

He was right. It couldn't possibly be as bad as the time he met her father's ambassadors. "Then I'm ready."

His parents were lovely, of course, smiling and curious about her and what brought her to Paris. They didn't seem concerned with the details of her association with their son and spoke very kindly of Charlotte Deveraux when Guillaume mentioned they were housemates. They'd recently met her through Guillaume's friend Antoine.

"Oh, Guillaume, darling, I almost forgot. Has Antoine sorted things with his fiancée? His mother has been so upset."

Based on Antoine's short letters, he was trying to untangling himself from the engagement his parents arranged for him. "No, not at all. In fact, I believe he's hoping to marry Charlotte instead."

"Oh, my." Madame Allard, who had her arm linked loosely around her husband's, looked up at him and squeezed in tighter. "Young love can be quite messy, can't it, dear?"

Monsieur Allard smiled down at her in agreement with such a deep, knowing admiration in his eyes that Diane nearly melted. It was a quick moment of solidarity between two people who had loved each other for a very long time, through life's turmoil and joy. In a flash it was gone; arm in arm, they returned their attention to the conversation, which then carried on in a different direction. Their obvious affection for each other squeezed Diane's heart. Seeing this adorable moment, she remembered what Guillaume had said about his parents' marriage. That they weren't miserable, and marriage had made their lives better instead of worse. And Diane understood, perhaps for the first time, exactly what Guillaume had been talking about. Is this what her parents would have if her mother had lived? For Diane, who didn't like being alone, it seemed like a lovely ideal. Growing with someone over so many years, a long-term partnership. But it was bittersweet, knowing her parents didn't get it.

Throughout the brief meeting, Diane put her best, most charismatic self forward. They spoke for nearly twenty minutes without it ever feeling like a chore. It was much less stressful than Diane imagined it would be. Her parents were not so easy to introduce to anyone. They could be so difficult that the best place for them was on the other side of the Atlantic. Diane kind of regretted that the Allards weren't really becoming her in-laws.

"They liked you," Guillaume said to Diane when his parents had gone to talk with the hosts.

"That's because we didn't tell them about the fake engagement. And they didn't find us in bed together."

"That's true." He laughed, a shallow, dry laugh that made Diane's whole body tingle. Then he said earnestly, "But I think they would have liked you even if we had told them."

Over the next few hours, Diane met several of Guillaume's friends and acquaintances. And the whole night was just as wonderful. She genuinely liked his people. She fit so naturally by his side, assisting his jokes and telling hers when he set her up. Her hand kept finding his. And every touch they shared, no matter how small or casual, sent a flurry of warm, fluttering desire through her whole body. It all felt so easy and so real that Diane wished it was.

Later that evening, as the party was winding down and guests were starting to say goodnight, Guillaume and Diane were alone on a balcony smoking cigarettes. They were standing side by side, leaning against the balustrade and looking out at the garden. Diane had been to balls and parties back in America, and they were nothing like a Paris event. The energy and people were more glamorous. Woollett, of course, was a rustic, small, completely different world. But even fashionable New York City didn't quite compare. When Guillaume mentioned calling up his carriage, she sighed. "I almost don't want it to end. That's a real testament to your people, Guillaume."

"I appreciate that," he said. "But it doesn't have to end. We could see if anyone has any opium."

He craned his neck, comically looking around.

"Stop. This isn't that kind of party."

"You're right. But perhaps I could find one."

"No, that's okay."

He watched her but didn't say anything for a moment.

"What?"

"Well, speaking of opium… I was just thinking that I still can't remember how we decided that you were going to sneak me into your room."

Diane raised her eyebrows. "Why do you want to remember that?"

"Because I'd say the same thing right now."

"Oh, would you?" She slid closer to him, leaning against his arm. She melted at the edges into his sturdiness. When he didn't answer right away, she looked up at him, close enough to his face to see his shave had started to grow out. His blue eyes sparkled like warm, welcoming seas.

"Yes, I would." His eyes fell from hers down to her mouth.

"You could start by kissing me."

In an instant, he dipped his head and kissed her. He inhaled deep, and parted her lips with his, taking firm swipes with his tongue. The kiss was sensuous and intent, a request for more. The whole night had been the most wholesome foreplay, and Diane lit up against him. Urgency surged through her.

When he freed her mouth to kiss a line down the edge of her jaw, she said, "And you could ask me to come back to your place."

He stopped short and pulled away to look at her. "Could I?"

"You could."

Without hesitation, he whisked her back through the house. He asked the butler to call up his carriage, and when it came around he helped Diane inside. As they started off, Guillaume pulled her onto his lap and held her firmly.

Looking her in the eyes, he said, "I am not nearly as drunk as I was the last time we spent the night together."

"Does that mean you won't pass out again?"

"It was you who passed out! I even tried to wake you."

"Oh, you did not." She kissed him before he could argue, and she kept kissing him, intensifying the waves of desire and building the ferocity of her storming urges, until the carriage rolled to a stop in front of a stately, gray stone mansion.

Like many of the wealthy families in the city, the Allard home was laid out in the hotel style with several separate apartments. Getting into Guillaume's apartment didn't require scurrying through any corridors past sleeping parents' bedrooms. Diane followed him through a semi-private entrance in the back and they were alone inside within minutes, far more discreet and much less of a hassle than sneaking into the pension for respectable women.

As soon as they reached his room, Guillaume slipped out of his shoes and lit a lamp. Diane marveled at being immersed in his space. The walls were a somber, stern gray with dark wood paneling. It was elegant and masculine, but also spare. The only decoration that stood out were a collection of paintings of dogs in various landscapes and settings. Hounds running in a pack through a green and gold autumn field. A whimsical brindle French bulldog wearing a jeweled collar and posed in front of an elegant, fluted marble fireplace. A serious-faced woman in a powder-white wig seated with three little brown poodles fluffed into balls. A portrait of a slim, grand dog that looked as big as a horse. She laughed as she took them all in. Guillaume's collection was physical proof of the silly streak running under his particular type of manliness.

Then she saw it and gasped. He had a gramophone! "Is it too late to put music on?"

"No, darling. In fact, I have something you must hear." He went to the machine, placed the needle, and turned the crank. Then familiar notes filled his room.

Diane gasped again, clutching her chest. "It's Debussy."

"All piano."

"Oh, it's incredible." She swayed to the tender first notes of "Nocturnes" and looked around his room. Two of the four tall windows were open to let the night air in. The bed was draped in curtains held back with gray tassels, and it was covered in dark blue cotton bedding. There were neat stacks of newspapers on both side tables. The room had been straightened, probably by a maid, but it was a peek into

Guillaume's life. His real life. When she turned to him, he was watching her.

"Would you like a drink?"

"I would. Whatever you're having."

He poured them each a glass of whiskey and then came to stand next to her by the window.

"Thank you," she said. She took a sip and shuddered at the burn in her throat. She always did that, even though the burn wasn't unpleasant. "What now?"

Guillaume raised his eyebrows. "I prefer to follow your lead."

"Oh, really?"

"I do."

"And why is that?"

"Because I want to go along with what you want."

"What I want?" She smiled seductively. "I guess I want you to do whatever got Marielle so hooked."

His brow furrowed when she said the other woman's name, but then he seemed to take it as a challenge. His blue eyes darkened, and he smiled wickedly. Grabbing her hand, he pulled her toward the bed. He took the whiskey from her and set it next to the pile of newspapers. Then he pushed her slowly onto the bed until she was fully in repose. He stood above her and lifted her skirts out of the way. As he moved the fabric, he also lifted her legs onto his shoulders and knelt before her.

Her view was obstructed by the fabric of her dress, but he made swift work of pulling her underthings off and moving everything out of the way. His hot breath, and then finally his mouth was on her.

Diane quivered and cried out when he took her gently into his teeth, and then soothed with his tongue. Just as everything was starting to blur, he slowly slid in a finger. With that, she was gone, shooting through the air in arcs of shining pleasure. When she landed moments later, she was gripping the dark fabric of his coverlet and panting. Guillaume stood up then, reappearing from between her legs.

"God, that was fabulous," she said as she caught her breath.

"I agree."

"Now what?" He lay down next to her on the bed.

"Whatever you want."

"It's your turn to choose."

"I prefer to let you choose."

"I choose to let you choose. Hurry, before the haze of sexiness wears off."

"Anything?" The word suffused with urgency.

"Well, not anything."

He considered her for a moment, or maybe considered his words. Then, matching her earlier playfulness, he said, "What if I told you that I want you to do whatever had Alvin Monroe so willing to wait?"

She smiled. She felt the urgency too. Like she was rushing to catch a boat or a train. Or like she had to hurry or her chance would pass. Like if they didn't do it now, they'd never get to. "Then I'd say you need to get me out of this dress."

Now he was smiling. "I've been hoping for the chance to do that since you started planning it in the shop."

He helped her up and turned her around, where a line of buttons started between her shoulders and went all the way down to the curve of her waist. One by one, he released the buttons and finally her from the garment. Her skin tingled from every movement of his hands. She turned around and began work on her corset, untying the strings and loosening the lacing. Her breasts heaved when they were free, and as if he couldn't resist, Guillaume's hands were on them, fondling and squeezing. She continued working to undress herself, untying the ribbon on her slip and stepping out of it. Naked now, she started unfastening Guillaume's pants. With each button, her desire built. He was hard and tense, which made her even more desperate. It had been a long time since she and Alvin had been together. And despite all her flirtations and talk with her housemates, there hadn't been any other men since she'd been in Paris. She pushed his pants down, and his hardness grazed against her. She pulled his shirt up over his head and ran her hands across his bare chest.

"Wait," he said, as she pushed him back onto the bed. "I have a rubber, if you like."

"Oh, Guillaume, do you? Because I do like." They were illegal in the United States. She'd always been so worried with Alvin that she'd get pregnant. Fear of pregnancy was part of the reason she left, or part of the reason she felt relieved to be away from him. These weren't thoughts she wanted to be having right now. Thoughts were not what she wanted at all. She wanted only impulse and instinct and pleasure and Guillaume.

She lay down on the bed and waited while he got up and carefully sheathed himself. He was statuesque in the flickering lamplight with sculpted limbs and a muscled torso. The music trembled in the air. Then, when he was ready, he crawled back over her, parting her legs and settling atop her. When they were face to face, she reached between them to guide him to exactly the right place and then she wrapped her legs around him as he slowly pressed inside.

Diane breathed out a sigh of pleasure. Then his mouth found hers, kissing her deep, splitting her lips with his tongue. Guillaume's skin was so soft and warm, and his muscles so firm underneath. His athletic legs kept the rhythm steady. His stomach was curved and flexed. His eyes closed, and his head fell back. She tightened her grip on his neck. And then Diane exploded again in a million pieces. He clenched as his orgasm rippled through him. Then his body loosened and settled onto hers. They lay there for a while, him resting over her, both of them fully spent. It was the sexiest thing she'd ever experienced, and they'd only just begun.

Then he pushed up and kissed her, deep and sensuous. Slowly starting the whole thing over again. By sunrise, they'd done it with her on top riding him like a horse, him on top again, him gripping her hips from behind, and her on top one more time. And no matter how many times she experienced Guillaume, she only wanted more. Every time felt like an adventure.

Chapter Eleven

The next morning, when Guillaume opened his eyes, Diane was still sleeping on the pillow beside him. Her rich brown hair spilled over her shoulders and fanned out on the bedding. Her breath slow and soft. They'd been up most of the night, so he didn't want to wake her. He slipped out of bed and dressed silently. He left the room to find coffee and something to eat. The ladies in the kitchen fixed him a tray. And when he returned to his rooms, Diane was awake, humming to herself, and tying her corset into place over her chemise.

"You should hold off on that," he said, setting the tray on a side table.

"What? Getting dressed?" She laughed and then kept humming.

"What song is that?" Guillaume smiled seductively and moved behind her. He put his arms around her waist. With her hair wild and everywhere, he wanted to push her back onto the bed.

"It's an old love song. You tell me your dream, I'll tell you mine…" She sang the words. When he kissed the lobe of her ear, she stopped. Her small shoulders slumped. "I'm sorry I can't stay. I have to work."

Dipping his face to her neck, he inhaled her sleepy, flowery scent and let his hands wander around her front. Sometime between last night and now, an idea had taken root in his mind that Diane was perhaps exactly what he was looking for in a wife and a lifetime. Someone light with a sense of humor, beautiful, smart. He'd always assumed he'd marry a French girl, but perhaps he hadn't considered alternatives. Now he definitely was.

She moved away from him and picked up her petticoat where it had been discarded on his armchair. She stepped into the thin, white garment and tied the delicate ribbons at her waist. She paused when it was finished, her gaze on something on his side table. The newspaper, probably yesterday's.

"You read the wedding section, Guillaume?"

She held up the paper, folded open on one of his favorite pages. The paper underneath it was turned to the same page as well. His daily reading of the wedding announcements wasn't something he usually discussed. "Everyone reads the wedding section."

"I don't. Well, I stopped years ago."

"Why?"

"Because it got to be all my friends from school. As girls we'd look because it was aspirational gossip. But as I got older and started knowing all the people in the headlines, it didn't feel as fun anymore."

"I read it every day. Right after the front page."

"These days, I'm most excited to look at the help-wanted ads." She smiled and put the paper down, returning to her dressing. He'd never watched this part before, at least not with so much interest. Her strawberry red dress had been lying in a pool on his floor. Scooping it into her thin arms, she shifted the garment into the proper position, held it aloft, and let it slide down over her.

"Can you help me with my buttons?"

She held her hair out of the way while Guillaume fastened her dress. Memories of doing the reverse the night before fluttered through him. The pale skin of her shoulders and neck was just as silky as the fabric. Guillaume pictured them exactly like this every morning, waking up together, watching her mundane, intimate routines, assisting. When he finished, he put his arms around her again, holding her there. She willingly tucked herself against him and purred. He didn't want her to leave. He didn't want her to work. And with all this in his head, his tongue became reckless.

"You know, if we really were getting married, you wouldn't have to work anymore."

She stiffened in his arms; a subtle and yet cataclysmic shift. He immediately regretted the words. Not because he hadn't meant it, but maybe it was too soon. He hadn't read her affections right.

Something.

"That's very funny." She stepped out of his arms and sat on the armchair to put on her shoes. "But I think we both know that would be a disaster."

The feel of her body moving away was like a kick to the chest. "Why do you say that?"

"Because, Guillaume, I didn't come all the way from America to avoid a marriage only to get married. I am not interested in being tied down."

"The way you say it—tied down—is not necessarily the same as marriage." He turned to the tray and poured each of them a cup of coffee. He passed her one.

She smiled and sipped the hot drink. "For a man, maybe not. A marriage is less constricting. But as a woman, legally binding myself to a man is considerably more so. All my friends at home are so busy keeping house and serving their husbands that they've practically become different people."

"Maybe what you're used to in America is not the way it is here. The way it would be with me." He pulled his mouth into a line and watched her intently for a reaction.

"I don't see why you and everyone else are so stuck on marriage."

"You know, Diane, some people see marriage as an adventure. Spending every day, growing old with someone. Getting to know them so deeply. Making a life together. Marriage is when the adventure starts."

"Marriage is a trap, Guillaume. One that I intend to avoid." She took another drink of her coffee and set the cup down on the tray. She was fully dressed now and ready to go. Then she came to him and put a hand on his chest. "But this isn't goodbye, is it? I may still need you again for dinner or another outing with Ada. Just to keep up appearances."

"I enjoyed last night immensely."

"I did too." She lifted up on her toes and put her arms around his neck, bringing her face to his. She paused there for a second, looking for something in his eyes maybe, and then she kissed him. She tasted like coffee. The kiss was brief, but it was also a promise that this wasn't the end. And when she pulled away, she was smiling. "So I will see you later."

"Okay."

Guillaume walked her back downstairs and sent her off in his carriage. As she waved goodbye through the window, Guillaume was confident that this wouldn't be their last time together, even though she had thoroughly rejected his suggestion about making the fake engagement real. He'd had enough petite amies to know when an affair would continue.

But for the first time, he wasn't so sure that an affair would be enough. Not with this woman.

Later that morning, Guillaume walked into the locker room at the tennis club. He and Antoine had a court reservation for ten. The club was full of people taking advantage of the cooler morning temperatures. Any later in the day, and it was almost too hot now to play. The city could be unbearable in the summer, even here at the club.

"Glad to see you in one piece," Guillaume said when he found Antoine on their usual bench. Guillaume hadn't seen Antoine in a few days because he'd been on a lovesick chase for his writer.

"Bonjour," Antoine said. "And she didn't kill me."

"She had every reason to, you know?"

"I do."

"And so it's over now with Louise?"

"It is. She's gone to her family chateau in the Loire Valley to wait out the gossip."

"What did Charlotte say when you arrived at her doorstep?"

"She was surprised and still mad. But after ensuring her that I am the dumbest man alive, I think she can forgive me. I'm taking the train back up there tomorrow so I can take her to dinner."

"She's still at home?"

"Yes. In Vernon."

"So what are you doing?"

"Everything I can to entice her to be with me." He tipped his head toward the doors that led out to the courts. "Shall we?"

Guillaume nodded and followed Antoine outside. He hadn't told anyone about Diane yet. Well, his parents and sisters met her briefly, but those introductions had been largely without explanation of her actual role in his life at the moment. After last night, though, he was compelled to talk and get an outsider's perspective. When they reached their court on the far side of the long row, both men swung their rackets a few times to warm up. The sun was bright and the sound of rackets hitting against rubber balls echoed all around them.

"You know," Guillaume said, "I've been seeing Charlotte's housemate, Diane?"

"I thought you said that was over."

"Well, we're actually pretending to be engaged."

"Wait, what?" Antoine stopped stretching to give Guillaume his full attention.

"Her father sent his fiancée from America to try to convince her and her sister to come home, and I happened to be in her company when they arrived. So she told them all that we're engaged."

"Why on earth would she do that?"

"She wants to stay in Paris, and she thought an engagement would be the perfect guise."

"You're announcing it?"

"No. No way. This is just to put off her family. No one else knows. Though Diane did go with me to the Prévot's ball last night. And… well, her housemates know it's fake. Her sister doesn't. And neither does the woman who owns the house where she stays. They think it's real."

"And her family believes that you're engaged?" Antoine's brow was deeply furrowed with disbelief. The whole situation was admittedly absurd. It was getting hard to keep track of who knew what. And the more people who heard about the engagement, the greater the chance that everyone would. Guillaume's father was often in the papers because of his business dealings, and his sister's wedding announcement had recently been plastered all over the society pages. The papers wouldn't hesitate to write up some rumors about Guillaume too.

"As far as I can tell. We've spent some time together, you know, to keep up the ruse."

"Shit. That sounds really complicated."

"Complicated doesn't even begin to describe the mess I'm in right now."

"It's quite a web of lies."

"That's not the worst of it. I actually like her. Diane. I think I could even fall in love with her."

"Isn't that what you told me about Marielle?"

"No. Not at all. I said I could get used to Marielle. With Diane, I think she could really be the one."

"So what's the problem then?"

"Well, she came to Paris to escape an engagement back at home, something her father arranged. And so she's not so keen on getting married here, either."

"But if she doesn't, she might end up on a boat back to America with her family?"

"It seems that way. Unless I can entice her."

"That is messy, my friend. Welcome to the club, I suppose." Antoine swung his racket through the air. Then he stopped, and, like it was an afterthought, said, "Some messes, though, can't be cleaned up."

"What do you mean?"

"I mean, I would be careful with Diane. I'm sure she's great. But you're talking about her being the one, and knowing you, you'd do anything she asks to help her. But this is an elaborate falsehood you're engaged in, and your heart is worth guarding. If I were you, I'd be careful."

Guillaume pursed his lips and considered this. But he didn't say anything. Antoine wasn't wrong, but he didn't really get it either. The situation was complicated. Instead of addressing this with his friend, Guillaume held up his racket. "Are you ready?"

"I am."

Guillaume trotted to the other side of the court. But Antoine's words echoed—not the part about guarding his heart, but about enticing her. The same strategy might work with Diane. If he could entice her to reconsider her ideas of what a marriage could be, then maybe she'd give him a chance. That was what he wanted, after all. A chance. Because no woman had ever puzzled and intrigued him in this way. Because he'd never spent the night with someone and not wanted her to leave. Because the thought of her leaving France or not seeing him again after her family left made his chest ache. Now that he knew her, living without her would be unthinkable. And then with all this swirling around in Guillaume's mind, he nearly missed Antoine's serve.

Diane worked long, exhausting shifts for the next three days. And she managed to avoid Ada's company, if not her letters and requests. Ada wrote daily, asking Diane to come for dinner, to bring Guillaume along, to come stay at the hotel for a few days. Work gave Diane an excuse to beg off, which was the only thing she liked about going to work. Even with the satisfaction of supporting herself, sort of, she didn't love her job at the restaurant. Although she wanted to like her coworkers and was curious about their lives, they seemed suspicious of her. They stopped talking when she came around. Not having any work friends didn't exactly make the job feel stable or good. Going from several days of that to lunch with Ada on her day off was not Diane's first choice for spending her time. But Diane reluctantly agreed to meet Ada for another tête-à-tête.

When she didn't see her in the hotel lobby or the dining room, Diane took the elevator up to their rooms and found Ada's door slightly ajar.

"Hello," she called as she stepped inside. Ada turned in surprise. She was standing across the room by the window with that same younger man from the dining room. He turned and looked at Diane too. For a second, Diane didn't know what to do. They were drinking wine. She got that same gross feeling of having caught someone in some devious act. Exactly how much time was Ada spending with this man? And what was he doing in her room?

"Oh, Diane," Ada said. "I must have lost track of time. You remember Mister Glover."

"I do." Diane gave him her hand.

"A pleasure to see you again, Miss Talbot." He smiled harmlessly. "But I won't keep you from your lunch."

Ada followed him toward the door, smiled and thanked him for the company. It all appeared to be above board, but he was always hurrying off. Diane could smell romance. The whole scene was eyebrow-raising.

"Again with the gentlemen, Ada?" Diane asked when he was gone.

"Don't be a child, Diane. Are you ready for lunch?"

"I am."

"What if we have it brought up? Since you're here already."

"Whatever you want is fine with me, Ada."

After the business of ordering lunch, the two women sat across from each other to wait for the food to arrive.

"I'm glad you could come, Diane. How are things going with Guillaume?"

Diane hadn't seen Guillaume since leaving his house the morning after sleeping over. But he'd written to her, and she would see him again soon. "Wonderful."

"Can he join us for dinner tonight?" Ada bobbed her shoulders and smiled. She seemed more smug than usual.

"I'll ask." Diane, to stop herself from fidgeting with her dress, folded her hands in her lap. The truth was, Diane was both dying to see Guillaume again and dreading it. She had revisited their time together over and over in her mind. The feel of his hands on her. His long body tangled in sheets. But his words were there too. One in particular: marriage. Guillaume may have had a lot of girlfriends, but he was looking for a wife. She needed to remember that and keep an appropriate distance. Because she didn't want to be a wife, not even Guillaume's.

"I heard from your father."

"And what did my father have to say?" The words dripped with exasperation. Diane hadn't heard a word from Daddy, and she was getting sick of Ada playing mediator.

"He's still hopeful you'll reconsider Alvin."

This only made her exasperation worse. "I've already written to him and told him it's over. I'm not marrying Alvin. I'm not coming home."

"What about your friends? All the girls you grew up with are back there, making lovely lives for themselves, and you're over here working in service and…" Ada trailed off with a shrug.

"And what? Sleeping around?"

"You said it. And based on the situation I discovered you in, that might be an accurate description. I'm not entirely sure."

A knock on the door interrupted them. It was their lunch. While the server came in and served, neither woman spoke. They busied themselves with unwrapping their silverware, placing napkins in their laps, and examining their sandwiches.

When the server left, Ada picked the discussion back up. "I'm not so sure it's over in Alvin's eyes."

"What do you mean?"

"I mean that it's not so easy to throw something away. Someone. He was very important to you before your extended vacation. He is important to your father. And now you're throwing it all away on a lark." Ada bit into her ham and brie sandwich.

Diane wanted to say that Guillaume wasn't a lark. But she stopped herself and ate a bite of her sandwich. Arguing about Guillaume was beside the point. The point was that she wasn't coming home. She wasn't marrying Alvin. "It's my choice."

"It is. But when your choices affect other people, they can be called into question. Particularly by your father."

"What if I prefer to keep my options open? What if I don't want to choose right now."

"No one can keep their options open forever. That's what life is. Life is about making choices and making the best of the results of those decisions."

"You make it sound so bleak."

"It's not bleak, Diane. It's life. The point is that you get to decide."

"I'm tired of having this argument. Can I choose not to have it?"

"I suppose you can for now. But not for long." Ada took another bite of her sandwich.

"What's that supposed to mean?"

Ada chewed and swallowed, leaving the question to dangle and taunt Diane for a moment before responding. "Your father is on his way to Paris. He has Alvin with him. They'll be here in three days."

Diane's food, which had been so delicious moments ago, became inedible in her mouth. What the hell? She forced herself to swallow. "You must be joking."

"No. I tried to tell him not to, but he's got it in his head that his presence is necessary."

"What did he say?"

"That he wants to meet Guillaume and his parents."

"And he's bringing Alvin? How could he do this?"

"As I said, it doesn't seem to be over in Alvin's eyes."

"He hasn't even responded to my telegram."

"I think you could count his impending arrival as a response."

Diane wanted to slap Ada then. Or at least swear at her. But it wasn't Ada's fault. It never was. Ada was, as always, an easy scapegoat for Diane's anger at the world. She pulled herself together. "Did you ask him to come?"

"No. I tried to discourage it, in fact. But your father seems to think I'm failing at my mission to return you and your sister to New York. Which perhaps I am. In any case, I told him everything was fine, that I was working on it. I told him he didn't need to come. But he seems to disagree."

Her father was coming.

To meet Guillaume.

And his parents.

Diane covered her sandwich with her napkin. She couldn't eat another bite.

This would never work. Faking for Ada and Harry was one thing, faking for Daddy and Alvin entirely another. So then what? Tell the truth, and she was on a boat with the family heading back to America.

"I have to go," Diane said. "If Daddy's on his way, then I'll need to get some time off work."

"Okay. Well, I'll see you and Guillaume tonight for dinner then?"

"Yes. Of course." Diane left the hotel room and took the stairs down because the elevator couldn't get there fast enough. She wanted out of that hotel. She'd underestimated her father's position on her going home to America. But this was just like him. She wasn't doing what she was supposed to do, Ada couldn't handle her, and so he would come take care of it himself.

Diane, by not returning home from her vacation like a good girl, had fallen out of line, and they were coming to put her back. And she wasn't just going up against her ex-boyfriend and her father, she was going up against everything her world had always revolved around.

Diane understood Daddy—his mother had been a wife and mother, his own wife had filled the same traditional role, and so he'd raised his girls the same way. To be someone's wife. To be Alvin's wife, his best friend's son's wife. Their marriage was an integral piece of her father's dynastic visions. Daddy and Alvin's father were close business associates. A marriage between their children would only strengthen all their mutual interests. Well, everyone's interests but Diane's. Daddy didn't seem to care about those.

Ada had merely been the scout; now, the real calvary was arriving. There was no way Diane would be able to hold them off. Holding her skirt in one hand and the handrail in the other, she descended as fast as she could without getting dizzy. When she reached the ground floor, she burst out of the stairwell. She made her way through the lobby and out the front doors of the hotel, waving off the doorman's offer to assist her with a carriage. She needed air. She needed to clear her head. And so Diane started walking, heading toward Rue de Fortuny.

After all this, she couldn't just get on a boat and go home to the life she didn't want. No, thank you. No way. She refused. She walked faster, as if she could flee the whole idea of it. As her dress boots chomped at the pavement, her resolve strengthened. She needed Guillaume. She needed to pull off the fake engagement. There was no other way to hold off their pressure and persuasion.

With Guillaume, she didn't have to face her father and Alvin alone. She didn't have to listen to their persuasions. If her father would be there in three days, she would need to talk to Guillaume and make sure he was ready.

But things were different now. Her feelings for him were more complicated. She really liked Guillaume. At the same time, the stakes were higher. She needed him more than ever. She'd need to broach the subject carefully. Appeal to his sense of duty, to his affection for her. And she'd have to do it without promising him anything she couldn't deliver, especially after what he said about wanting to fall in love and get married. She didn't want to give him the wrong idea. And she had a feeling that he wasn't going to like being involved in her increasingly messy mess.

Chapter Twelve

Later that evening, Guillaume was pinning a red rose to his lapel when a knock came on his door. He called out that it was open, and his mother entered.

"A messenger brought this for you," she said, holding an envelope up to show him. Maman was dressed for dinner in a pale green gown and her favorite diamond earrings. Her gray hair was pulled into her signature sleek updo. She and Papa were going to a fundraiser.

"Thank you for bringing it up." He recognized Diane's handwriting on the envelope but didn't stop what he was doing to take it. The pin slipped through his fingers and missed the stem. He pulled it out and started again.

"I haven't seen you all day, so I seized the opportunity to talk." She set the envelope on the dresser then nodded at the pin. "Do you need a hand with that?"

"Yes, merci."

Maman stepped forward and took the rose. She slid her small hand under his lapel and deftly pinned the flower. When she was done and admiring her work, he smoothed his hands down his front.

"Anything in particular you'd like to talk about?"

"Not really. Is this letter from your American friend?"

"It is."

"There have been quite a few from her lately."

"There have."

"I know better than to ask if that means it's getting serious." She smiled.

"Oh, do you you? I'm surprised you even noticed."

"I'm your mother. I notice everything. Even if you don't notice me noticing."

"Oh?"

"For example, I noticed the way you looked at the American was certainly different from the way you've looked at the others. At least the others I've met."

"You talk like I've had a hundred girlfriends."

"You've had a few. And lots of friends. I'm not judging. You're a young man, and I want you to enjoy your life. But I thought I saw a little something more in this latest one."

Guillaume's chest tightened. His mother was right. But the situation was not so easy, and he needed to take it slow. Entice her. "I am enjoying her company immensely."

"Yes. I thought so. So I came up here hoping you'd tell me more about her."

"More? Well, she's fun and bright. And being with her feels different from all the others in a way I haven't quite pinpointed yet. I feel like an improved version of myself, or maybe a more complete version."

His mother's smile widened as he talked about Diane. Was he that transparent? Probably it didn't matter. He'd had enough girlfriends to know that, when you liked one, you needed to show it.

"Well, that's wonderful. I look forward to seeing her again. Are you having dinner with her tonight?"

"I am."

She stepped back and admired him from head to toe. "You look handsome. I'll let you finish. And I'll look forward to an update tomorrow."

"Of course. Oh, and Maman?"

"Yes, dear?"

"I might not leave for the beach with you and Papa. I might stay here for a while longer."

"Does Diane go to the beach?"

"No, she has some friends visiting from America. I'd like to spend time with them while they're here, get to know her better." He didn't have time to explain Diane's almost-family, nor did he want his mother extending any premature invites. But the sentiment was true. Although her family wasn't easy, he did want to make a good impression on them. He wanted to win their favor.

"That's wonderful, dear. Just let me know."

As his mother left the room, Guillaume's eyes fell on the envelope on his dresser. He carried it to his desk and cut it open with the letter knife.

Guillaume,
I need to speak with you before dinner tonight. Please meet me in the hotel lobby.
Thank you,
Diane

So simple, and yet so evasive. Had something happened? Was it urgent? It must be important if she'd sent a messenger only minutes before he was to leave to meet her. He tried not to think too much about it as he left the house and took his carriage to the hotel.

Inside, Diane was waiting for him in a chair under a giant arrangement of white flowers. She was wearing the same blue dress that she wore the first time he met her family at the hotel, and she looked even more worried than she did that day. Her brow was furrowed and her smile, when her eyes met his, was weak. Guillaume's tender hope sank in his gut.

She stood as he approached. "You got my note."

"I did." He kissed her hello on both cheeks. "Should I be worried?"

"Maybe. Let's find somewhere private." He followed her toward the back of the lobby. She found a set of armchairs arranged in a corner by a window and sat in one of them.

When they'd settled in, she smiled and asked how he'd been.

"Fine until now. What's going on?"

Diane's face scrunched as if saying the words were agony coming out. "My father is on his way here. To Paris."

"Oh. Okay." Guillaume sat back in the chair. That wasn't so bad, was it? Almost expected, considering he'd already sent his fiancée.

"He's coming to try to convince me to come home." Her brow knit tighter. "And he's not coming alone."

"What does that mean, exactly?"

Diane straightened in her chair, obviously steeling herself for whatever she had to say next.

"Just tell me, Diane."

"Alvin is coming with him."

Guillaume recoiled. Why was her ex coming to Paris with her father? There could only be one reason, and it wasn't to finalize the breakup. He slumped into the bench. "I don't understand. I thought it was over between you."

"It was. It is. I wrote him and told him. And now he's on a boat heading this way with my father."

"Why?"

"To try and change my mind?"

"But you broke it off. In certain terms?"

"My terms were quite certain. I'm not sure why he's wasting his time."

"And your father is on his side?"

"My father wants me to come home. So, in that respect, yes."

Guillaume didn't respond for a moment while he absorbed all this new information. "So what does that mean for us?"

Diane sat forward, leaning closer to him. "It means that I need you more than ever to help pull off this fake engagement. And I'm telling you now so you aren't ambushed by my familial mess."

"When will they be here?"

"They're due in three days. They'll want to meet you as soon as possible."

"I see."

"I'm sorry, Guillaume. This whole situation is perhaps considerably deeper than you may have thought at the start."

"Yes. Things are getting trickier by the day, aren't they?"

"We should go to the table. Ada's waiting. But I wanted you to know before someone else brings it up."

"Okay."

"Like the time my almost-stepmother brought up Alvin and nearly ended our whole charade. Surely you remember."

"Surely I do." She was making light of it, but Guillaume felt like everything weighed a ton. He wanted to get to know her family, spend time charming her, not compete with her ex-fiancé or almost-fiancé or whatever he was. And he didn't like the way she'd reduced their situation to a charade. It may have started like that, but it wasn't a charade for him anymore. They'd slept together. It had been meaningful to him. If she could reduce it to a charade after everything that had happened, was she ever going to take it seriously?

Guillaume was the kind of man for whom things tended to come easy. His father had made so much money that he didn't have to worry about it. He was a natural on the tennis court. He easily won friends and influence. But people had also told Guillaume that sometimes he gave up on things too readily. He'd heard this from his mother and father. He'd heard it from teachers and friends. He liked things to be easy. That's how he knew things were right: they were easy. But this thing with Diane, as much as it ached to admit, was getting harder and harder every time he thought it should be getting easier.

"Let's get out there before Ada has a fit about us being late." Diane stood and so did Guillaume. As he followed her back out through the lobby to the dining room, his feelings kept mixing. He was going to have to pretend to be her fiancé for her father and other fiancé, when more and more he wanted her to take him seriously as a real potential suitor. He wanted to entice her. Not block some other guy. Of course, with her whole family pressuring her to choose the other man, there didn't seem to be much hope for Guillaume.

He smiled and greeted everyone at the dinner table warmly. And as he settled into his seat, Guillaume reassessed the situation. He wasn't quite sure what to think or what role to take, especially with this audience.

Ada stole an apologetic glance. But no one would look at him. When Catherine's eyes momentarily met his, they flicked away just as fast. Everyone at the table was aware that Diane's father and almost-fiancé were on their way. And likely everyone was rooting against him. By extension, that meant they were also rooting against Diane. Unless they all knew something that he didn't.

He hated to admit it, but that seemed likely. He wanted to believe Diane, that her family was working against her best interests. He wanted to trust Diane. But she'd hidden things from him before. He couldn't help but wonder if she was doing so again. He'd come tonight intending to make their relationship real, or at least get closer to it. Now it was looking more and more like his heart would wind up broken. Because Diane wasn't exactly rooting for him either. She'd told him that she'd never marry him.

No one spoke for several minutes, and the silence thickened. Guillaume cleared his throat, attracting everyone's expectant looks. But he didn't know what to say.

Then Diane rolled her eyes and said, "I may as well clear up what everyone is wondering. I've told Guillaume the news. So we can all speak openly about the fact that Daddy is on his way to break up our engagement."

"Guillaume," Ada said, visibly relieved that the subject had been breached. "I want you to know I discouraged it."

Guillaume nodded. But she'd discouraged what, exactly?

Two servers arrived carrying trays of the first course. Steam rose from the bowls as they placed the soup in front of each person at the table. When everyone had been served, Guillaume returned to the conversation.

"Perhaps, Madame Beall, I could ask you… Why is Monsieur Talbot so determined for Diane to marry this gentleman?"

"The young man's father is Daddy's best friend," Diane cut in. "Alvin and I grew up together, and we were friends. Such good friends that everyone has always assumed we'd marry. I told you all of this, Guillaume."

"You made promises to him, Diane. Don't forget to mention that," Catherine chimed in.

"Whose side are you on, Catherine?"

"I'm not on anyone's side, Diane. It's the truth." Catherine's eyes widened with indignation and righteousness. "And it seems disingenuous to Guillaume to brush it off as anything less than a promise to your best friend."

"He was quite shocked to learn of the engagement to Guillaume, Diane," Ada said.

"Because she's been stringing him along this whole time."

"Stop it, Catherine. You don't know what you're talking about, and what you're saying is certainly hurtful to my fiancé, who is sitting right here." Diane reached a hand across the table to touch his arm. "I'm sorry, Guillaume, that my family is so rude."

The conversation fell away while they all ate their soup. In his mind, Guillaume had minimized the fiancé or almost-fiancé because Diane had assured him it hadn't been significant. Diane was a woman who had a life before she knew Guillaume. There was no reason to fault her for that. But would a man cross an ocean for an insignificant attachment? What exactly was she throwing aside to play engaged with him? And just how entangled in all of this should he allow himself to get? None of the fathomable answers led Guillaume to a particularly good place. He'd come tonight looking forward to seeing her again, to winning her over. But the evening was unfolding in quite a different way. And Guillaume didn't like it. The longer he sat there with them while they stole pitiable glances at him, the more foolish he felt. When it was just him and Diane, everything between them was so easy. But there was nothing easy about sharing this meal with Diane and her family. Suddenly, he wanted nothing more than to be at the beach, away from all of this.

Tension swirled through the rest of dinner, but the conversation was subdued. They talked about the news from America and not much else. Then when the meal was mercifully finished, Guillaume thanked them and excused himself. "I have to get going."

"Oh," Diane said with surprise as Guillaume rose from his seat. "I was going to have dessert."

"Don't let me stop you. Au revoir." He turned and walked away.

"Guillaume, wait a second."

Guillaume didn't wait. He pretended not to hear and walked briskly through the dining room. As he reached the lobby, Diane caught up with him.

"Guillaume. Stop for a second. Why do I feel like I'm always chasing you through this hotel lobby? What's going on?"

"Just like I said, I have to go." He slowed his pace but didn't stop, and Diane fell into step with him. With his considerable height advantage, she had to work to keep up. He didn't hate that she was chasing after him.

"Oh, well, I thought we would perhaps spend some time together after dinner." Her miraculous brown eyes were wide, on the verge of pleading. They'd reached the door now.

"Can you bring up my carriage?" Guillaume asked the concierge. The older man nodded and hurried to pass the message along. The faster the better. With all the feelings in

Guillaume, he needed to be away from Diane. He had to be strong or this whole situation would get worse. Diane was still looking at him like that, like she desperately wanted him to stay. That would likely be a mistake. "I have other plans."

"I see." Her pretty face crumpled. "Well, can you give me a ride back to Rue de Fortuny? Like always?"

He didn't want to give her a ride because he desperately needed space to clear his head, but he couldn't exactly decline her either. Not when she was standing here looking at him with her pleading eyes. Like usual, those eyes cut straight into something within him that couldn't tell her no. And his resolve faltered, the way it always did.

"Fine."

Chapter Thirteen

Within minutes, Diane was settling herself into Guillaume's carriage. She hadn't bothered to go back and explain to Ada or Catherine, but she left a message for them at the front desk in case they troubled themselves to ask. This whole situation was devolving into disaster. And now Guillaume was upset with her. She couldn't exactly blame him for that; she kept asking him for more and more when he was getting so little from her in this arrangement. It was supposed to be mutually beneficial, not her taking advantage of him. He was, at this point, doing her a huge favor. There was nothing left in it for him. And everything was a mess. So much so that it almost seemed getting on the boat back to New York would be easier than facing it all when her father and Alvin arrived.

Because Alvin was coming. To Paris. And the most shameful part of it all was that she was actually looking forward to seeing him. It had been almost a year. And when she'd said goodbye to him, it had been passionate and filled with promises. Promises that she now knew she'd never be able to keep. She both didn't want to face him and couldn't wait to see him again.

But that didn't mean she wanted to be done with Guillaume either. She hated that he was upset with her.

When Guillaume got in the carriage, he put his hat next to Diane and sat on the opposite bench. He pushed his long legs toward the wall to avoid resting them against hers. And then he shifted away from her and toward the window.

Diane sighed. "You're upset because my father is coming."

"On the contrary, Diane. I was thrilled to hear your father was coming." His eyes flashed with bitterness, then he turned away from her again. "I look forward to meeting the man. It's his traveling companion who has me puzzled."

"I thought we were past all this Alvin business." Diane, hands in her lap, played with the smooth blue fabric of her dress, commiserating rather than arguing.

"So did I."

"But you haven't really forgiven me for not telling you about him. And now that he's coming, you're upset."

Guillaume cleared his throat but didn't speak. He was still looking out the window.

"I don't know why he's coming here, Guillaume."

"Diane, be honest with yourself and with me. You do know why he's coming here. We both do."

She did know. She knew exactly what Alvin was doing. "It doesn't matter what his reasons for coming to Paris are. My position hasn't changed. And I still need you to help me."

"The game is getting old, Diane." He let his head fall back against the carriage wall.

"It's not a game. It's my life. You have to believe me that I don't want to go home."

"And you've made it perfectly clear that you don't want me either. Not seriously. So I'm not sure why I should care."

"Is this because of what I said about never marrying you?"

He shot her another sharp look. His blue eyes cold, his mouth hard.

"Guillaume, I've only known you for a few weeks. How can I possibly know if I want to marry you."

"It's pointless if you won't even consider it." His tone was dismissive and cool.

"I thought I made it clear the other night when I came over to your place that I do want you." She tilted her head, pouted playfully, and arched her back, mustering all her sultriness, hoping to lighten his mood with innuendo.

"It's not the same thing. I don't think the other night was wise, considering your current predicament. And it won't happen again."

Chastened, Diane sunk deeper into the seat. This was all going sideways. "Guillaume, I don't understand. Why is everyone so attached to the idea of marriage anyway? You know what happened between your friend and Charlotte, don't you? Did he tell you about that? Charlotte is in love with him. But they can't get married because she's poor and doesn't come from the right kind of family. Marriage is an empty, flawed institution. Even when it's real!"

"Antoine is actually trying to win her back. He's broken it off with the marquis's daughter. He wants to marry Charlotte."

"Well, that's fine for them. But it's not what I want."

"Either you don't know what you want, or you're so afraid of what you want that you won't do anything about it. And in either case, I'm not going to be here for it."

"What do you mean?"

"I'm done talking about it, Diane. Really." He shifted on the seat, still keeping his distance even though it had to be uncomfortable with his legs pushed in that direction. "You're welcome to keep up the ruse. Tell your family whatever you need to. Maintain the fake engagement. But I'm afraid I won't be there to meet your father. Or your best friend."

He said the best friend part like he'd found a hair in his mouth.

"I thought you were going to help me."

Guillaume shrugged. "I'm leaving with my family for the beach. I mentioned it, I'm sure. We go every summer. I won't be around."

The carriage pulled up outside 77 Rue de Fortuny. When it stopped, Guillaume practically leaped from its confines. He turned back, ever the gentleman, to offer her a hand. But Diane made no move to get out. "Guillaume, please, what am I supposed to tell my father?"

"I'm sure you'll come up with something."

"We had an agreement, Guillaume. We are supposed to be fake engaged. I am counting on you."

"Diane, this was supposed to be a simple, mutually beneficial arrangement. It's no longer that. Now it's just a disaster. Like I said, you are welcome to tell them we're getting married. Tell them anything you want." Guillaume offered his hand again, but he didn't look her in the eye.

She still didn't move to disembark the carriage. Without him there bolstering the engagement, she'd never be able to stand up to her father. She'd never be able to hold Alvin off. "What if I told you I'd consider marrying you, for real?"

He shook his head. "You and I both know that would be a lie."

He was right. She'd said it as a last resort. Something deflated inside Diane; she wasn't getting her way and desperately needed it. So as she stepped down onto the sidewalk, she continued arguing.

"Guillaume, please, we can talk about all of that again after my family leaves. But for now, can't you help me for a few more days? If my father doesn't see you and meet you, he'll never believe me that we're engaged. Or that I belong here in Paris. Just one meeting? Then you can go." They were facing each other on the sidewalk now. She stomped her foot for emphasis, like hitting a beat on a dance floor. "I can't do it without you. You make me feel stronger, and you make me seem more settled."

She was pathetic for begging, but she was desperate. Guillaume leaving town at all wasn't ideal, but hopefully, if he could delay for a few more days, she wouldn't need much time to convince her father that she was happy and comfortably settling in Paris. She could promise they'd come home for Thanksgiving, maybe. The fake engagement could still work. It would have to.

Guillaume scraped both hands through his hair. When he looked up at her again, it was disheveled and draping over his left eye in the most appealing way. Turmoil burned in his blue eyes. "Fine, Diane. Fine. I'll do it. But this is it. I can't do anything more for a woman who is just going to leave me."

His words hit her like a bolt of lightning in the heart. Was leaving the only alternative to marriage? Diane didn't know what to say. Guillaume made her stronger and better than any other version of herself. Even if they were faking being in love, having him around made her feel more whole. But she wasn't going to marry anyone, and he ultimately wanted a wife, and so she had to be careful about what she said.

"Guillaume, do you honestly believe that after all of this there could ever be nothing between us? Not even a friendship? Let's just take it one step at a time, please."

"I said I'd do it. I'll help you when your father comes."

"Oh, thank you, Guillaume. Thank you. You are a wonderful, kind man." She considered reaching up for a kiss, but before she could, he stepped into his carriage and closed the door.

Diane watched from the sidewalk as Guillaume's carriage pulled off. And when he was gone, she went inside. The house was quiet, and so Diane went to her room and closed the door. As she undressed, her mind replayed the conversation with Guillaume. His words. The pained look on his face as he said them. And her own deep sense of relief when he finally agreed to keep helping her. She cared about him very much, not only because he was helping her stay in Paris, but because he was a wonderful man. He valued her opinion. He never called her a mess or insinuated that she was. He was protective without being possessive. Everyone always said Diane was a good time, lots of fun. But there was more to her than that. Guillaume seemed to see the quieter parts of her that everyone else overlooked. She liked herself the way he saw her. He was the perfect man.

She rolled her own words around in her head as well. Somehow, waving her anti-marriage flag at Guillaume this time hadn't given her the usual thrill of empowerment. Now it felt like a loss. A silly hill she was dying on. All alone.

The next morning, Diane came down to the dining room for breakfast at the usual time. Room and board at the pension included meals. Breakfast and dinner were served family style and lunch usually meant poking around in the kitchen for whatever Cook had available. Today's spread was coffee and croissants with apricot jam.

Madame Tremblay was seated at her spot at the head of the table; meals were one of her prime opportunities for keeping an eye on her renters. But Nadine and Vanessa were the only other housemates present. Catherine was still at the hotel being traitorous. And Charlotte was still in Vernon, recovering from Antoine's engagement drama. Which was good reason for Diane to be suspicious of the whole marriage enterprise, even if they were, as Guillaume had argued, working it out.

"Bon matin," Madame said when Diane pulled out her chair.

"Bon matin," Diane said. The others, between sips of coffee and mouthfuls of pastry, greeted her as well.

"I was just telling the ladies here that I heard from Charlotte," Madame said. "The vicomte found her in Vernon, and he's been trying to reconcile."

"Has he succeeded at all?" Vanessa asked tentatively. "She won't be so mad at me for putting their affair in the papers if he proposes."

"Wait! What?"

Nadine nodded while Vanessa explained to Diane that she'd used Charlotte's private life in a gossip column.

"Wow. That's treacherous, Vanessa. Do you think he will? Propose?"

"He better."

"He's friends with Guillaume," Diane revealed. "And Guillaume says Antoine wants to marry her."

"Well, that's good." Madame gave a tight, curt nod of approval of the situation.

"Is that what Charlotte wants?" Diane asked. "To marry him?"

"I think she loves him," Nadine said.

"Is that a reason to marry him? Into an aristocratic family with all those traditions and expectations."

"That and money." Nadine sighed dreamily. "Love is the best reason to marry someone."

"He's in line to be a vicomte, and so she will become a vicomtesse," Madame said. "That's another reason to marry someone."

"That would make Charlotte the luckiest girl in the world, wouldn't it?" Nadine said.

"I'm not sure any married woman is the luckiest girl in the world. I don't know why any woman would willingly shackle herself to a man, who will then have all the power over her."

"Diane, you sound so cynical. Especially for someone newly engaged." Nadine cocked her head in Diane's direction.

"Are you worried, dear?" Madame asked thoughtfully.

Diane cleared her throat. She did sound cynical, and she should tread carefully because she wanted Madame to believe her engagement to Guillaume was sound and real. "Maybe a little. But more so for Charlotte than for me."

"It depends on who you're married to, of course. It can be a shackle, but if you do it right, it can make everything in your life more meaningful and grand."

"That's very romantic. But what if Antoine decides he doesn't want Charlotte to write anymore." Diane tipped her nose into the air and affected a high society demeanor as she said, "It wouldn't be proper for a vicomtesse."

"The vulgarity!" Nadine, adept at playing aristocratic on stage, feigned aghast.

"A decent man won't hold a woman back," Madame Tremblay said. "He'll help her do whatever she wants. You just have to choose the right man."

"Did you like being married, Madame?" Diane asked, refilling her cup of coffee.

"Oh, I loved it, dear." Madame smiled warmly and patted Diane's arm. "I married my best friend. We had a lot of fun together. And I still miss him."

"Would you get married again?"

"I would, dear. If I found the right man. That's the tricky part. Choosing the right one. You have to be careful."

The conversation moved onto neighborhood gossip, but Diane was still stuck on the idea of choice. Diane understood what they were saying, but she still didn't fully believe it. Make a good choice. Ada had said much the same. *Life is about making choices and making the best of the results of those decisions.* But Diane didn't like having Ada's words in her head or taking Ada's advice on anything. And no matter what she chose, that choice eliminated other choices. It left something behind or closed a proverbial door. Doors enclosed people. Every choice was a trap in a way. That's why she had no intention of making one—not as far as marriage was concerned.

It was too much to properly consider when her father's arrival was imminent. Guillaume would be with her, which was a relief. That he'd said he was going to the beach the following day wasn't ideal. She'd rather have him by her side for the duration of her family's visit. He was the perfect shield from their expectations. She was also fairly confident she could convince Guillaume to forgo the beach trip altogether. With him, all she had to do was ask. This, she was pretty sure, was also not a reason to marry him. Though perhaps not as sure as she once was.

Two days later, Diane was waiting on the platform with Ada, Catherine, and Harry when Daddy's train from Calais pulled into the station. Diane, wound tight with tension, shifted on her feet and watched as passengers began to disembark. Unfamiliar face after unfamiliar face streamed onto the platform. Then she recognized her father's stern profile and broad frame as he stepped down, briefcase and cane in hand.

"Daddy," Catherine squealed.

"Hello, dear. Or should I say bonjour?" Daddy was dressed in one of his tailored dark gray suits and bowler hat, exactly the same in Paris as he'd been in Woollett. His brown beard was whiter on the sides than it had been when she'd seen him last.

"I don't care what you say, I'm so glad to see you." Catherine wrapped her arms around him the way they'd done every day as little girls when he came home from work. Diane and Catherine would race to meet him at the door, eager to be engulfed in his warm, worldly presence.

"I'm glad to see you too, dear." His misty blue eyes found Diane's then. "And you too, Dini. Give your travel-weary father a hug."

Diane smiled and stepped into his arms. He enveloped her in warmth and familiar smells of sandalwood and smoke. Diane's knees weakened with the kind of relief that could only come from a parent's embrace. She had underestimated how good it would be to see her father again. After a long hug, he released her and stepped back to admire her.

"You girls are as beautiful as ever," Daddy said. Then he moved on to hug Ada, who was waiting patiently for the sisters to have their turn.

Ada, smiling girlishly, held her hands out for Daddy. He stepped into her arms and wrapped his around her. Diane scrutinized the moment for weakness or hints of trouble, but there was genuine warmth from both parties. Was there also a hint of resignation in their greeting? Or shyness? Maybe that was always there.

That's when Diane saw Alvin. He was stepping down from the train, dressed in a light gray suit that had rumpled from sitting for so much of the day. His light hair was trim and neat under his gray bowler hat. He was exactly the same in Paris as he'd been in Woollett too. When their eyes met, he smiled. He set his bag on the ground and opened his arms for her. She practically jumped into them, and when he caught her, he lifted her off the ground.

"Diane. Diane. Diane," he whispered, burying his face in her neck. "I have dreamed of this day since you left Woollett."

He smelled familiar too, cologne with a hint of cigarettes. They'd probably spent most of the trip on the smoking car, knowing him and Daddy. Alvin pulled away to look at her, as if he couldn't believe she was really here. He smiled and then went in for a kiss, but she turned her head to avoid it. His shoulders slumped, like he'd only just remembered that this was not the reunion he'd been hoping for. His bright eyes dimmed slightly with understanding. "So it's true then? You've found someone else."

For Diane, the ruse had never been so flimsy as it was in that moment. This was Alvin. Not Ada. And it wasn't as easy to lie to him, especially not to his face. But she'd written, and so much of the lying was already done.

"I have met someone else," she admitted. "Though I never thought it would be possible to top you."

Sadness tinged his smile. "I should have never let you go."

Let. As if he had given her permission. As if she needed it. Sadly, she was never more certain that he was wrong for her. She maybe didn't know what was right, but she knew it wasn't Alvin. "Perhaps not. But no matter where I live, I will always be your friend. You know that, don't you?"

"Diane, that's what I'm here to find out." He spread his arms and opened his hands, offering himself.

"It was bold of you to come. Especially after my telegram."

"I've tolerated your absence all this time. Barely." He set his hands down on her shoulders, gently shook her, and looked her in the eyes to emphasize his point. "Your telegram only solidified for me what I suspected all along."

"What's that?"

"That I needed to come here myself if I want you back."

"But what if you can't have me? There's another man, you know. I'm engaged."

"I've only just arrived."

He hugged her again, quick and friendly, and then moved away from her to greet Ada, Catherine, and Harry.

Even rumpled and tired from traveling, he was a handsome sight. But as happy as she was to see him, Diane's stomach didn't flutter at his flirtations. Nothing stirred within her besides nostalgia. The memories that bubbled to the surface were of their friendship, not their romance. He was not the man for her. She was sure of that. She wasn't so sure he was going to take no for an answer.

Chapter Fourteen

When Guillaume walked into the dining room at the Grand Hôtel, he spotted Diane right away. How could he not? She was wearing a bold blue dress that made her skin glow. Her hair was done up in loose curls that spilled around her neck and shoulders. Her presence was like a magnet. Like a moon in a night sky. She was seated on the far side of the room, near an oversized bouquet of white roses and carnations and feathers, and it appeared her whole family was there with her. There was a large man with a beard and small, penetrating eyes next to Ada. This must be Diane's father. Another blond gentleman with his back toward Guillaume was seated next to Diane. This was undoubtedly his rival Alvin.

Guillaume stopped short. Not because he didn't expect to see these other men at the table. Diane had sent word earlier confirming that they'd arrived and requesting his presence at dinner. Reluctantly, Guillaume had come. But now, his last chance to hesitate, he slid onto a bar stool where he could watch them for a few minutes before throwing himself at their mercy. The bartender greeted him promptly, and Guillaume ordered a whiskey.

Diane laughed and smiled so brightly that Guillaume's breath caught—until he realized that the recipient of this smile was undoubtedly her American. Seeing her affection for him, seeing her so thrilled with his presence, made Guillaume wonder yet again why Diane was so averse to going back to America, back to the life that obviously suited her so well.

Just then, a hand fell on Guillaume's shoulder. Harry.

"Bonsoir, Guillaume."

"Ah! Bonsoir."

"Have I caught you plotting your escape?" Harry nodded at the table where the Talbots were sitting as he slid onto the barstool beside Guillaume's.

"You could say that."

Harry gestured to the bartender that he'd also have a whiskey. "I don't blame you. Tonight's a big night for you and Diane. I could use a warm-up myself."

"Why's that?" Guillaume asked.

"Mister Talbot is an intimidating man. Friendly enough, but intimidating. Particularly when one is involved with his daughter."

Guillaume laughed. "I've heard this is a situation that you can understand."

"Yes."

"But our engagement, Diane and me, it happened fast." Guillaume had to choose his words carefully. He wasn't exactly sure how much Harry knew about the realities of this particular mess, but he assumed little. Diane was still keeping the fake part of the betrothal a secret from her sister.

Harry raised his eyebrows and took a drink.

"Not that it's unsteady..." Guillaume rushed to correct himself. Despite their fake engagement, Guillaume's feelings were real. He had fully and completely fallen for Diane. He worried that if this other man, with the support of Diane's father, had come to win her back, then there was no way Guillaume was getting out of this meal with his heart intact.

But Guillaume also knew Harry had a mess of his own, pretending not to be in a relationship with Catherine. Harry could be a sympathetic ear. "Our engagement is new. Delicate by nature. And the ex-boyfriend or ex-fiancé or whatever—him being here isn't helping to strengthen it."

The bartender arrived with Harry's whiskey, and they drank from their respective tumblers. It pleasantly seared Guillaume's mouth and throat as he swallowed.

Diane's boisterous laugh carried across the dining room, drawing Guillaume's eyes back to the table. Harry, noticing Guillaume's apprehension, said, "I wouldn't take it too hard, all this mess."

"No?"

"Diane and her sister are tricky. Headstrong, if you know what I mean. And I'm not exactly sure what's going on with her and Alvin. They used to be close, and they seem to have fallen back into step since he arrived this afternoon. I'm not saying this in support of your endeavor or to discourage it. I don't know you well enough to say whether you're right for Diane or not. And I'm not Diane." Harry paused, sipped his whiskey thoughtfully.

Guillaume waited for him to continue.

"But I can say that it will all work out right in the end. No matter what happens. If Diane latches back onto him," Harry said, pointing in the direction of the table, "then it was meant to be, wasn't it? There's no way to tell what she's thinking, or what she's going to do. You've made it this far, my friend. There's nothing else you can do at this point but try to enjoy dinner."

Guillaume laughed, but the situation was clearer. If Harry was talking about Diane getting back with her ex, then that was likely on the mind of everyone else at the table as well. This wasn't exactly a surprise, but it also meant Guillaume's fears were warranted. There was a chance Diane would rush back into this other man's arms.

They finished their whiskeys and rose from their stools. With the booze burning in his gut, Guillaume was as ready as he'd ever be.

"Guillaume, darling," Diane said when he reached the table.

Guillaume nodded and kissed her on the cheek when she stood to greet him. Her father and suitor stood as well.

"This is my fiancé." Diane's words tripped slightly on the fiancé part, and small as it was, the reaction pricked another hole in Guillaume's confidence. What was he doing here?

"Guillaume Allard," she continued, "this is my father, Maxwell Talbot."

Guillaume shook firmly and made eye contact. Monsieur Talbot was a tall man, but not quite as tall as Guillaume, with a graying beard, suspicious eyes, and a broad hand. As the older man sized him up, Guillaume recognized the quirked eyebrow. There was no doubt Diane was this man's daughter.

"It's a pleasure to meet you, son. A surprise, for sure. But a pleasure nonetheless."

"I could say the same about you," Guillaume said. He smiled, tapping into what he hoped was his most charming self. And hoping that his English wouldn't betray him in this crucial moment.

Monsieur Talbot patted him hard on the shoulder and turned to Alvin. "I've brought Diane's friend Alvin Monroe with me."

Diane stepped in then. "Guillaume Allard, this is Alvin Monroe."

He had the blond, corn-fed appearance of so many Americans. But when Alvin squeezed his hand a little too hard, Guillaume didn't squeeze harder. He had a firm, solid handshake, but he wasn't going to compete with this man in petty gestures of dominance. And his quarrel wasn't with Alvin Monroe. His quarrel was with Diane, the woman who had ensnared him in her plot and to whom he couldn't seem to let go.

Both seats next to Diane were taken by Ada and Alvin, and so Guillaume sat across from her, between her father at the head of the table and Catherine.

"So, Guillaume, tell us about yourself. Diane says you grew up in Paris?"

"I did. I've been here all my life."

"And what does your father do?"

"Investments now, but before that he built and sold a shipping enterprise in Marseille."

"Ah! Logistics."

"Yes."

"Fantastic. I rely quite heavily on my shipping partners. I'm in toothpicks, surely Diane has told you. Manufacturing."

"That's fascinating, monsieur. Diane has told me a little about your operation. But I would love to hear more."

"Wonderful." Diane's father beamed at her, obviously proud of his daughter, even if he wasn't so keen on her current choices. "Ada tells me that you met my daughter in a cabaret?"

Guillaume gulped. Is that what Diane had told Ada? It hadn't been seedy or unrespectable, at least not by Parisian standards. But it sounded terribly untoward coming from her father in such blunt terms. Of all the times not to embellish.

Perhaps sensing his hesitation, Catherine jumped in and said, "I was there. She didn't like him at first."

Guillaume cringed, remembering it. Their meeting had been initially unfortunate, this was true, but again the blunt terms stung. Was this how she'd described things to Catherine after he'd tried that whole evening to redeem himself? "You didn't like me?"

"Oh, it's nothing. You remember," Diane said sweetly. Then she turned to her father. "We were arguing, and Guillaume butted in to tell us that I should go back to America. He was terribly rude. Then he turned out to be our housemate's friend. I was hungry, and I let him buy me dinner, and now here we are."

"Getting married?" Monsieur Talbot raised his hands in question.

"Getting married!" Diane nodded as if she were also trying to convince herself. She looked at Guillaume, disbelief in her eyes. "So it all worked out because you were adorable and charming. And I've liked you ever since."

Diane's face flushed guiltily. How much of all of this had been purely for show, to keep up appearances? In an attempt to steer the conversation away from their relationship, Guillaume asked, "How was your trip?"

And while Monsieur Talbot chattered on about the food on the ship, Guillaume set his gaze on Alvin, who was leaning into Diane's ear and saying something. She laughed then and looked at him adoringly. Every drop of attention she paid this other man was like torture for Guillaume. And she was giving it so liberally that Guillaume couldn't stop wondering why he had even bothered to come. He wanted to spend the next few weeks dipping his feet in the English Channel, not watching while his heart was slowly sliced from his chest. When the server put a glass of red wine in front of him, Guillaume swallowed half of it.

Finally, Diane looked at him, and the smile she'd been giving Alvin faltered slightly. Guillaume nodded. And she smiled at him then too, but something else passed over her face. Guilt, maybe. Or, sorrow.

It had to be hard for her to see Alvin after so much time. And Guillaume couldn't exactly fault her if his presence drummed up some confusing feelings. He knew how tricky love could get. He wanted the best for her, ultimately, even if it was another man. But Antoine was right—his heart was also worth guarding. And his emotions were a mess.

Dinner was served and conversation ebbed and flowed. Guillaume told them all about the metro and the work the city had done to build the tunnels. He brought his most magnanimous self to every topic the Talbots raised. And he avoided looking at Alvin through most of it. Diane, on the other hand, was quite attentive to Alvin.

"Daddy got us tickets to the opera," Diane said at the end of the meal. "*Les Barbares*, tomorrow night at Palais Garnier."

"That sounds fun." Guillaume shrugged noncommittally.

"See, I told you he'd be happy to come along," she said triumphantly to Alvin.

"You did." He smiled just as triumphantly, obviously chuffed at being the focus of Diane's attention even if he was wrong.

"The show is at eight, Guillaume. We can meet you there."

Guillaume's skin warmed to an uncomfortable level. He didn't want to blow Diane's cover, but he'd told her he wouldn't be around. Had she forgotten? Guillaume would rather walk across a desert than see a show with Diane and her family. He couldn't say that, of course. He'd already told her he was leaving for Cabourg. Maybe she wanted to keep up appearances tonight and make excuses for him later when she could explain everything to her father. Guillaume was losing the plot. So he didn't tell her otherwise.

When dinner was finished, and they rose from the table, Guillaume begged off for the evening. An early day, he said. No one questioned him further.

He'd also come to a decision. Diane had made promises to this other man, and he'd come from America to settle those promises. Guillaume, although he'd promised to help Diane, should step aside so that whatever needed to happen between Diane and Alvin could play out. It was the respectable thing to do in this situation.

"I'll walk you out," Diane said as they were leaving the dining room. The Talbots were all headed upstairs to have drinks their rooms.

"Okay." Guillaume offered her his arm and they crossed the lobby. Diane swayed a few steps, and then she leaned into him. She was softly humming that same song she often did. When they reached the desk at the front of the lobby, Guillaume asked the concierge to call up his carriage.

"That went well, I think," she said while they waited.

"Your father is more intimidating than you let on."

"Really? Well, he's terribly old-fashioned. So I suppose, as his daughter, that's always what I talk about first. But it's good to see him. I missed him. And…" She stopped talking, Guillaume suspected, before she said anything about Alvin. But the fact that she had feelings about seeing him again, or maybe just feelings for him, was obvious. She didn't need to say it.

"I won't be at the opera tomorrow. You know I'm going to the beach."

"Oh, you can't. I won't hear of it." Diane slurred her words, and Guillaume realized how drunk she was. He hadn't been paying attention to that. But her eyes were glassy and cantankerous. Guillaume loved this version of Diane. It had gotten him into trouble before. Now, however, his spirit for playful argument couldn't be riled. The most painful prospect Guillaume saw in Diane's eyes right then was the real possibility that her night was only beginning. She might forget everything he was saying to her now. She might go back into that hotel and reconcile in any number of ways with Alvin. And there was nothing Guillaume could do to stop it.

His carriage arrived. "I better go."

He hesitated to kiss goodbye, but she didn't. As naturally as if they were truly betrothed, she put a hand on his chest and rose on her toes for a chaste peck. Then before he could put his arms around her or press for more, she was walking away.

"Until tomorrow," she said over her shoulder. If she'd forgotten about him leaving town, it was because she was so wrapped up in her company. Or she hadn't forgotten at all and just assumed he'd do whatever she asked.

"Au revoir, Diane." Guillaume got in the carriage and set his hat next to him on the seat. His ride pulled away, and he watched through the window as Diane disappeared back into the hotel. His instinct was to go along with whatever she wanted. He cared about Diane, loved her, he was coming to realize. But the warning signs of trouble were too blatant to ignore. His heart would end up broken if he continued carrying on with this woman. Breaking it off now, before his feelings got any more entangled, would prevent him from certain emotional death. As hard as it would be, he had to do it. Threading his hands through his hair, he said aloud to himself, as if for reassurance, "My heart is worth guarding."

After dinner, Diane and her family made their way from the dining room, across the lobby, and over to the elevator. The attendant ushered them inside—Ada, Catherine, Diane, Alvin, Harry, and finally Daddy, who requested the third floor. While the attendant worked the controls and the elevator car rose through the building, Diane's stomach turned. She was tipsy and needed to stop drinking alcohol.

Alvin, who was standing next to Diane, brushed the back of his hand against hers to get her attention. When she looked at him, he smiled and took her hand in his. It was a sweet gesture, meant as a secret intimacy between them in the presence of her parents, like so many they'd shared before she came to Paris. Because their families were friends, they'd spent many social hours plotting how to get away in some secluded place for a kiss or, when they got older, more than kissing. These stolen encounters used to fuel her adventurous spirit. Now they were fond memories. And it was clear from the gleam in Alvin's eyes that he was remembering them too.

As sweet and familiar as it was, it didn't move Diane or fill her with longing. She felt admiration and genuine affection, but it wasn't a great love returning or a passion reigniting. It was platonic.

When the elevator car stopped, they disembarked and made their way to the rooms Daddy was now sharing with Ada. Ada sent for more coffee and two bottles of dessert wine. And when it arrived, they all sat together and continued the same sort of conversations they'd had at dinner, mostly about people from Woollett. Diane declined to drink anything but water, and as she sat there, trying to sober up, she became keenly aware of how different it felt to be in the room with them all. Something had shifted since she left America. These were her people, her loved ones, but they were no longer her home. She no longer belonged with them back in Woollett. Paris was home.

When Diane separated from the group and perched near the window to smoke, Alvin followed. He lit her cigarette and leaned against the wall next to her. "I have been hoping to get you alone all night."

"I'm sorry, monsieur, but I'm spoken for," she said teasingly. She passed him a cigarette, but he didn't light it yet.

"That's what you keep saying, but your fiancé is nowhere to be found."

"That's because you drove him off."

"I was perfectly polite." Alvin puffed up his chest, no doubt feeling victorious that he was the last man standing next to her.

"Yes, I suppose you were. But your possessive air canceled out all of that politeness."

"Again—why isn't he here putting on possessive airs of his own?"

"Maybe Guillaume trusts me?" Her cigarette tasted good and the cool air from the window was reviving her from all the champagne.

"I'd say that perhaps he shouldn't, at least not in my company."

It occurred to Diane then that she'd imagined this moment, or an early version of it, in a hotel room very similar to this one. Back when she was living at the hotel, she had daydreamed a handful of times about Alvin coming to Paris for her. That had stopped though. Since moving to Madame Tremblay's and getting to know her housemates and working to support herself, she hadn't imagined Alvin. Now that she was back in the hotel, and he was there with her, there was something perversely karmic about it. She was getting exactly what she'd wanted, only she didn't want it anymore. "I've told you that it's over."

"Maybe your airs say otherwise." Alvin lit his cigarette.

"Maybe you're misinterpreting my airs."

"Come on, Diane. Don't tell me you're really going to marry him."

Her chest tightened. She'd created a situation where she couldn't be frank with Alvin, and it was hard. Guillaume was right: this was a complicated mess. And Alvin wasn't making it any easier by asking her to repeat the lie. "I think what's most important for you to understand is that I'm not coming back to America, Alvin. I want to stay in Paris. And Guillaume is helping me do that."

"So you admit it's a marriage of convenience?"

"Aren't they all just business deals when you really think about it?"

"Diane, you sound so cynical." He moved closer to her then, put a hand on her arm. Looking straight into her eyes, he said, "You and I used to set the world on fire. We were going to marry for love. The distance may have tamped down the flames, but if you'd let me, we could rekindle it. I'm here for you, Diane. I've come all this way. Let me show you how much it would mean to me if you became my wife."

"Alvin, please." She started to move away, but he held her forearm tight enough to stop her.

"And I get that you love Paris. I love it too. How could I not? Now that I've been here, I think we could spend a season here every year. Maybe even buy a place. An apartment with a view of the Seine. What do you think?"

"I've already told you." Diane slipped free and put her cigarette out in the ashtray. "I'm marrying Guillaume. And you deserve someone who will love you more than I ever could. Someone who wants the same things as you."

"I know you think you've fallen out of love with me. And maybe you have. But not so far that we can't find that passion again."

"I love you like an old friend. Not like someone I want to marry."

"And you love Guillaume like that?"

"I do." The words rolled out without hesitation. And they didn't feel like a lie. Not like the others she'd told. She certainly loved his company. His humor and way of seeing the world. She loved his body. Craved it, in fact. She loved the way he made her feel better and more herself in every situation. But before she allowed herself to reach the logical conclusion of all this, she reminded herself that it wasn't worth it. She didn't want to marry, and Guillaume was looking for a wife. It would be unfair to love him as anything more than a friend. And she'd likely end up as hurt as he would when things didn't work out between them.

"I feel like a fool for coming all this way."

"You are a fool for doing it. But love is always messy." Diane put a hand affectionately on his shoulder. She hated to hurt him, but she had to do it. "And I suspect that, if you hadn't come, we'd both always wonder if we should have given it another chance."

"But you're sure we shouldn't?"

"I'm sure." She took her hand away, establishing distance between them. "But I'm still glad you came. That you're here. That we get to say all of this to each other in person rather than in letters."

"I am too, I suppose. And you're right. If I hadn't come, then I would have always regretted it."

"And now you're seeing Paris."

"And now I'm seeing Paris."

They rejoined the group then, and everyone was saying goodnight. It had gotten late, and a wave of exhaustion hit Diane. "Instead of getting a carriage home, do you mind if I stay with you tonight, Catherine?"

Catherine looked suspiciously between Diane and Alvin, completely misunderstanding the situation. A sly, misinformed smile spread on her face. "Of course."

Diane rolled her eyes. She'd just have to straighten Catherine out when they got to their room. She hadn't spoken to her sister in days, and Diane obviously had to fill her in on quite a bit.

Chapter Fifteen

The next morning, sun streamed through the windows of the hotel room. Catherine was already up and dressing, but Diane lingered in her bed, still trying to shake off her luxurious sleep.

"It's like when we first arrived, waking up here together," Catherine said.

"Just like old times." Only so much had changed since they were on vacation.

Catherine cinched her corset and wrapped the strings around her waist, tying them at her front. Diane had watched her sister dress thousands of times over the course of their lives. Sharing rooms, getting dressed together—it had all been a part of her daily life. Coming to Paris together, staying together, had extended the last vestiges of their girlhood. But they weren't little girls anymore.

"I sent for coffee," Catherine said, checking her work in the mirror. "I won't make it down to breakfast if I don't have it."

"What time is breakfast?"

"We have an hour." Catherine sat at the dressing table and picked up her hairbrush. Her long, golden brown hair was crimped and bent from sleeping in braids.

"So how is it going with you and Harry?"

"It's complicated." Catherine rolled her eyes and brushed her hair. "What about you and Alvin? He's here to win you back."

"That is his goal. But he's not succeeding." Diane smoothed the crisp white sheets over the top of her.

"He isn't?" Her surprise was genuine.

"Did you think he would?"

"I suppose I didn't. But maybe I hoped he would."

"It was romantic of him to come, though, wasn't it?" This was part of the fun, Diane supposed, fiddling with the end of the bedsheet. Getting to see Alvin come all this way and fight for her, even if there was no way he could win. She was admittedly flattered.

"It was romantic of Harry to come as well, even though he assures me he's here for the cultural experience."

"So you're together then?"

"I wouldn't say that. Discussions are ongoing."

"Are you going to tell Daddy and Ada?"

"It's too soon for that." Catherine could hold onto a secret indefinitely. But sitting at the dinner table with her and Harry —seeing them together in any context really—their mutual affection was hard to miss.

"But you're going back to New York with them?"

Catherine sighed. "I am. Any chance you are?"

"Not if I can help it. But I do have a confession to make."

"What's that?"

"I'm not really engaged to Guillaume. When you all came into my room that morning, I said it to get myself out of trouble. And we've been pretending this whole time so that everyone will be convinced that this is where I belong." Diane, embarrassed by her confession, pulled the sheet up over her head.

"I assumed it was a marriage of convenience, especially considering you barely know him." Catherine didn't sound shocked. "Fake is a little surprising. So you're going to call it off then, as soon as we leave?"

"That was the plan. But now I think I'm falling for Guillaume." When she pulled the sheet back down to show herself, Catherine's mouth was hanging open.

"Really? Last night it was hard to tell, you know. You were giving so much attention to Alvin."

"I know. I feel deeply guilty that he's here, that Guillaume is witnessing it all." Their letters had been irregular for months, but she hadn't completely broken it off with Alvin until Ada arrived. When she was honest with herself, she'd strung him along. His coming to Paris was her fault. The whole mess was her own making. "But I'm not in love with Alvin anymore, if I ever was. I'm not sure love is moving across an ocean to avoid marrying a person."

"No, it isn't. But I did the same, and I'm pretty sure I still love Harry."

Diane gasped and squealed at this revelation. "You do?"

"I believe so, yes."

"That's good, right? I almost wish I still loved Alvin. Everything would be so much easier in my life if I did." Diane played with the bedsheets in her fingers. "It just feels different now, between us. I am a different person. I came here thinking that this trip would get something out of my system, but it seems to have changed the system altogether."

"And so why don't you just marry Guillaume? To stay in Paris?"

"You know I don't want to legally bind myself to a man for life."

"Not even a man you think you might be falling in love with?"

"I fled a country for the same thing."

"Then what do you want, Diane?"

"Adventure?"

Catherine rolled her eyes again. "You say that to avoid giving a real answer. What does it actually mean to you? Specifically?"

"I'm not sure I know anymore."

"Mama once told me that love is the greatest adventure of all."

"Did she?" Diane flung back the bed covers and stood up. She'd miss breakfast if she didn't start getting ready for the day.

"She did. I was probably eleven or twelve, so a few years before she died, and I asked her if it was boring to be a mother and a wife."

"You did?"

"Yes. And she said she was too busy to be bored. But that love could never be boring. She said that being with Daddy and having us girls was a new adventure every day."

"Why haven't you told me this before?"

"I don't know. I've been thinking about her a lot lately. And you've been digging in your heels about going home, using some nebulous idea of adventure as an excuse. When you used to talk about being here and staying, I understood when you said you wanted adventure—seeing Paris, dancing in the different clubs, eating at the different places, seeing the world. I got it. But there will always be something more to see, and something more to experience. And there are other adventures besides experiences. There are emotional adventures, depths to plumb, feelings to have with another person that are so big and scary and just as enthralling as seeing a new city."

"Haven't you become wise since your return to the hotel?"

"I've had a lot of quiet, alone time in this big room." Catherine was fully dressed now. "So what are you going to do about your feelings for Guillaume, if you're not going to marry him?"

"What do you mean?"

"Are you going to tell him how you feel?"

"I suppose I better think about it. Maybe tonight at the opera."

She got dressed, and they met everyone downstairs for a hearty breakfast of crepes, summer berries, and the most delicious whipped cream Diane had ever had. Then Daddy took Ada, Diane, and Catherine to the department store next door.

Inside the store was a marvel of merchandise. Diane and Catherine knew the place well, having stayed right next door when they were still on vacation.

"Ladies," Daddy said, taking it all in. "I'll be in the café if you need my opinion. I want to see everything before I buy anything."

It had been so long since Diane had been properly shopping, and she'd forgotten how much she loved shopping with her father. He could be so grumpy and stern, but something about shops softened him up. Their mother had always overseen their selections when they were little girls, but Daddy let them make all their choices. He noticed clothing and offered solid opinions. He always enjoyed seeing what they'd chosen, and he rarely set limits. At least not until Diane and Catherine didn't come home when they were supposed to.

The three women fanned out, staying close and reconvening frequently, but keeping to themselves while they wandered through the departments. And so Diane spent the time examining her feelings for Guillaume and anticipating seeing him at the opera that evening. Dress shopping brought back memories of their trip to the modiste. It felt like ages ago, but it had been less than two weeks. His generous spirit and willingness to participate by offering his opinions actually reminded her of shopping with her father. The two men weren't that different.

Diane chose a new red dress for the occasion, one that she was excited to show off for Guillaume. The night of the ball he'd said red was his favorite color. She also chose a new corset, chemises, stockings, and lacy underthings in each color they had. She got new red satin shoes for the opera, black leather boots for everyday wear, a hat with red feathers, and four more dresses—two for daytime, and two for going out in the evenings.

After visiting the seamstresses to have everything fitted, she met Daddy in the café.

"Did you find everything you need?"

"I did, thank you. It's been a while since I've shopped, and so I must say I needed quite a bit."

"Guillaume hasn't taken you shopping?"

"Well, he did buy me a dress for a ball. But not like this. It wouldn't really be proper, would it?"

"Probably not until you're married."

"I hate to admit it, but money does make life so much easier. It was hard not shopping for all those months."

"You poor thing." He laughed because they both knew that not shopping wasn't much of a hardship. Diane was lucky even when she couldn't afford new dresses. "But you won't suffer for much longer? Guillaume has money. And when you marry, you'll take control of your inheritance."

"I will." Diane gulped, but her father didn't seem to notice. Her deception inflated sitting face to face with her father like this. And lately she felt more and more like she didn't want it to be a lie anymore. Guillaume had suggested they make the engagement real. Would he give her another chance? Did she want it?

She'd written him that morning to ask him to dinner. But she hadn't heard back. Last night he'd mentioned going to the beach, and he had already delayed his travel. So tonight might be her last chance to speak with him in person for a while. It wouldn't be ideal with her whole family there, but she could maybe get him alone for a few minutes before the show.

After shopping and lunch in the café, they returned to the hotel with boxes and bags by the armful. Because she had everything she needed there, Diane didn't return to Rue de Fortuny before it was time to get ready for dinner and the opera.

When Guillaume didn't show up for dinner, Diane dismissed it. He must not have seen her letter. Or maybe he'd written to her at home instead of at the hotel. But she'd used the hotel stationery. Had this upset him? Maybe because Alvin was there too? Diane, admittedly, wouldn't want Guillaume staying the night down the hall from an ex-lover who'd come to town to reclaim him. But no. Guillaume had left her at the hotel, so he couldn't have been too worried about where she might sleep. Whatever this was between Guillaume and Diane, it was tenuous. And she'd resisted it for a long time. But there was something there. It wouldn't dissipate because of Alvin's presence.

She tried to think back over their last conversation the night before. The exact words were fuzzy because she'd had four glasses of champagne, but she distinctly remembered standing outside the hotel saying goodnight. She remembered kissing him. The way the streetlight shadowed his kind, handsome face. He'd said he was coming, she was sure of it. Guillaume had come through for her every time, never refused her anything. He'd be at the opera house as planned.

They walked from the hotel on Boulevard des Capucines around the corner to the opera house. The sky was darkening, and the fancy people were out in their gowns and silk top hats and lacquered carriages, heading to this or that event. Diane linked arms with Harry and Catherine, while Ada, Daddy, and Alvin followed behind them. Alvin had been distant all day. More distant than he'd been the previous day, certainly. It pained Diane. She wanted him to keep his distance, but she also didn't want to lose his friendship. Though if she stayed in Paris, she wasn't sure what that would look like beyond letters at birthdays and holiday greetings. It wasn't like she'd never see him again. She'd travel to Woollett at least once a year. Her whole family would be there. So perhaps his distance now was how it had to be.

She genuinely wanted him to enjoy his time in Paris. He was a young, handsome man in the city for the first time. He should take advantage of everything Paris had to offer.

Diane had passed the Palais Garnier many times, but seeing it in passing was quite different from seeing it up close. A statue of Apollo stood like a crown at the building's peak, and he was flanked by statues representing poetry and music. The facade was built like a display for a sculpture collection, with a row of bronze busts of the great composers and statues embodying the various artistic aspects of opera, such as dance and music and drama, at the base of every arch. Everywhere she looked, she found something eye-catching and beautiful.

They all oohed and ahhed when they entered the opulent foyer. Every surface from the ceiling to the floor was designed and decorated in the maximalist, Napoleonic style. Paintings on the ceiling depicted scenes from mythology, and intricately carved marble columns and trim made the walls into fine sculpture. The white marble staircase rose and diverged at the main auditorium entrance where sculptures of tragedy and comedy stood guard. It was breathtaking. Diane had never felt more like a tourist, gaping at the sights, but she embraced it. The building was too pretty not to.

Small groups of people mingled here and there, meeting up and socializing before the show started.

"I'll wait for Guillaume here," Diane said when her family headed upstairs.

"Are you sure he's coming?" Catherine asked tentatively. They'd all been giving Diane sympathetic glances since Guillaume didn't show up at the hotel.

"Not entirely, but I'll wait anyway."

Daddy had gotten them a box on one of the upper levels, and so he gave her two tickets and said he'd see them inside.

Diane stood at the base of the opulent stairs, admiring her surroundings and watching the people, all dressed in their best evening wear, file in, find their friends, and make their way up. Heels clicked on marble, and murmured conversations echoed through the space. She admired the statues and the ornate lanterns. She leaned against the red and green marble balustrade, the glossy stone cool on the backs of her upper arms. She fiddled with her gloves and smoothed her dress countless times. She checked every face that passed her for

Guillaume's. Soon, the crowd tapered off to a trickle of late arrivals. Everyone had gone into the auditorium. Still no Guillaume.

The muffled sound of the orchestra starting up filled the empty foyer. And every possible scenario explaining Guillaume's absence passed through Diane's nervous mind. Miscommunications. Emergencies. Tragedies. The echo of hurried footfalls approaching came then, and her hope rose. But it was some other man in a top hat and black tails, rushing to get to his seat. He nodded politely when he saw her and then took the stairs two at a time.

Guillaume wasn't coming. And with all the explanations swirling in her mind, one sinking realization began to culminate for Diane. She'd taken Guillaume for granted, and now he wasn't here.

"Mademoiselle, can I help you?" An usher approached.

"Oh, no. I was waiting for someone, but now I'm not so sure he's coming."

"I can leave a message at the box office, if you like."

"That's kind of you, but I'm sure it won't be needed." She showed him her ticket.

"Upstairs and to the right, mademoiselle."

"Merci." Diane climbed the stairs then, each step echoing her ascent. But her stomach had fallen to aching depths. Over and over again, her mind rolled over all the words they'd exchanged, all the words she could remember. And the one piece she kept landing on, the one that now glared in its obviousness, was when he said, "Au revoir, Diane."

The first act of *Les Barbares* was nearly half over by the time she reached their box. The auditorium was covered in red velvet and trimmed in ornate gold. And the biggest chandelier she'd ever seen hung above the stage. When Catherine and then her father looked at her quizzically, Diane whispered that something had come up. Guillaume couldn't make it after all. She sat next to Catherine and pretended to be entranced in the performance. Onstage, against a backdrop of ancient ruins, the virginal Floria was falling in love with the leader of her city's nordic invaders. But Diane had missed so much of the setup that it was nothing more than romantic voices singing in a foreign language against aching string music.

Perhaps she should leave and go to his house. Try to talk to him. But it would be a waste. Guillaume wasn't going to be there. He was probably halfway to the beach.

Diane begged off after the performance, making vague excuses for both herself and Guillaume. Then she caught a cab back to Rue de Fortuny. The house was dark when the carriage dropped her off, and Diane let herself in through the front door. On her way upstairs, she passed the table in the foyer where Madame often put the mail. A white envelope practically glowed in the shadowy hall. It was from Guillaume. She took it upstairs, carefully navigating the dark house. When she reached her room, she lit the lamp and found the letter knife on the escritoire. Then she sat on the settee, opened the envelope, and began reading.

Dearest Diane,

I won't be at the opera tonight because I have decided to head on to the beach after all. I would make excuses, but the truth is that, last night with your family, I realized that continuing to play the role of your fiancé would lead to my own emotional demise. To put it simply, Diane, you are going to break my heart.

Nothing between us has felt fake for me since the night of the Prévot's ball. Since then, I have carried on with the hope that you'll come around to me, despite the fact that you've told me on numerous occasions that you will not. I love you, Diane. And I suspect you love me too, though I could be wrong. In any case, I have speculated on your refusals—telling myself that you felt the same and were only afraid of commitment. But the fact is, sitting there at dinner, I realized that my situation is no different from Alvin's. Neither one of us, it seems, can take no for an answer. Though you have made yourself perfectly clear.

For the sake of my heart, I cannot continue to pretend as your fiancé. I will end up hurt, and I cannot face the father of my beloved and perpetuate a lie. We want different things in life, and despite chemistry or emotional connection, this makes us wrong for each other. There is no reason for me to pretend anymore, especially not for the wrong woman.

It has been a pleasure knowing you, Diane, and I wish you the best in all your endeavors. I understand the point of our arrangement was to hold off your family's persuasions to go home. Perhaps you might consider the possibility that, if you do cave to the pressure, then it was meant to be all along despite your resistance.
Guillaume

Diane read the letter three times, and then she crumpled into tears.

The next morning Diane's face resembled a smacked bottom, red and puffy from crying herself to sleep. And it reflected the rawness inside her. She went to work, seating lunch guests at the restaurant and serving drinks until she was exhausted. She swept the gross floors and took the garbage out to the disgusting bin in the alley. She went home after her shift ready to collapse. But she'd promised to have dinner with her father, and so even with her sluggish spirit, she cleaned up, dressed, and caught a cab to the hotel.

The idea of telling everyone that the engagement was off between her and Guillaume made her heart race. And it weakened her case against going home to Woollett. If she wanted to stay in Paris, she'd need to hold her father off for the duration of his stay. And he intended to stay in Paris for three more weeks. His subtle brand of pressure and persuasion was how she ended up making promises to Alvin in the first place. So she decided to tell them that Guillaume was at the beach for his annual vacation, a trip that had been planned long before their arrival, and he'd sent his regrets. All of this was true, of course, except for the part about the engagement. A sham she would now have to hold up all on her own.

"You're joking," her father said when she announced Guillaume's departure at the dinner table.

"I'm afraid not." They'd all just sat down, and Guillaume's continued absence was apparent. Diane wanted to get the difficult news out of the way first thing.

"He couldn't have put it off while we are in town?" The server was there pouring wine; Daddy passed him his glass but otherwise ignored him.

"He's made commitments, Daddy. And your arrival was a bit of a surprise, if you remember."

"Is everything okay between the two of you?" Ada asked, looking down her nose at Diane.

"It's fine. Everything's fine. I don't know why you would suggest it isn't."

"No one's suggesting anything, Diane. We're asking. Because we care," Daddy said.

"I know." Diane sighed. She had to hide all her negative feelings about Guillaume's departure because she didn't want them to think her engagement might be in trouble. Even though it was both fake and very much in trouble. Lies had a way of compounding themselves, making everything more difficult.

"It seems to me that nothing could be more important than spending time with one's fiancée's family," tutted Alvin.

"We're engaged, Alvin, not joined at the hip. And if you wanted his full attention, then you should have planned this trip with us, not to ambush us."

"Ambush?" Daddy said, voice raised in indignation. "My dear, your engagement was as much an ambush to us as our arrival was to you."

"Fine. But can we please talk about something else," Diane said. "Besides picking apart my life."

"Yes, please," Catherine chimed in. At least she wasn't working against Diane.

The conversation moved on, thankfully. But Diane stopped following it.

She had become a different person in Paris. A more independent person who could work for a living, kind of. A person who had moved on from the man she'd thought she wanted to marry.

But Guillaume's presence in her life had changed her too. He appreciated her whims and big ideas in a way that no one in her life ever had. With Alvin, her chaos was something to fix or improve upon, while Guillaume seemed to marvel in it. He'd made her feel loved. And she missed him. She missed his presence, his thoughts and perspectives on the world. The sound of his voice. The feel of his hand on her the small of her back or his arm in hers. His presence made her a better version of herself. Perhaps the best version that had ever existed. He didn't make her feel like a fickle, flighty person the way her family did. He made her feel valid and clever and strong. He'd done all of this for her, while his lasting impression of her was that she was the wrong woman. The wrong woman.

She'd practically memorized his letter. His words, while harsh, cast her situation in a stark light. *If you do cave to the pressure, then it was meant to be all along despite your resistance.* She'd like to argue with him about that. As a man, he didn't understand that a woman couldn't control her own money. He didn't understand what it would be like to be attached to someone who could change his mind about his affection for her and leave her with nothing. Divorce caused scandal and gossip that was disproportionately hard on the wife. She wanted to tell him that it was more complicated as a woman. That everything was harder. But she couldn't. He was gone. And she desperately wished he wasn't.

When dinner was served, she moved her food around on her plate. There was nothing wrong with it, but she couldn't eat it. Her emotional mess had hijacked her appetite. The wine, landing on her empty and churning stomach, only made it worse. As soon as coffee and dessert were being served, she excused herself from going upstairs after dinner. She caught a cab back to Rue de Fortuny and went upstairs to her empty rooms without bothering to see what her housemates were up to.

Chapter Sixteen

"Coucou." Guillaume's mother knocked and then entered his room before he could respond.

Guillaume was lying on his stomach atop his made bed, halfway dressed, with his face to the wall. The patterned wallpaper he'd been staring at for some time now blurred and shifted as his eyes focused and unfocussed.

"Yes, Maman," he said without moving.

"I've brought company."

Guillaume closed his eyes and sighed, wishing that she hadn't. He'd been in no mood for company since leaving Paris five days ago.

"Guillaume," a familiar man's voice called.

Guillaume, who hadn't lost quite all of his self-respect, pushed up off the bed and faced them. Next to his mother stood Olivier Arnaud, Guillaume's old friend. He hadn't seen him since his parents' party, the night they all went to Moulin Rouge. The night he met Diane. That felt like ages ago now.

"I ran into your mother on the promenade and thought I'd come see if your tennis game has improved at all."

"Probably not." Guillaume said, wiping at his mouth in case he'd drooled on himself lying there. Guillaume's tennis racket sat untouched in the closet. He rose from the bed creaky and stiff, like a man who hadn't risen in years. Then Olivier pulled him into a firm embrace.

"You're right, Madame Allard. He's in a pitiful state if he can't even defend his serve."

Guillaume laughed, despite himself. "To be honest, I haven't felt like playing."

His friend regarded him quizzically, while his mother poked around the room. She pulled open the window curtains, letting in the glorious view of the gunmetal blue sea and pale, cloudless sky. Then she went to the desk and straightened a stack of newspapers. When she came to the untouched lunch tray, which she'd sent up even though he'd said he wasn't hungry, she clucked her tongue. "Why didn't you eat?"

"I wasn't hungry."

"You're always hungry, Guillaume."

"Not today."

His mother and friend exchanged knowing looks, and Guillaume wondered if she'd plucked him off the promenade and drug him up here to try and liven up Guillaume. "I've hardly seen you eat a thing since you arrived."

"Just not feeling myself is all." He hadn't left his room more than a handful of times. He'd begged off all invitations, only going out once to walk down to the beach alone. The palatial hotel faced out toward the sea. The lobby on the ground floor opened onto the wide esplanade that lined the beach. As a teenager, he'd spent hours prowling the promenade, making friends and watching the groups of girls pass. But instead of prowling, this time he crossed the esplanade and took the stairs down to the beach. The waves of the cold sea lapped at his feet. The gulls screamed. The wind blew, salty and cool on his face. But none of it refreshed him or lifted him in any meaningful way. Every experience, tactile or intellectual, only brought longing.

None of this was like Guillaume at all.

He'd been through rough breakups before. It was always hard to let go of a girl he liked. But this felt different—not like he was going through something and would eventually emerge with minor scarring, but like he was irrevocably damaged and would never be the same. Paralysis of the spirit, brought upon by heartbreak.

"All this over a girl?" Olivier said.

Maman shrugged and looked questioningly at Guillaume.

"I suppose it is."

"Get out of bed, man. I've got something to show you. Something you're going to love."

"What's that?"

"Oh, you have to see it. Get dressed. We're going to take a ride."

Guillaume protested, but Olivier insisted. And Guillaume's mother couldn't have been happier when he relented.

Twenty minutes later, Guillaume was outside, standing next to Olivier and his sleek new automobile.

"It's the Mercedes Phaeton, a passenger version of the race car model." Olivier beamed at his toy. "It runs on petrol and can go four times as fast as the fastest horse and carriage."

"It's sure flashy." The black paint on the hood was so shiny that Guillaume could see his reflection in it. He needed a haircut even more than usual.

"How about a little adventure to forget about your troubles."

That word. Adventure. Would he ever not equate it with Diane? Despite himself, Guillaume laughed at his friend's look of complete and utter glee. Guillaume couldn't resist. "You talked me into it."

While Guillaume got in, Olivier cranked the engine until it rumbled to life, vibrating the seat and Guillaume. Olivier climbed into the driver's seat, where a steering wheel rose from the floor. He shifted the engine into gear with a stick mounted to the side of the car body, and then Olivier pulled away from the hotel and onto the street. Guillaume had ridden in motorized vehicles twice. Once at the World's Fair last summer. And once when he was a kid, a friend of his father's brought his Renault to their country house.

Getting out of town was slow going, maneuvering around carriages and narrow streets. But when the landscape opened up with farmland and fields, Olivier sped up. Guillaume removed his hat and held it in his lap. The wind whipped his hair across his face and back with every movement of his head. The ground whizzed past underneath them. And it was hard not to smile at the sheer exhilaration of going so fast.

They took a winding road up a green hillside outside of town and parked at the picturesque little twelfth-century church. The medieval stone building sat next to a pond and had a pleasant view of the rolling hills and town below it. Guillaume had come here often during other summers at the beach to look around and marvel at the fact a building could stand for so many hundreds of years. As Diane said, France had plenty of old things, but the age of this particular building was remarkable. Parts were covered in thick ivy, but the pitted stones and narrow doors and windows evoked a sense of time's passing and the meaning of permanence. Had the industrious people who'd placed these stones ever considered it would still be standing nearly seven centuries later? Had they even considered so many years?

Life was short. Guillaume had been a child not so long ago, standing in this same churchyard. He was but a blip in time. And he'd only get one chance to enjoy it.

"Do you ever think about marriage, Olivier?" They were walking around the side of the building now. Bees lingered in the tall spikes of fox glove, and the grass was soft under Guillaume's feet. The sun was shining and warm, but the cool sea breeze made it tolerable.

"You mean doing it? Of course. We'll all have to do it sooner or later, right?"

"Well, yes, but I mean about marriage in a general sense. Like what it means to people in their lives."

"I don't know. I mean, people have been doing it for so long." He raised his hands to indicate the old building they'd come to see. "Probably since before this church was built."

"Probably. But do you ever consider that it's unfair in a way? Especially to women?"

Olivier shrugged. "I suppose it is. The arrangement does generally favor men, at least in the legal respects. Women can't vote. They can't control their money. Marriage is the only real way for a woman to be secure, unless she has generous and understanding family to take care of her. Is this about your petite amie?"

"Diane. Yes, I suppose. She doesn't want to get married. She's adamantly against it."

"So have you asked her?"

"Not exactly. But she won't marry me. She came to France to avoid marrying someone else, in fact."

While they walked around the church, Guillaume explained everything to his friend—about the fake engagement, the father and ex coming to Paris, and how Diane kept refusing him despite their obvious connection. Olivier listened and nodded encouragingly, asking questions for clarification and letting Guillaume get it all out. They reached the bank of the pond. The blue sky and scant, wispy clouds reflected in the flat mirror of water.

"So all of this has you reconsidering marriage as an institution?"

"I suppose it does. Yes."

"Well, I've certainly heard of women resisting the marital yoke. Lesbians and old maids, that sort of thing. But if she doesn't want to marry, what does she want?"

"She says she wants adventure. To not be bound by anyone's desires for what her life should be like."

"But you love her, right?"

"I do."

"So why would you do anything to make her miserable in marriage?"

"I wouldn't. I would let her do whatever she wants."

"Does she know that?"

Guillaume wasn't sure how to answer. Did she know?

"Look. Marriage is legally binding, but inside of that it is a personal relationship. The two people involved can make it anything they want it to be."

"I suppose you're right." After all, Guillaume's parents weren't miserable.

"Of course I'm right," Olivier said smugly. Then he put a hand on Guillaume's shoulder, giving him a single firm shake. "Maybe you've been focused too much on the fact that she says she doesn't want to get married, when you should be focusing on showing her what a marriage with you could be like. That it could be different from anyone else's marriage. That's if you really want to marry her. If not, then perhaps we should spend the evening in the casino meeting all the pretty mademoiselles."

"It's not that simple. Her family came to Paris to take her back to America. She could be on her way there now for all I know."

"That is trickier. Have you written to her?"

"No."

"Then I would start there. And go to the casino with me tonight."

When they'd had their fill of the historic building, Guillaume and Olivier drove back to town, and Guillaume returned to the hotel, windblown and with a clearer head. He did feel decidedly better. After cleaning up, he wrote a letter to Diane, apologizing for his abrupt departure and assuring her that he wanted to help her stay in France. Then, for the first time since coming to Cabourg, Guillaume went out with friends and enjoyed himself.

Diane sat across from her father and Alvin in the hotel dining room. Catherine, Harry, and Ada were going to one of the tamer cabarets. And so Diane was having dinner with her father and Alvin. She'd taken off work as much as she could, and taken off early on the days she couldn't, so every day since their arrival, she'd had dinner at the hotel. She liked seeing Daddy after they'd been apart for so long, but it was no longer fun. The hotel had morphed from the place where her family ate dinner into the stage for her deceit.

A discontentedness had descended on her since Guillaume's departure. But she couldn't express it or let on that she was upset about anything because she was still trying to maintain the appearance of her engagement. So far, the best she could come up with was pretending to receive letters and telling them all about Guillaume's experiences in Cabourg, which she made up as she went along.

Diane knew absolutely nothing about Cabourg. She had even made the mistake of telling Daddy that it was in the south of France. She'd later been paging through the guidebook that was in every room of the Grand Hôtel and discovered that Cabourg was actually in Normandy, to the north. She'd promptly and discreetly removed the incriminating guidebooks from both the room her father and Ada were sharing and Catherine's room, just in case. The thought of Alvin or Harry discovering it had kept her up on multiple nights. Devising a plan to slip into their rooms for such an errand was harder. But it distracted her from missing Guillaume, at least a little.

To Alvin's credit, he hadn't been around so much. Diane suspected he'd discovered the pleasures of Paris. They weren't hard to find. This was both an uncomfortable truth and to be expected. She was happy for him.

More troubling was the fact that Catherine was definitely leaving France. Diane would soon be alone. The finality of this arrangement was more uncomfortable than Diane had expected. She'd never been without her sister before. Every time she thought about Catherine living on the other side of the Atlantic, dread filled Diane. Not only would her sister be far away, but there was a fair chance she'd not be able to pay her rent and have to move to some seedy hovel in an unfashionable or even destitute part of the city. If it were out of walking distance from work, this would make it more difficult to keep her position at the restaurant. The metro promised to help transportation throughout the city, but it didn't serve all parts of Paris yet. She could lose her job without reliable transportation. Her lot in life would continue to degrade from there. She wanted to stay in Paris. But did she want to stay in Paris if she was living in squalor?

She'd never felt quite so alone, and she wasn't yet. She always had someone around to keep her company and provide moral support. Catherine or Alvin. Guillaume. But this aloneness was also of her own making. She'd chosen not to be with Alvin. She'd chosen not to go back home with her sister. She'd chosen not to be with Guillaume. And by choosing not to marry, to be completely free, she was choosing not to go through life bolstered by a partner. But she had never been the type of person who preferred to be alone. She didn't even like eating without company. The idea of eating a lifetime of meals alone sounded like torture. So why was she choosing to be alone for the rest of her life? It was almost like she hadn't fully thought through her convictions.

The server arrived with a bottle of wine. He poured it, took their dinner orders, and then disappeared back into the swirl of restaurant activity. People all around them were eating and celebrating and living life. Instead of their usual place, they were seated at a much smaller table off to the side of the dining room because it was only the three of them tonight.

While her father and Alvin talked about baseball, Diane let her eyes wander around the room full of people, which was how she spotted Monsieur Glover, Ada's friend from the boat. He was with two other gentlemen at a table near the bar, laughing and talking like he knew them well. When he noticed Diane, he nodded and smiled and then went back to his conversation.

The gross feeling of having caught Ada with this man had faded, but she still hadn't quite figured out his motive. Or Ada's for that matter. She was obviously capable of attracting attention. Monsieur Glover was not near as handsome as Daddy. But he was young, and he was obviously, if strangely, interested in Ada. He could have been some swindling fraud, but he didn't strike Diane as that smart or malicious. Ada, despite Diane's feelings for her, was a woman. Prone as anyone to flattery and persuasion, particularly on vacation. And could she really fault Ada for engaging in flirtations with another man when her father still hadn't married her? Relationships were so complicated.

A pianist started playing on the other side of the dining room, a familiar tune that Diane should have been able to name but couldn't. The delicate notes trembled over the usual din of restaurant sounds and conversations. The server came around with the soup course—a lovely vichyssoise that was perfect for such a hot summer night. Her father, speaking with a higher than appropriate volume and attention to enunciation, said it looked wonderful and praised the service. The server departed, and the table fell quiet aside from the sounds of soup spoons scraping the sides of bowls. But Diane was still thinking about Ada.

"Daddy, why aren't you and Ada married yet?" She'd never asked this before, which now struck her as strange.

"What?" Her father recoiled at the question. "What business is it of yours?"

"Well, you have no problem making a marriage for me into your business."

Alvin raised his eyebrows at this, but didn't say anything.

Diane continued. "And Ada's been around for years. You've given her a ring. So why haven't you married her?"

"I suppose the timing hasn't been right, maybe. Or it hasn't felt necessary yet."

"What do you mean it hasn't felt necessary?"

"Well, we've both done all of that before, and I'm busy."

"It's a simple ceremony, Daddy. A trip to the courthouse."

"I know that." He was thoughtful for a moment, sipping his wine. "But people need different things out of legal arrangements like marriage. For you, you can't control your inheritance until you're married. So this is why I'm so relieved about your engagement, even though I will have to get used to the idea of you not being married to Alvin."

Daddy looked at Alvin, who was now intently eating his soup, no doubt to avoid engaging in the conversation. Then Daddy turned his full attention back to Diane. "I don't know all the details about how things work here in France—I have a lawyer looking into that, in fact—but marriage is important for you and your sister, so that you have those legal protections. Ada is a widow; she's got control of her money. And she and I have always had the kind of relationship where, if she needs anything, she can ask me."

"Still, she has to ask you for it. And she doesn't have that much money of her own."

"I'm not stingy, if that's what you're implying, Diane. And the arrangement, such as it is, works for us."

"Does Ada see it that way?"

"Why? Has she said something to you?" Daddy's heavy brow creased. He seemed genuinely surprised by the question.

"Not really, but I do get the impression that she perceives her relationship with you to be... not unstable, but not as stable as it could be."

He waved a dismissive hand. "Well, of course, it isn't. I'm not legally beholden to her."

"But she also doesn't have the security of your fortune, if something were to happen to you."

"Believe me, dear, Ada will be fine. What's this all about?"

"I don't know." She couldn't exactly explain it to him without revealing the falsity of her engagement. "Just curious, I guess."

"Well, marriage as an institution exists primarily for security. But it's also about love. I loved your mother dearly, and perhaps that hasn't been so easy for me to overcome. Ada too. As a young woman, she lost the man she thought she'd spend the rest of her life with."

Diane considered this perhaps for the first time, at least in terms of how it affected their relationship. Both her father and Ada had lost their first loves. They'd both been through so much. The fear of losing another spouse was probably visceral and real. Grief so vast it was difficult to cross. And them being together now was, in a way, a triumph of the spirit.

The server arrived with their main course then, and the conversation dropped. Everyone got busy with their food, and Diane ate her steak tartare. She might never understand why her father and Ada hadn't married yet. But she did understand what he'd said about every arrangement being determined by the people involved. She liked the idea of a permanent—or at least semipermanent—companion. A traveling companion. A companion to her life. A friend in the house to talk to and all of that. There were legalities, and those legalities were unfair to women on the whole. But maybe it wasn't marriage she was so afraid of; maybe it was marriage to the wrong man.

Chapter Seventeen

The next morning, Diane awoke with a vague sense that she was forgetting something and no idea what it might be. This wasn't an uncommon sensation, and she trusted that it would eventually come to her, if it was all that important.

She spent a leisurely few hours in her room, writing in her journal and writing to Guillaume. She'd written to him every day since he left. At first, she'd asked him to reconsider and come back. But she didn't know where to write to him in Cabourg, so she'd sent the letters to his house like always. There was a chance someone might forward them along, but there was also a chance that her letters were piling up somewhere unread, waiting for him. So she kept writing about all the conversations she wished they could have. Not only big ones, but also small ones. She wrote to him like she was sitting next to him in a carriage, chatting about this or that.

He hadn't responded, and so perhaps it was a pointless exercise. But that somehow only made her want to write more. It was like she was writing in her journal but also sending out a signal. She missed him. And even if he wasn't there to reply, she got comfort from writing her thoughts to him anyway.

As she sealed and addressed the letter, that thing she'd forgotten came to her like a strike on the head. She was supposed to work at ten. It was now after eleven.

She was missing work!

She'd been so distracted by her father and Guillaume and everything else that she'd forgotten what day it was.

Diane rushed to get ready, haphazardly fixing her hair and dressing in her standard black skirt. She picked her white shirt and tie up off her floor. Then she ran from her room, down the stairs, and out the door. She always walked to work because it was a few blocks and not worth the effort of catching a cab ride unless it was raining. Running down Rue de Fortuny, she wished more than anything that an empty cab would appear. How had she forgotten something so essential to her survival? How could she have been so foolish? Since her father arrived, Diane had taken off work more days than she'd worked, almost like she was sliding back into her old ways. She hadn't grown up with parents who had to get to work on time, and she'd never worked until coming to Paris. It wasn't exactly the easiest thing in the world to get used to. It was the hardest thing she'd ever done, in fact. And now she was screwing it up again.

Never had the restaurant felt so far away as when she was running toward it. Never had she wanted to be there so badly. Sweat pooled under her clothing, between her breasts and under her arms. Her feet hurt from pounding on the pavement and a cramp ached in her side. When she reached the front door of Bouillon Juillet, she flung it open. Inside, standing at her station, was her polished and sleek boss. His hair was greased into place, and his uniform clean and pressed. When he looked up and saw her sweaty, red face, wrinkled shirt, and messy hair, he shook his head solemnly and pulled out his pocket watch.

"I'm so sorry," Diane said, smoothing her hair as best she could. "I completely forgot what day it was. I've had family in town. I ran all the way from my house to get here."

Her boss held up his hand. "I don't want to hear your excuses, Diane. The only thing that matters is that you weren't here this morning to get ready for our important event this afternoon. But Celine was."

"Celine?" The young woman standing next to her boss, who Diane just now noticed, smiled sheepishly. She waved to Diane the way a child who'd been caught staring might.

"Yes. Celine came in looking for a job, and I gave her yours. Because you weren't here."

"But you can't do that. I need this job. And I'm here now. I'll work late to make up for it. I'll take extra shifts."

He pursed his lips hatefully. "If I can't count on you to show up for your existing shifts, then why would I assign more to you?"

Diane started to speak, but he held up his hand again.

"It was a rhetorical question. You're fired, Diane." He came around the counter then and placed a gentle, firm hand on her back between her shoulders. It was warm and oddly comforting. Then he steered her to the door, pushed it open for her, and nudged her out of it. As the door swung closed, he dusted his hands together, like he'd taken out the trash. Then he went back to training Celine, who was staring blank-faced at Diane through the large pane of glass.

"Shit!" Diane stomped her foot on the pavement so hard that it hurt. Her hands tightened into fists at her sides. Could a person lose a job for something like this? She wasn't even two hours late.

But after running for so long, she barely had the energy to maintain a fist. She hadn't even fully recovered her breath. And so she turned back the way she came and started walking.

Now she remembered the last time she'd been in. She had wanted more time off, and her boss had told her about the party scheduled for today. He said he needed her and couldn't give her today off. He'd told her how important it was. It all came back to her. Yes, one could get fired for this sort of thing.

The timing could not have been worse. Her father was in town. Her fake engagement was falling apart. All the tethers holding her in Paris were snapping like flimsy twine. And now she had to pretend to have a job. Or tell her father she got fired. Or find something else fast.

If she didn't find anything, she'd have to ask her father for money to pay her rent. If she asked him for money, it was only a matter of time before he'd wonder why she needed it when her wedding was imminent. And everything about her engagement story would fall apart from there.

She went home because she had nothing else to do. By the time she was climbing the stairs to her room, Diane's spirit had plunged. She was the flightiest, most frivolous person to ever live. And there was no way she was going to be able to get herself together. It was as if everything in her life was aligning to tell her that Paris was not meant for her. She was not meant for Paris.

Then Catherine's distinct cackle carried through the hall. Her sister was here. Upstairs talking to Nadine.

Instead of going up to see them, Diane went to their rooms and removed her work shirt and tie. At least she'd never have to wear those again. She had just started getting used to the job. She'd actually thought her boss liked her. And now the job was gone. Like all the others. There was a crude impersonality to the working world that both puzzled her and put her in her place. No matter how important staying in Paris was to her, no one cared whether she could pay her rent or hold off her father's persuasions or avoid marrying this or that man. No one cared, even if they liked her.

She was sitting on her bed when Catherine came in. "You're back from work already?"

Diane nodded. How was it that Catherine remembered Diane was working today when Diane hadn't remembered herself? "What are you doing here?"

"I do live here, you know."

"Do you?"

"Well, not for long, I guess." Catherine started tidying the sitting room, putting the coffee cups in a pile to go down to the kitchen, and stacking up the newspapers that littered seemingly every surface. "Why are you back from work so early?"

A sudden, unexpected rush of tears stung Diane's eyes. "I got fired."

"No, Diane. For what?"

"I forgot my shift. They've already replaced me."

"I'm sorry." Catherine crossed the room and hugged Diane. Then they sat together on Diane's bed. After a quiet, supportive silence, Catherine said, "I've been ready to go home for a while now, you know."

Diane did know this, but it was still so hard to believe. "Why? Is it just to get married? You could do that here if Harry is willing to stay."

"I'm not going back just for Harry. I'm not sure what's going to happen between us, to be honest." Catherine picked up a brush off Diane's nightstand and turned it in her hands.

"So how could you give up Paris for Woollett?"

"Honestly, Paris doesn't remind me of Mama. Woollett does."

Diane had never considered this. But it was true; her mother had never been to Paris. Every street in Woollett held a memory. Maybe that was why Diane didn't want to live there. Maybe she and her sister were more different than she realized.

She might never understand her sister wanting to go. Catherine had had no trouble holding down a good job. They'd made friends here. And yet after all that work, Catherine was willing and ready to leave. Such was the pull of home.

"It just feels so surreal. Everything has changed so much since they arrived, and it's never going to be the same. You're leaving, Catherine."

"What will you do?"

"After this morning, I might have to go back too."

"What about Guillaume?"

Diane sighed and fell back on the bed. "I think I'm in love with him. But he's not speaking to me. There was a letter waiting for me when I got home from the opera. He's broken it off with me."

"Why?"

"Because I don't want to get married, among other reasons. I've treated him poorly."

"Diane, I don't think you're truly afraid of marriage. Or not just marriage, anyway. You, my dear sister, are afraid of commitment."

"Commitment, in general?"

"Commitment, broadly, generally, universally. Definitely. You're afraid to make choices."

"I make choices."

"Sometimes, about small things. But you're terrified of committing to staying in Paris because I'm not, which is why you argue with me about it all the time. You crossed an ocean so you wouldn't have to decide whether or not to marry Alvin. And you've been wishy washy sticking to that decision since he arrived. You say you want to stay in Paris, but you don't want to do the things that will actually allow you to do so. Like hold down a job, or marry the man you obviously love. You and I both know that if Daddy forces you on that boat, deep inside you'll be relieved because it gets you out of another decision."

Although her instinct was to protest, Diane stopped herself. She had more or less crossed an ocean to get out of making decisions about Alvin. "I never thought about it that way."

"Of course, you didn't. Yes, every decision is a trap. No matter what you choose, you have to give something up. But you'll never have anything if you don't choose something. That's what life is. Choices. Paths taken and not. It's foolish to think you can avoid it and ever have a chance at happiness."

Diane didn't say anything for a moment, letting her sister's words sink in. It was true that all the impermanence she cultivated in her life was starting to wear on her. Sounds of life carried through the house. Footfalls of one of their housemates heading downstairs. The front door opened and closed again. Diane's favorite part of living in the women's pension was that she was never alone in the house. Whether she needed an ear or a warm drink or a little guidance, there was always someone around. "Do you think I should tell Daddy what's happened?"

"I don't think you should lie. Not to Daddy. And not to yourself."

"You know as soon as I tell him about Guillaume, he's going to book my passage home."

"So what if he does? Just because he buys a ticket, doesn't mean you have to get on the boat. You are the one who gets to decide your life. Not Daddy."

"We do know all about not getting on boats, don't we?"

"Absolutely."

"So how do I make decisions? How do I know what I really want when everything feels so complicated?"

"You know, I read in an advice column in the paper the other day about this very thing. And the advice was to make a list of pros and cons for whatever decision feels hard to make. Like fold your paper in half and make the lists side by side, so you can see them both on the sheet."

"And then it will be obvious which list is longer?"

"Yes. You should try it." She patted Diane on the leg, and then stood up. "I am meeting Ada. So I can't stay while you do it."

"It's okay. I can do it alone."

"I know you can." Catherine pinned her hat onto her hair and checked the time. Then she kissed Diane on the forehead and said goodbye.

"I'll be at dinner."

"See you then."

When Catherine was gone, Diane sat on her bed for a long time, considering what she'd said. Was that why she argued with Catherine about staying in Paris? Because she couldn't decide to do it on her own? Making the list almost seemed too easy. But without work, she truly had nothing better to do but try it. And so she went to her room, flipped to a clean spread of two sheets in her journal. On one side, she wrote, "Stay in Paris," and on the other, she wrote, "Go home." Then she started her list. One by one, she emptied her head of all her worries and concerns. By the time she set the list aside, the right decision was obvious. She went to the escritoire for a sheet of stationery and wrote to Guillaume for the second time that day.

When she'd finished, she folded the paper, fitted it into an envelope, and addressed it. She was on her way down to put it in the post when she noticed an envelope on the table in the hall. It was from him. He'd written to her.

Diane picked up the envelope and tore it open right there.

Diane,

The beach has not been as refreshing as usual because the cloud of our attachment shadows it. I was harsh in my last letter. And while I haven't heard from you here, I know that your response is waiting for me at home. Perhaps in the form of no response at all. In any case, I haven't changed my mind about things entirely. But I do believe I've pled my case in the wrong way. So I would like another chance.

I cannot lie anymore. I cannot play at something untruthful. But I can be honest and open with my feelings. I have had to acknowledge their importance in my life, and I am prepared to stand up for them.

Some time has passed, and I don't know what has happened with your family in Paris since my departure. But I hope very much that you'll still be there when I return in a few weeks. I have searched my soul and keep arriving at the desire for your happiness. Whatever that looks like. And so I had to write and tell you that if happiness is on a boat back to America, then I wish you well. If it is still in Paris, then I will help you however I can to achieve it. Please know that you won't be alone there or unsupported, even without your family. You are more than you often give yourself credit for. I have suffered so much without you. I want very much to be in your life. Your friend, at first. And know that I will be working for more until the endeavor runs its course.

I will be back in town on September 15. And I hope to see you then.

With love,
Guillaume

Chapter Eighteen

Elated by Guillaume's letter, Diane arrived for dinner at the Grand Hôtel that night with renewed confidence. She smiled at the now-familiar concierge and waitstaff. When she reached their usual table, Daddy, Alvin, and Harry stood to greet her.

"Dini, dear, you look lovely as always," Daddy said. He was wearing a new dinner jacket in the latest cut, no doubt procured since coming to Paris.

"Thank you, Daddy. You look nice too. Good evening." Diane sat, and everyone settled in. Then, before the server came or the conversation picked back up, she cleared her throat and said, "I have something I need to tell you, Daddy. Everyone."

When all their eyes landed on her, her bravery drifted away like smoke. Diane gulped.

"What is it?" Her father looked worried. After the engagement surprise, he was probably afraid to hear whatever came out of her mouth next. He had reason to be.

She took a breath and consciously loosened her shoulders. The only way out was through, but on the other side was freedom. "The engagement with Guillaume is off. Not that it was ever really, truly on."

Catherine pressed her mouth into a line and nodded solemnly in support.

Diane forged ahead. "He was tired of faking it, and so he left to go to the beach. There's nothing more to it than the fact that it was all a lie."

For a long moment, everyone at the table was silent. They all stared at her. Daddy's mouth hung open. Catherine fanned herself, a combination of surprise and respect showing on her face. Harry slowly shook his head.

"I'm so sorry, dear," Ada said with self-righteous concern.

"I'm sorry to hear that too." Alvin smiled like his horse just won the race.

"How could you lie to us like this?" Daddy's face crumpled with hurt.

"I don't know. It started off innocently enough, a way to get out of trouble. But then the more adamant you and Ada were about me coming home, the more I felt like I needed the fake engagement with Guillaume to help put you off. It just kept getting more and more complicated."

"So who is he then? Is he anyone to you?"

"He is, Daddy, of course. He started out as a friend. And through all of this, I realized that I do love him. And I want to try to repair things."

"So you plan to stay in Paris still? Even though the engagement is off? Or was never on."

"Yes, Daddy. My whole life doesn't revolve around marriage. We have that in common."

Ada shifted in her chair and sipped her wine.

"So you'll keep working at the restaurant then? And how long can you keep that up?"

"Actually, no. That's the other thing. I got fired from the restaurant today. I've been so busy that I forgot about work."

"You forgot?"

Diane nodded. It was such a foolish thing to do, and yet she'd done it. No use hiding it when she was being honest about everything else.

"So your rent money..."

Diane steeled herself. In addition to making her list of pros and cons, she'd done a lot of thinking about what she needed to really make her choice and live it. "I'm hoping you'll give it to me, Daddy. I'm asking for your help. I got fired in part because I've been taking so much time off this past week. And now that you're taking Catherine back to America with you, I won't have a roommate to share my rent. I need your help so I don't end up on the street before I find another job."

"I plan on putting in a good word for her at the law office," Catherine chimed in. "They need someone because I'm leaving. And she's already trained, so I think they'll take her back."

"Even if that doesn't work, I should be able to find something quick. But a roommate will be harder. It can be an early Christmas present, if you like. But I need help."

"You knew about this, Catherine?"

"She told me last night."

"Diane, I understand you like it here." Daddy shook his head. "But you'll be all alone. We're all leaving."

"I know that. And I won't be alone. I have Madame Tremblay and all my housemates. And I have Guillaume."

When Catherine raised her eyebrows, Diane explained. "He wrote to me. I got the letter today. He'll be back in a few weeks, and he assures me that I can rely on him for friendship and support. I hope it becomes more than that. But in either case, I won't be alone, even though I will be on my own."

Saying these words to her family was like standing in front of a crowd naked. But even baring herself, her resolve strengthened. She was doing exactly what she was supposed to be doing. She was staying in Paris. She was working it out with Guillaume. She was making a life for herself exactly where she wanted to be.

Her father leaned back in his seat, considering everything she'd said. He pursed his lips, puffing his mustache out the way he did when he had something to say. But then the server came for their dinner order. Everyone asked for the mussels except for Ada, who ordered beef.

As soon as the server had gone, Diane pressed him again. "So, Daddy? Can you help me?"

"I think you should, Daddy," Catherine said.

"Of course, I can, Dini, if that's what you really want. I should have been more supportive this whole time. And I don't say it often enough… I haven't said it in a long time. I'm proud of you girls, coming over here and working so hard. I couldn't be prouder." He covered Diane's hand with his giant one and dipped his head to catch her eye. "But I'm also buying you a ticket home. I'll keep it open, so you don't have to leave when we do. Then no matter what happens, you'll be able to come home."

Diane's eyes filled with tears. "That's fine. If you want to leave me a lifeboat, then I'll take it. But I'm still not ready to leave Paris, even if it does mean staying here on my own."

He squeezed her hand. "I'm proud of you for coming clean about the engagement. I'm sure it wasn't easy."

"I figured this would be better than just not getting on the boat."

"Ha. I appreciate that."

Their train from Paris to the port in Calais departed on a hot, bright mid-August day. Diane stayed at the hotel on her family's last night in town, and in the morning she accompanied them to the station without any pretenses about getting on the train herself. After going through the ticketing lines and navigating through the crowds of travelers, they gathered together one last time on the platform.

Travelers moved around them, and a train on a different track pulled away. Every conversation they had was about the logistics of travel and the anticipation of being on the boat or being home. Small things, like appointments to make and friends to see. These exchanges gave Diane little pangs of regret that she wouldn't be included. But she had her own list of things to do now that she would be on her own in Paris.

Their train rolled in and emptied out. Soon the porter called for all aboard.

When Daddy looked at Diane, it was with the same expression he had when he'd dropped her and Catherine at the dock in New York the day they'd left for Paris. Like he was losing her. Back then it had seemed silly, like he was a sentimental man, and she was merely traveling for a vacation. Now he really was losing her, and Diane no longer dismissed his feelings.

She hugged and kissed her father, inhaling his familiar scent of sandalwood and smoke one more time to imprint it on her memory. They'd all said everything they needed to say in the days leading up to this departure. Now all that was left was goodbye.

"I want you to know that when you left New York, you were a young girl with a head full of desires." His eyes were damp. He'd cried at their mother's funeral, with agonizing tears streaming down his cheeks. That was the only time she'd seen him so overcome with an emotion that wasn't anger. This was different, sadness tinged with pride. "But now you are a strong young woman, and I have no doubt that you'll do just fine here in Paris. It's a beautiful city, and I understand why you want to stay."

"Do you, Daddy?"

"Of course. I was young once." He squeezed her one more time. "Just remember that you'll always have a home in Woollett, no matter what happens."

"Thank you, Daddy. I'll come visit soon."

Next, she hugged her sister. Both were teary as they held each other tight. "I'll miss you," Diane said into Catherine's hair.

"I'll miss you too."

"There's still time, you know. To not get on the train."

Catherine laughed. "This time I'm getting on it. But I'll be back. And you'll come visit."

"I will. And know that, if you get to the port and change your mind, you're welcome to come right back."

Diane hugged Ada—stiffly, but a hug nonetheless. They'd achieved a truce of sorts. An understanding. And Ada seemed more relaxed now that everything had worked out to everyone's satisfaction.

Then it was time to say goodbye to Alvin. When she put her arms around him for a hug, he lifted her into the air and swung her gently back and forth.

"I'll miss you, Diane. Again."

"I'll miss you, too, Alvin. But you'll be all right without me."

"I will." He set her down and stepped out of her arms.

"I'm sorry about everything. Again," Diane said.

"No reason to be sorry. Good luck with your Frenchman. And don't forget to write." He seemed to be getting over their breakup well; it had been in the works for almost a year, after all. All the discomfort between them had dissipated, and they were parting as friends. But he'd also met a woman from New York who was visiting Paris with her family. And it was serious enough that they'd already made plans to meet back in America. Her name was Philippa, and her father was a state senator. Alvin would be fine. He kissed her on each cheek and said he'd see her soon. "Not because you won't make it here. But because you—and maybe your husband—will surely come visit."

"Thank you, Alvin."

And then came the shuffle of boarding the train. Diane watched them file into the line, bags in hand, with the crowd of fellow travelers. They waved from inside the train car. Diane wiped her eyes with a handkerchief. She was scared to death that they were leaving, but she also sensed that everything was unfolding as it should, at least for now.

Finally, as the train slid away from the platform, she waved and cried a little more. She'd miss them. But instead of letting herself feel alone, she returned to the house on Rue de Fortuny and had a glass of whiskey with her housemates.

In the following weeks, Diane continued to write Guillaume daily. But she didn't bother explaining about all the letters she'd already sent to his home. From his letters, he didn't seem to know about them, and rather than waste ink and time rehashing everything she had already said, she just kept the conversation going and sent her messages to the hotel instead of his house in Paris. And she liked the fact that her pile of letters was maybe there waiting for him when he came home.

In the meantime, she had to work. She couldn't hop on a train to Cabourg because she'd taken over Catherine's job at the law office. And Diane didn't want to get fired again. While she waited for Guillaume, she had to be responsible and establish herself independently, or at least somewhat independently, in Paris. As much to prove that she could to her family as to prove it to herself.

Her father agreed to pay her rent, including Catherine's portion until she found a suitable roommate or living situation, which she was in no hurry to do. In fact, Daddy seemed thrilled to help her with money. He gave her two hundred francs before he left Paris. He also paid Madame Tremblay for two months rent and asked that she send him the bills and receipts from now on. Perhaps he felt guilty about not sending them anything for so long, and he was compensating for it with generosity.

Diane returned to the law office seven months and three weeks after being fired. Catherine put in a lot of good words with her boss about how much Diane had changed and how worthy she was of another chance, and she'd managed to get Diane back in. With Catherine leaving, they needed Diane almost as much as she needed the job. That she was already trained and readily available helped for sure. And Diane was apologetic. She was a different person now. That pride that had been so insulted by menial tasks was now wise and quiet. There were always indignities to suffer, especially in employment. Now she knew better than to take the indignities of serving coffee and pulling files personally. This was why people had aspirations, so they could get out of the work they couldn't endure. She was even learning to type.

With a skill like typing, Madame Tremblay assured her, she'd never have to rely on a man for anything. Diane liked the sound of that, but she was also beginning to understand the benefits of relying on people. The way one's life could expand. The right people, of course, were essential. Guillaume was the right kind of person to rely on. And she wanted to be the right person for him to rely on as well. The right woman.

Chapter Nineteen

On the day Guillaume was to return to Paris, Diane used the new telephone at work to call the train station and ask about arrivals from Normandy. And, with permission from her boss, she left early to meet the train at Gare Saint Lazare.

She had confirmed Guillaume's travel plans by letter, but she hadn't told him that she was planning to be at the station. She needed him to step down off the train car, see her there, run into her open arms, and swing her around in a passionate embrace. This was unlikely to happen. He'd be arriving with his family; Diane had met them all once, but that felt like ages ago. Although she was fairly sure she'd recognize them, she wasn't sure she'd made enough of an impression on them for recollection. The point was that she'd be there as soon as he arrived. She needed to do that. To show him that she meant everything in all her letters.

The station was busy with travelers coming and going, and after checking the arrivals board, she made her way down to the platform. Other people milled about, reading newspapers and their pocket watches. The afternoon light shone through the paned glass ceiling. A pigeon pecked at something on the ground near a trash can. Then a distant chugging rattle grew louder and louder.

The train arrived minutes later, filling the terminal with puffs of screeching steam. There was no way to know from where on the train Guillaume and his family would emerge, so she positioned herself near the platform exit where everyone arriving would have to pass her. The cars opened and passengers began to descend. In moments the station was crowded with people home from vacation, sun-kissed and toting bags with sand in the crevices.

Diane took a deep breath when she spotted Guillaume's sisters. They were engaged in conversation, so they didn't notice Diane. Then one—Josephine, perhaps—looked right at her. Her brow furrowed slightly, like she was trying to place Diane, but the foot traffic swept her along before she could.

Diane rose onto her tip-toes and searched for Guillaume. Then there he was, ten paces in front of her, coming her way. He didn't see her yet, and so Diane watched him make his way through the crowd. His hair was a little lighter from the sun, and his sideburns were a little longer. His chiseled jaw was set with exhaustion from travel. He towered over everyone around him, and looked very much the returned vacationer in his straw fedora. His gaze was pointed down, watching his step. But then he looked up, and his blue eyes landed on her.

Diane's heart thumped and her throat tightened with anticipation. His reaction to her presence would surely betray his true feelings. She smiled tentatively. And to her relief, he smiled with surprise and genuine delight. Holding her gaze, he picked up his speed and cut across the flow of pedestrian traffic to reach her.

Diane walked toward him too. And then, within seconds, after all that time, they were face to face.

"Bonjour."

"Bonjour."

"What are you doing here?"

"I couldn't wait any longer to see you. I left work early."

"You didn't have to do that." He gestured with his arm for her to walk with him, and they started moving toward the exit.

"I did." She didn't want to tell him in a crowd of people like this, but she also didn't want to wait. She put a hand on his arm. "I need to say something, Guillaume. I came here because I can't wait to tell you."

Nodding, he stepped out of the flow of traffic and led her to a more secluded spot by the stairs. His tan linen suit was rumpled, but not in a bad way. Diane had waited so long for this moment, and now here he was. Standing right in front of her. Her chest swelled with affection, and she was just so very happy to see him. She could burst. But there were all these people around them, noticing and moving along. She wished they could be alone.

"What is it?"

She felt silly now, for not thinking this romantic reunion all the way through. A crowded train platform was not the right place to profess her love. But what was done was done. She couldn't change the setting now. Saying what she needed to say was most important. "I want to make the engagement real. I regret not doing it when you asked me before. And I wish I could go back and change it. I want to fix that mistake now."

He raised his eyebrows in surprise, but he didn't say anything. His silence was palpable.

"You're hesitating."

"I'm surprised, Diane. I'm sorry. I just—"

"Let me guess," Diane said. "This feels like a trap?"

"Ha. A little, maybe." The shock on his face softened. "But maybe I'd like to go back a little further than that."

"You want to do opium again?"

273

"Well, maybe. But no."

"Moulin Rouge?"

"Yes, when we were just a man and a woman meeting through mutual friends in a cabaret."

"Back to the very beginning."

"Yes. I want to buy you dinner."

"Ah, of course. You know there was a time when I would have let anyone buy me dinner if I was hungry enough."

"So I've heard. But I have reason to believe that you'll find me charming."

"Okay. Then you can buy me dinner."

"Tomorrow?"

"Tomorrow is fine."

"Great. I'll pick you up at seven."

"Seven." She nodded. And when he offered his arm, she took it.

They walked together out of the train station. Outside, the sky had clouded over, like it might rain later—a welcome reprieve from the lingering summer heat. His family was gathering with the porters and all their things to wait for their carriages. One of the sisters—Diane would have to learn how to tell them apart—stared curiously at them. Before reaching his family, Guillaume stopped. "Let's say goodbye here, where we won't have an audience."

Diane was relieved. She wasn't sure she was ready to reunite with his family, not quite yet. Guillaume seemed to be thinking the same thing.

"Thank you for coming, Diane." He set his bag on the ground next to his feet to free up his hand. Then he touched her hand where it was resting on his arm.

"I couldn't help myself." They stood there for a moment, gazing at each other. And despite her uncertainties and any awkwardness of their public reunion, Diane knew everything would be okay.

"I better go." He tipped his head toward his family. The carriages were pulling up now.

"Okay."

"Tomorrow at seven?"

"I look forward to it." With that promise of tomorrow between them, they went their separate ways.

After a month away, Guillaume entered his rooms with relief. He set his bag down and removed his shoes. His room was exactly as he'd left it. The servants had put his trunks in a pile outside the door to his dressing room. They hadn't even had time to unpack yet. And there was a pile of mail on the table between the sitting room and his bedroom. A big, unruly pile… of pale pink monogrammed envelopes spilling all over the table. Every one of them from Diane.

Where to start with that many letters? Most of them were pink, but some were white and bore the Grand Hôtel's seal. She had to have written more than once a day. He had another substantial stack of the ones he'd received in Cabourg in his suitcase.

Guillaume lit a cigarette and chose an envelope at random. Then he slid a finger under the flap and removed the letter. It was only a few lines of text.

Guillaume,

*I keep thinking about your head between my legs, the feel of your
exquisite mouth. Can we do that again?*
Yours, Diane

He laughed and desire zapped through him. That was quite
a hook. He picked up another letter and opened it.

Guillaume,
    *My family makes me crazy. I have spent the day with them
and so don't want to continue the saga here. Cook made chicken
for dinner. It was slathered in oil and rubbed in rosemary. I
thought of you. And I am thinking of you now, as my lamp burns
low, and Paris is still awake below my window.*
    *I think the ladies in the house next door—rumored to be of ill-
repute, according to Madame Tremblay—are having a party
tonight. If you were in town, I would arrange to meet you in the
shadow between our doors where we could kiss and go in together.
Parties like that, I've realized, are much more fun with a partner.
If I went without you, I'd only look for you in every person. And
so I am writing instead.*
    *I haven't heard from you, Guillaume. Still. And I think it's
because my letters aren't being forwarded to wherever you are.
You aren't home, and I don't know anything more than the name
of the town with the beach where you've gone. Will you come
home to my letters? Will you come home to me?*
Yours, Diane

He read that one a second time, then picked up another.

Guillaume,

I miss you. I had not anticipated feeling this way about you or anyone ever. This emptiness in the room where I want you to be, this gap in my thinking that comes from considering yours. I am as unprepared for the feelings as I am for knowing what to do about them. But when you come home to Paris, I hope that we can experience the feelings together.
Diane

Guillaume read the whole stack of letters, twenty-nine total, all sent in the week or so between his departure and when she must have received his letter to her. When he was done, he put them in chronological order according to the dates she'd scribbled into the corner of each one. And he read them again, all the while a deep, encompassing pleasure swelled within his chest. He would never not love this woman.

The next day, Diane was waiting in the drawing room on Rue de Fortuny when Guillaume arrived promptly at seven. Madame Tremblay, who was waiting with her, went to answer the door. Diane liked the idea of doing everything properly this time. No getting caught in bed together. No lies. No faking. And so his coming to the door and passing muster with Madame made it even more proper. Madame's footfalls down the stairs carried up through the hall, followed by the door unlatching and their voices. Diane couldn't make out what they were saying, but Madame's laugh reassured her.

A moment later, Guillaume strode in on Madame's heels. His eyes swept the room, and he smiled when they landed on Diane. He was dressed sharply in a black suit, and his blue cravat made his eyes brighter. Again, his presence was a relief and a thrill.

"Bonsoir, Diane." Guillaume took her hand and raised it to his lips.

"Bonsoir." A wave of pleasant heat went through her.

"I can serve a drink, if you have time for one," Madame offered. She liked him; offering the drink was a sure sign. This was important, considering there was a good chance Madame knew that he'd once been snuck into her house for respectable ladies.

"Unfortunately, we have a reservation. But another time?"

"Another time." Madame smiled up at him. He did have a forgivable face.

"Shall we?"

"Yes, please." Diane followed him down the stairs and out to the carriage. After helping her inside, he climbed in and the driver set off.

"I read your letters. The ones at my house."

"Oh. And?" She'd been half-hoping someone had tossed all those.

"And they were nice to come home to."

"Nice?"

"Very nice." He covered her hand with his. "But did you mean it all?"

"Of course. Some of them were written in fits of panic. I hadn't heard anything from you from the beach, you know. So I was afraid I might never hear from you again."

"I did sense some hints of desperation in a few of them."

Diane laughed and blushed. Although her letters were honest and heart-felt, they were also mildly embarrassing now that she was on the other side of her emotional crisis. "Well, it's been a few weeks. And there have been many letters since. So I hope that you can regard them as both honest, but also outdated in the fact that I think I can better articulate my feelings and the lessons I've learned through all of this much more eloquently now."

"I see. More eloquently?"

"Yes," she smiled and put her other hand atop his, making a hand sandwich with his in the middle. "For example, I have a better understanding of my tendency toward chasing experiences, and how it sometimes prevents me from experiencing true depth."

Guillaume nodded. "Impressive."

"And I have also come to believe that love is also a kind of adventure."

"Really?"

"Absolutely. Emotional depth, commitment—these can be as amazing and confounding as visiting a new city."

"Interesting." He was smiling like a cat that had caught a mouse.

"Yes. Very. And the most important thing is that, no matter where I am—Woollett or Paris or wherever—it's really all just scenery when you are experiencing it, experiencing life, with someone you love so deeply."

"And so..."

"And so I've learned quite a lot from all this, Guillaume. I was afraid before. Afraid of many things. But even though we were pretending, I was completely lost without you. I fell in love with you. I am in love with you. And I want to make it work between us, despite everything that's happened."

"I fell in love with you too." He bent down to kiss her. His mouth was warm and soft. And his kiss was gentle and loving.

She opened her mouth and tilted her head to the side, pressing for more. And he gave it to her, putting a hand behind her head and holding her in place. His body was firm and solid against hers, and she melted into him. It was like she'd arrived home. The best kind of home that she could take with her wherever she went.

Then he pulled away and looked at her. "I want to make it work. But I have learned some things too. And I want you to know that I missed you too much to care if we ever get married at all. I just want us to be together, whatever that looks like for us."

"Thank you, Guillaume."

There was so much she wanted to say, dreams for a future she wanted to start dreaming, but they were almost to the restaurant now, and so she chose more kissing instead. Guillaume didn't seem to mind.

Epilogue

June 1902

"*Has it come* yet?"

"What?" Cook jumped. She was standing at the long table in the center of the kitchen, chopping onions, and she wasn't used to interruptions at this hour. The kitchen at 77 Rue de Fortuny, which had stone walls and small windows along the top of the ceiling, was still cool and dim in the dawn light. Cook put a hand on her chest when she saw Diane standing there, dressed in a long sweater and hair loose. "Goodness, no, mademoiselle. And I thought you were joking when you said you were getting up early to get the paper."

"My announcement should be in there today."

"I know, mademoiselle. Everyone does. It's not much of an announcement anymore."

Diane laughed. The announcement had been submitted to all the major Paris papers and the one back at home in Woollett. Diane had been endlessly excited about it. "But now it will be in print!"

"Indeed."

"Is there any coffee?"

"Help yourself." Cook tipped her head toward the percolator keeping warm on the stove.

Diane was fixing her coffee with milk and sugar when a knock came at the service door. She turned to look so fast that she almost spilled the hot liquid. Then, in the shadowy morning light, Guillaume's face appeared in the window.

"Oh, goodness." Cook sighed. "The party is starting awfully early. I don't have anything ready for breakfast."

"Don't worry about us. I'm too excited to eat," Diane said as she rushed to the door.

"Yes, but he never is."

Diane pulled the door open and smiled expectantly. He hadn't told her he was coming, but she wasn't surprised that he had.

"Special delivery," Guillaume said, producing the morning paper from behind his back.

"Is it in there! Did you see it?"

"I had to look before I dared come over this early." He winked at Cook, who rolled her eyes. "It's in there."

Diane squealed and pulled him inside. "Let me see it."

He passed the paper to Diane, and she spread it out on a clean spot on Cook's counter. She flipped to the weddings section, and there it was, right at the top along with their photograph. They'd posed sitting close together on a settee in his parents' drawing room. Diane was dressed in a sensible new suit and ostentatiously feathered hat. She was looking up at Guillaume, smiling. And Guillaume, who insisted on putting his arm around her shoulders, was beaming at the camera. His broad smile filled his handsome face with joy that was clear even in the black and white newsprint.

She'd seen the picture, of course, but seeing it in the paper, she marveled again at how perfect they looked. And knowing that all her friends back at home would see this photograph of her and her adorable beloved thrilled Diane. Her Frenchman!

She could practically hear all her girlfriends squealing with delight.

"Read it aloud for us," Cook said.

"Yes, I want to hear it in your voice."

"I'm sure you do! Okay." She lifted the page and turned to face them. Then she started reading.

Allard & Talbot

The marriage of American Mademoiselle Diane Talbot of Woollett, New York, to French Monsieur Guillaume Allard of Paris will occur on July 1 in a small morning ceremony at Saint-Eustache Church. The bride's and groom's families will be in attendance. Afterward, the couple will celebrate with friends at the Allard family home. Monsieur and the new Madame Allard will leave immediately following the festivities for a tour of Italy and Greece before traveling on to the United States. Their friends and families wish them many years, all the happiness, and never-ending adventures together.

"It's perfect, dear. Absolutely perfect," Cook said, sniffing and wiping a tear that could have been caused by her onions, but probably not.

"It is perfect," Diane said. Guillaume smiled at her. Hadn't stopped smiling since he walked in the door, in fact.

"It's official."

"It is."

"I've officially trapped you." He put his arms around her and pulled her close.

"My dear, Guillaume," Diane laughed. "Marriage is most definitely a trap, and it's one I'm happily falling into."

About the Author

Melinda Copp is a writer based in Bluffton, South Carolina. Her work has been published in newspapers, magazines, and literary journals, including *HuffPost*, *The Rumpus*, *The Cleveland Review of Books*, and *The Petigru Review*.

Melinda has a bachelor's degree in journalism from West Virginia University and a master's degree in creative writing from Goucher College. She writes essays about books, culture, and life in her monthly e-mail newsletter, *Melinda's Letter*. Like a note from a friend, new essays arrive on the first Tuesday of every month. Subscribe for a free short story and other extras here: melindacopp.com.

Antoine de Larminet is the last surviving son of an aristocratic family. In line to inherit a title, he has promised his parents that he'll marry a peer and carry on the centuries-old tradition. He was raised in an antiquated world where love was often found outside of arranged society marriages. Even as the French aristocracy is losing relevance to modernity, Antoine never questioned this commitment to this family legacy—until his chance meeting with clever and beautiful Charlotte.

Their attraction is immediate, and the more they bump into each other at the clubs and salons of Paris, the stronger their attachment grows. But Antoine can't marry Charlotte because she's as proletarian as they come. And Charlotte will lose all credibility as a writer and social critic if she becomes the mistress of an aristocrat.

The world around them is changing, but if love is to win, one of them will have to give up everything they stand for.

Love and the Downfall of Society is available now in paperback and ebook everywhere books are sold.

strangely compelling companion. But is falling into the arms of another man really the answer to Louise's trouble?

Against the stunning backdrop of the Loire Valley, Louise tells her side of the story as you've never heard it. And she gets another chance at happily ever after.

For a free copy of Louise's story, subscribe to *Melinda's Letter* at melindacopp.substack.com.

Let's Keep in Touch…

Follow Melinda Copp for updates about forthcoming books, new writing, and promotions!

On Substack: melindacopp.substack.com/
On Instagram: instagram.com/melindacopp/
On Facebook: facebook.com/melindacoppwriter/
On Threads: threads.net/@melindacopp

And please consider reviewing this book on all your favorite book review sites. Your review will help new readers discover Melinda's books.